TIME RAIDERS

Only they can cross the boundaries of time;
only they have the power to save humanity

Meet the team of Project Anasazi, a secret military
unit sent through time to save the world, as they
discover dark and dangerous new passions.

Available from Mills & Boon® Nocturne™:

The Seeker by Lindsay McKenna
21st May

The Slayer by Cindy Dees
21st May

The Avenger by P.C. Cast
4th June

The Protector by Merline Lovelace
18th June

D1079959

Available in June 2010
from Mills & Boon® Nocturne™

Time Raiders: The Seeker
by Lindsay McKenna

Time Raiders: The Slayer
by Cindy Dees

Time Raiders: The Avenger
by P.C. Cast

TIME RAIDERS

The Seeker

LINDSAY McKENNA

⊚™ MILLS & BOON®

All the characters in this book have no existence outside the imagination of the author, and have no relation whatsoever to anyone bearing the same name or names. They are not even distantly inspired by any individual known or unknown to the author, and all the incidents are pure invention.

First published in Great Britain 2010
Harlequin Mills & Boon Limited,
Eton House, 18-24 Paradise Road, Richmond, Surrey TW9 1SR

© Lindsay McKenna and Merline Lovelace 2009

ISBN: 978 0 263 88765 5

89-0610

Harlequin Mills & Boon policy is to use papers that are natural, renewable and recyclable products and made from wood grown in sustainable forests. The logging and manufacturing processes conform to the legal environmental regulations of the country of origin.

Printed and bound in Spain
by Litografia Rosés S.A., Barcelona

Lindsay McKenna feels that telling a story is a way to share what and how she sees the world she lives in. Love is the greatest healer of all, and the books she creates are parables that underline this belief. Working with flower essences, also gentle healers, she devotes part of her life to the world of Nature to help ease people's suffering. She knows that the right words can heal and that the creation of a story can be catalytic to a person's life. And she hopes that her books may in some way educate and lift the reader in a positive manner. She can be reached at www.lindsaymckenna.com or www.medicinegarden. com.

To the real Energy Hunters in my life:
Michele Burdet, shamanic facilitator and world-class
dowser, Switzerland; Marchien (Marty) Rienstra,
interfaith minister and author of *Eisha's Search*, USA;
Grahame Martin, author of *Chakra Prescribing and
Homeopathy*, and professional homoeopath, England;
Nicholas R Mann, geomancer and author of
Sedona: Sacred Earth; Dr Michael Smith, author of
Jung and Shamanism. Wonderful friends whom I have
shared marvellous mystical adventures with!
Thank you for being who you are. I'm grateful
to be your friend. May we have many more exciting
and fascinating adventures to come!

The Beginning

Fifty thousand years ago, after discovering that human females carried a nascent genetic potential that might one day develop into the ability to star navigate, the Galactic Council planted a dozen pieces of a bronze disc, known as the Karanovo Stamp, across the Earth, hidden in darkness until mankind advances enough to travel through time and find them.

And then, out of the ashes of the mystery-shrouded Roswell Alien crash in 1947 arose a secret research project called Anasazi. Its improbable goal: learn to use the recovered alien technology for the purposes of time travel. General Beverly Ashton was the last to command this project before a dozen time travelers were inexplicably lost and the project disbanded.

However, the recent discovery of an ancient journal, known as the *Ad Astra,* has given Professor Athena Carswell the information she needs to begin sending modern time travelers back through human history in search of the twelve pieces of the Karanovo Stamp. This stamp, when fully reassembled, will send a signal across the galaxy to the Council, indicating that mankind is ready to be introduced to the rest of the galactic community.

Project Anasazi has secretly been reactivated, and General Ashton, now retired, and Professor Carswell are continuing the project's work. They are carefully recruiting and training a team of military women and men to make the dangerous time jumps. But threats loom on the horizon, both from humans who would see the project ended— or worse, steal its work and use it for nefarious ends—and from the Centauri Federation, which will do anything to stop humans from learning how to navigate the stars...

Chapter 1

"Delia," Professor Athena Carswell said, her voice low with excitement, "I have fully decoded Argenta's *Ad Astra* journal!"

Delia Sebastian sat at the oval table in a conference room at Red Rock University in Flagstaff, Arizona. "That's awesome!" she exclaimed.

At her right elbow was retired Marine Corps General Beverly Ashton. The three women were discussing one of the greatest secrets on Earth—a time-travel lab.

The *Ad Astra* journal had been stolen from a museum in France. Argenta, a historian and Roman woman in the days of Pliny, had recorded information in this journal about star beings creating a disk and placing pieces of it on Earth. With the information from the journal in hand, they could now move forward with their mission.

Delia studied Athena's heart-shaped face and serious green eyes, which right now sparkled with happiness. In the world outside her lab, so secret it was known only by individuals at the highest levels of the U.S. government, Athena would not be recognized as a genius quantum mechanics physicist. Looks were deceiving, Delia knew.

Ashton stirred. "Better than awesome, Captain Sebastian. Professor Carswell has translated those lost pages you retrieved for her on your last time-jump mission."

Delia had left the Marine Corps, as had the general, but they maintained military protocol. They preferred its efficiency.

"Yes, ma'am," Delia murmured deferentially to the short, blond-haired woman. Delia could see touches of silver at Ashton's temples bracketing her square face with its stubborn-looking chin. When the general was tight jawed, she took on the look of a pit bull determined not to lose a fight. That's why General Ashton had been drummed out of her beloved Marine Corps. She had defended Professor

Carswell's time travel theories when everyone else wanted to let the professor disappear into history. Ashton had not agreed with the status quo, so she'd been forced to retire.

Undeterred, she had drummed up money from the civilian sector to build the Time Raiders lab here in Flagstaff. The general's belief in Athena's theories had been rewarded, and now they could, in fact, time travel.

Clearing her throat, Delia swung her attention back to the professor, who held a report in her hands. Despite her five-foot-three-inch height, Athena was a force to be reckoned with. Delia had nothing but admiration for the brilliant scientist who was so far ahead of her time.

The 1947 UFO crash in Roswell, New Mexico, had provided a treasure trove of unfamiliar items. The U.S. Army had tried for decades to identify and decode their secrets, but never could. Athena, while working at the Pentagon on the time travel project, had found out about the strange items. Since no one cared about the Roswell crash any longer, the odd collection was released into her care.

Among the items from the Roswell crash was a headband, or what some called a "navigation crown." Athena had cracked the mathematical formula found on a quartz crystal embedded in it, and discovered what the mysterious headband could do: send people back in time.

When she lost twelve volunteers to different periods and cultures, unable to bring them back to the present, the Pentagon quickly dumped her and the project like a hot potato, and more or less booted Ashton out of the Corps.

In the end, it had all worked out. Athena got to keep the alien headband and once the lab was built, was able to discover how to retrieve time jumpers, transporting them back to the present. Now, as a result of the professor's amazing feat, they were ready for some serious missions.

Managing a grim smile, Delia watched lights dance in Athena's narrowed eyes. "I know you've been trying to read Argenta's backward-Latin entries in her journal for some time, Professor. What did you discover?"

Grinning with pleasure, she leaned forward and said, "Where the first of the twelve pieces of the Karanovo stamp seal is located!"

Delia gasped. "You're joking!"

The general snorted. "The professor doesn't joke, Captain. You should know that by now."

"Er...that's correct, ma'am." Turning her gaze back to Athena, who was brushing her light brown curls off her forehead, Delia said, "I'm not going to bother to ask how you did it because I know you'd give me a formula I couldn't comprehend. The better question is where *is* the first piece? What time in history?"

"As always, Delia, you cut to the chase," Athena said. She tapped the papers beneath her hand. "We know the Pleiades constellation is a group of nine, not seven, star systems. This information comes from Argenta's journal, as well as from present-day astronomy. When we sent you to her villa in Pompeii in 44 B.C., you found the leather-bound journal in her study, and copied the pages that were later 'lost.' That's when I knew we were on to something." The lost pages had been stolen out of Athena's office. No one ever found who had done it or why. In order to find out what was contained on those pages, Delia had been sent back to photograph the originals. Excitement rose in her wispy, feminine voice. "Argenta, like Leonardo da Vinci, wrote backwards. It has taken me until just last week to finish translating the Latin text. In one passage, Argenta, who was considered a famous historian in her time, said she knew who had the first piece of the Karanovo bronze seal—Servilia, mistress to Julius Caesar."

"Are you sending me back to find it?" Delia's pulse began to quicken with that familiar sizzle of excitement. Because of her own Greek heritage, her favorite periods in history were the Roman and Greek empires. She had made three time-travel jumps for the professor after Athena had fine-tuned her use of the alien headband.

Waving her hand, the professor said, "Beverly and I have been working hard to map out this next Time Raider journey. And yes, you are being chosen to go back to 44 B.C."

Delia had been the first volunteer to be sent back in time once Athena thought she'd figured out the retrieval formula. No one had been certain that her tweaks would work. But the jump into the past, plus the return, had been successful.

Athena then sent Delia twice more to the historian's study in Pompeii to locate her mysterious journal. Delia brought the journal back, copied the missing pages and then returned it. Even then, parts of the journal had been missing. So Athena had sent Delia as a Time Raider to Argenta's villa to locate those missing pages.

The professor had been right: those critical passages contained information and a drawing with the twelve pieces of the Karanovo bronze seal, each carved with a different constellation. In the journal Argenta said a fake one would be left on Earth while the real one was cut into twelve pieces. When all were found and fitted together it would create the disk in the journal. The fake had been made, Argenta wrote, to throw off the enemy.

"And you're sure the bronze fragment is there?" Delia asked now.

Frowning, Athena scrubbed her brow and muttered, "Servilia is Julius Caesar's former mistress. She's powerful and savvy. She's been shunted aside for young, beautiful Queen Cleopatra of Egypt, who has, by the way, borne Julius a son. A son he's always wanted but never got—until now. Calpurnia, Caesar's wife, has been pushed aside, as well. But it is Servilia who has a piece of the seal, according to Argenta's journal."

"Where is it?" Delia asked.

"We don't know," Ashton said unhappily. "All we can do is have Athena set the course once she puts on that headband and sends you through time to Servilia's location. From there, you're going to have to put clues together like puzzle pieces. Follow the woman around like a cosmic bloodhound until you locate it."

The professor produced a colored photo of the Bronze Age stamp seal that had been unearthed by archaeologists in Bulgaria, near Nova Zagora. "This disk was discovered in 1991. There are twelve constellations emblazoned on it. The seal is solid

bronze, six centimeters in diameter and two centimeters thick. What is of great interest to me is that
a drawing of this very disk was found in Argenta's
journal, among those missing pages you copied. It
is an exact copy of the one found in Bulgaria. The
Roman historian said that the twelve constellations
represent twelve pieces of another seal that was deliberately cut apart by the Star people. When the
pieces are fitted together they make a round disk.
The twelve sections were scattered around the
world, in different cultures and different time
periods, apparently. According to my calculations,
the time line could cover thousands of years, from
Egypt onward to the nineteenth century."

Fascinated, Delia studied the round bronze
stamp, which reminded her of an old, worn copper
coin. "So I'm going after one of the twelve pieces."
She lifted her head. "You say it's the *first* piece?"

Athena shrugged. "I don't know. But in her
journal, Argenta did identify it as the first. And said
that Servilia was using it."

"How?" Delia wondered. "Does it possess pro-
perties like that headband you wear to send us back
and forth in time?"

Again the professor shrugged. "That's something
you'll have to discover once you and your partner
find it."

"Partner?" Delia swung her head toward the general. The dark blue business suit Beverly Ashton wore wasn't a uniform, but her squared shoulders and the proud way she wore it shouted of her military background. "General? What partner? I've always time traveled alone."

"Not on this mission," Ashton said. She glanced at Athena briefly and then went on. "The professor has created an ESC, or emergency signaling cuff—a metal armband with a quartz cabochon embedded into it. The crystal has been imprinted with your brain-wave pattern and frequency as well as the professor's. Information on our time and location are contained in it as well. Now that we know she can send and retrieve a time traveler, we needed to create better plans for future missions."

"Take a look," Athena said, pulling something from the pocket of her white lab coat. She held up a silvery armband, then set it on the table in front of Delia. "You can wear this on your wrist or your arm. It's made from titanium, so it's lightweight and won't break. Through it we will remain connected no matter where you are in time. Never take it off. When you're ready to come back, all you have to do is press the crystal with your finger and it will send a signal to me. I'll bring you home."

Delia raised both hands. "Whoa! Wait a minute. What's this about a partner?"

The former Marine Corps officer eyed her soberly. "As we move into Time Raider mission mode, we will try a team for the first time. That way, if one of you gets hurt or killed, the other can continue the mission and complete it."

Delia was aware that Athena had sent other volunteers besides herself back in time. After recalculating the mathematical formula and upgrading the headband's crystals, the professor had managed to ensure she never lost anyone again. "But," Delia sputtered, "you've always sent us alone."

"This mission is different, Captain," Ashton said. "We have an objective, a target, and it's a serious and deadly business. We have no idea what the pieces of the Karanovo seal really represent aside from what we've learned via Argenta's journal." She grimaced wryly. "Two heads are always better than one. Athena will time-jump a team for this trip, not an individual."

Delia shook her head in protest. "I don't want a partner, General. I've done everything you've asked of me on my other missions. And I did so alone."

"Don't go getting bent out of shape on this, Captain." Ashton drilled her with her blue eyes. "You don't have a choice in the matter."

Delia saw the pit-bull look appear on her face and knew there was no use arguing with the former Marine Corps officer. "Yes, ma'am, I hear you."

"You don't have to agree with our change of policy, but you do have to take a partner," Ashton growled. "I'm ordering you to team up with Captain Jake Tyler. He's U.S. Army Special Forces. His mother is a professor of history at Cornell University and his father a professor of medicine."

She pulled out a file and handed it to Delia. "Tyler has psychic abilities as a mind reader. He's got a degree in electrical engineering and a minor in Roman culture, which is why he was chosen. He knows all about the societal framework of that period and will provide excellent backup to your own psychic skills."

Shock bolted through Delia and she barely heard Ashton's words. The only ones that registered seemed to burn into her heart, filling her with rage. *Captain Jake Tyler…!*

Choking, she rasped, "There's no way in hell you're hooking me up with that Neanderthal bastard, General. No way!" She started to rise out of her chair.

Ashton's arm shot out like a snake striking. She gripped Delia's forearm. "Sit down, Captain. And let's just turn down the volume on this tirade, shall we?"

Delia sank back in her seat and Ashton released her arm, still scowling disapprovingly. Okay, so she wasn't behaving rationally about this, Delia admitted. But Tyler always stirred up that kind of violent reaction in her—from the aching need to be in his arms, to sharing his bed, to blinding anger. Glaring at the general, she growled, "Then tell me why you'd ever team me up with that caveman?"

"He might be a Neanderthal," Ashton retorted, "but he's got the right credentials for this mission. His background is exactly what is needed to find that bronze piece from the Karanovo seal."

After clearing her throat, Athena interjected, "Delia, remember what is at stake here. In the *Ad Astra* journal I translated, Argenta admitted she was a 'plant' from the Pleiades, *not* an Earthling."

"She's an alien?" Delia felt her eyes grow round as she snapped her head toward the professor.

"Yes," Athena said emphatically. "From what I can piece together from the recent journal pages you retrieved, she was deliberately planted here by the Galactic Council. As a mole to spy on our civilization. Argenta was from the constellation Pleiades and they were a part of that council."

Stunned, Delia stared at both women, who nodded almost in unison. "But…why? *Alien?* We knew from her journals that the Pleiadians were enlisted by the Council to embed some sort of message into the twelve pieces of the disk. But this is a new twist."

"Argenta was an alien monitor planted here on Earth," Athena told her. "I wouldn't be surprised if she was the one to give Servilia that section of the seal. I can't prove it. There's nothing in her journal to make my guess a fact, but my gut tells me so."

"This is a real shocker," Delia exclaimed, her mind running wild with questions. "If Argenta was an alien checking out our civilization at that time, doesn't it stand to reason that the Council might have planted a different monitor with another piece at another time and age? Twelve monitors? Twelve pieces of the stamp?"

"Exactly," Athena said, clearly pleased with Delia's lightning-quick deductions. "Of course, that is conjecture. It might not be so. But we've come to suspect that the Galactic Council dropped several 'bread crumbs' throughout Earth's history, over a very long period, to see if we would ever find them. If we did discover them, gather all twelve pieces and put the seal back together again, then we could contact this alien council directly."

Delia's shock over Tyler coming warred with the amazing news the professor had just shared with her. "And you already know that the Pleiadians are involved, from other passages in Argenta's journals. It appears that constellation was chosen by the Galactic Council to implement this plan on earth"

"Yes. But now," Athena said, "we have more of an understanding of why this alien culture is interested in us as a planet and people." She looked over at Ashton. "General, do you want to share the rest of the information with Delia?"

The woman gave a brisk nod, fixing her narrowed gaze on Delia. "Captain, I think once you realize the enormity of what we're going to divulge, you'll drop your objections to Tyler going along on this mission. According to the decoded text in Argenta's journal, the Pleiadians want Earth to join their galactic alliance, even though we humans are considered a backward and primitive species by their council. They decided to cut into pieces the Karanovo seal embossed with the twelve constellations—imagery representing the twelve star systems that comprise the council. They were planning to place a piece in each culture and age as Earth progressed over the millennia. They said that until we could become heart-centered and compassionate, a planet of peace, we could not join their alliance. But apparently they saw enough glimmers of potential, felt enough hope when they first met Earthlings long ago, that they 'seeded' the planet with these sections of the seal. If we can send specialists back in time to retrieve them, bring them together to the present era, we might reassemble the seal and send the message that we're ready to join the alliance."

Rubbing her brow, Delia said, "But how do we know if this is a positive thing, General? Maybe the Galactic Council wants to enslave us. If their technology is that advanced, they might very well do so. They could have some pretty dark plans for us, a situation that could be triggered if we find those twelve pieces and put in a call to them."

"We've talked it over," Athena assured her. "In fact, Argenta made note of one alien culture that *is* trying to take over Earth and its inhabitants. There's an entry in her journal where she names Kentar, lord of the Centaurian constellation, as an enemy to Earth. She speaks of Centaurian monitors coming to Earth to try and enslave us."

"So," Delia said, "you think the Pleiadians and the Galactic Council represent the positive side in this scenario?"

Ashton sighed. "It appears that way. We really don't know yet. We're hoping that as you hunt down the first fragment of the Karanovo seal we'll find out more about the council. Nowhere in the *Ad Astra* journal did Argenta say the Galactic Council had any diabolical plans for enslaving us as the Centaurians do."

Grimacing, Delia said, "Well, if Argenta was Pleiadian, she's not going to speak out against her own kind, is she?"

"Obviously not," Ashton said. "But the critical scenario before us is *why* we need you to team up with Tyler. He's already been briefed and is on his way here, by the way." The general shook her head. "There is just too much at stake, Captain. We need a team to handle this highly sensitive mission. We know that Centaurians are our enemy. Were they active in that era? What do they look like? Will they be easy to spot? We don't know. And are Pleiadians as friendly as they seem to be? Do they really hold us to a higher purpose and call? This new time-travel mission will be different from any we've experienced."

"Another thing we don't know is whether some other group might be aware of this disk," the professor interjected. "Argenta's journal was handed down through time, coming to me for translation after the university bought it in an auction. The journal could have been decoded by others through the centuries. Latin is easy to translate, even when written backward. It takes time, but anyone with a lot of patience can do it. So who else might possibly know about it? And might they have located the missing pages?"

"An even more provocative and worrisome question," Ashton stated, "is what if those missing pages are in the hands of someone else here, right now? What if they know the rest of the story, like we do?"

"Even if they did," Delia protested, "they don't have the ability to go back in time and find the pieces."

Holding up her hand, Athena said, "Not so fast. Remember, the segments are solid bronze, and survive through the centuries. You don't *have* to time-jump to find them, although we feel that it's an easier method than any other. Twelve pieces buried in twelve different time periods... If someone had enough money and a desire to track them down, they could hire archaeologists to do just that." She frowned. "If that is so, and a person or group with less than stellar principles gets to these seals first, the world could be in a lot of trouble. Maybe the Centaurians are here right now, working to find them with some greedy individual hungry for power."

"Which is why," the general growled, "it's imperative we get started with this mission immediately. As soon as you two discover the first piece and bring it back Professor Carswell will use it to determine where the second piece might be."

"That's right," Athena told Delia. "In her journal, Argenta hinted that when one piece was found, directions to a second segment would be on it. Everything is encrypted in a mathematical code. Once I break that code, we can send a second team out. Each fragment brought back should give us information about the next one."

"We are assuming there is another party looking for them," Ashton warned Delia gravely. "Plus these Centaurians may know about them. If that is so, then we potentially have two different enemies trying to find these pieces before we do."

The professor smiled. "I don't disagree with you, General, but an ace up our sleeve is that we *can* time travel." She looked at Delia. "And frankly, we feel you're the best candidate, along with Captain Tyler, to recover that first piece. You are Greek by birth. You know the Greek culture like no one else. I'll be sending you and Tyler back as Greek mercenaries. You speak the language fluently, although I will be imprinting both of you with all the language skills, social customs, historical information and anything else you might need to fade into this culture. Armed as you are with your present-day knowledge, Delia, we can think of no one else better suited for this mission than you two."

"Yes. The entire Time Raider project is resting

on your shoulders, Captain," Ashton warned. "Which is why you've got to put aside any personal baggage you have with Captain Tyler. It's going to take two of you to get this mission accomplished. Now do you understand?"

The weight of the world seemed to settle around Delia's shoulders as she sat there, hands folded on the table. "Yes, ma'am, I get it." Glancing at Athena, she asked, "Do we know what will happen if we get all twelve pieces and contact the Pleiadian council?"

"Argenta said in her journal that it would be a very good thing," the professor replied. "That Earth could join as a full member, with all the rights accorded to it. Whatever that means."

"Humph," Delia said. "Is their agenda any different from our known enemies, the Centaurians, then?"

"Good question," the general grumbled. "The only way to find out is to get through these twelve missions and see what happens."

Taking a deep breath, Delia stared at her clenched hands, noting how white her knuckles were. Inwardly, her heart was in chaos over the fact that Jake Tyler was going to time-jump with her. He'd once been her lover. Their breakup had been an emotional earthquake for Delia for she had loved him with a desperation she had never experienced before or since.

That had been two years ago, but she wasn't over it yet. Delia knew Jake was in the Time Raider program, but she had managed to avoid him completely.

Damn, how was she going to handle the mission *and* him?

Chapter 2

"Captain Tyler is here, Del," the lab assistant said from the door of the planning room. "He's with the professor and general in the main conference room."

Frowning, Delia closed the file she'd been looking at. It was time for the coming jump. "Thanks, Josie. I'll be there in a minute."

Delia drew a deep breath and let it out slowly as she listened to the familiar sound of Birkenstocks slapping the flagstones as the lab assistant walked on. Delia wanted to be alone for a few moments more to absorb the details of the mission. Taking the armband off the table in front of her, she slipped it into a pocket of her lab coat, then fingered the mission folder numbly, trying to calm her roiling feelings and wildly pumping heart. How to deal with Tyler? He was so damned arrogant.

Delia felt her body tingling in anticipation, in spite of her annoyance. She'd always responded that way before meeting Jake back when they had been lovers. Frowning, she smoothed her pink angora sweater as she got to her feet. January in Flagstaff meant freezing temperatures and snow. Grabbing the file, she forced herself to move toward the main conference room.

Heading across the lab, Delia eyed the huge glass cylinder that rose from the floor to the twelve-foot-high ceiling. Inside were two chairs. She'd sat in one and been sent back in time more often than any other volunteer.

Off to the left was Athena's brown leather chair. On a wooden stand next to it, locked in a glass box, was the precious headband that had been discovered by U.S. Army officials after the saucer had crashed in the New Mexico desert near Roswell.

Always fascinated with the object, Delia slowed her pace to look at it. The silver metal was shaped to fit Athena's head. It had two flaps that hugged the sides of her skull, each holding a beautiful, clear quartz crystal cabochon. The stones had a slightly lavender glow.

Delia's psychic gift was the ability to see auras and colors around objects and people. She gazed in wonder, watching the lavender color ebb and flow. So much magic was captured in those memory crystals, she knew.

Athena Carswell's genius was to break the mathematical code on the frequency contained in them and harness time jumping. Someone had been wearing that headband during the Roswell crash, the professor was convinced. Whoever it was must have had a stroke or some other kind of brain malfunction.

Pulling herself back to the challenge at hand, Delia walked on. The door to the main conference room was partly open, and she could hear Jake's deep voice. Her heart squeezed at the memory of his breath brushing across her sensitized body, and she bit her lip as she hugged the mission file to her breast. *Jake.* Oh, God, how was she going to handle this meeting? It had been so hard breaking up with him! But she hated his determination to control everyone he met—most of all her.

Pulling open the door, Delia saw Jake standing with Athena and General Ashton at one end of the long, polished table. He wore a suede blazer the same color as his dark brown hair, a light blue polo shirt that brought out the stormy hue of his intelligent eyes, and Levi's that showed off his long, powerful legs.

Swallowing, Delia met his gaze as he lifted his
head. She knew how adept he was at mind reading,
and she purposely set up a wall around her thoughts,
wanting to make sure he couldn't know how she
really felt.

"Hi, Del," Jake said in greeting. "Long time no
see."

Delia saw at once that Professor Carswell and
General Ashton seemed to be under the spell of the
ruggedly handsome soldier. "Tyler," she muttered
defensively. Turning, she made sure the conference
door was shut, and then sat down at the far end of the
table, as far as she could from Jake, who was standing
at the head of it. Delia nodded to the two women.

Placing the file on the table, she was glad when
Athena sat next to her, General Ashton opposite.
Everyone got to the business at hand, much to Delia's
relief. Giving Jake a quick glance out of the corner
of her eye, she found she couldn't ignore him any
more than the other women. His face was square,
with an aquiline nose and sensual mouth. Her body
flared to life as she recalled his strong, compelling
lips sliding across her skin. Biting the inside of her
cheek, Delia tried to forget. It was impossible.

And then Jake lifted his head, his gaze directed
at her. Feeling as if he'd read her thoughts, she
scowled at him. Whenever Jake sent out mental

probes to read a mind, her scalp always prickled in warning. That hadn't happened. So how had he known she was reliving those torrid, searching kisses he'd given her so long ago?

"How have you been, Del?" Jake asked conversationally. He gave her a smile of welcome as everyone opened their briefing files. It was too easy to lose himself in her golden-brown eyes, framed with those thick, black lashes. Her hair was shoulder length, slightly curly, and her Greek blood evident by her glowing olive complexion.

"Fine," she growled.

Jake remembered the first time he'd met Delia, on the plains of Afghanistan during a military operation. He'd thought she was a beautiful Greek goddess come to life. Even in a helmet, Kevlar vest and camouflage gear, carrying an M-16 on her hip, she couldn't hide the fact she was a sensual woman. Jake didn't try to push away the memory of that first meeting. Delia had been a Marine Corps captain in charge of her squad, and all business. But what a body! And what a mouth! On the field of battle no woman wore makeup, but Delia didn't have to. She was haunting to Jake, a fever that had never left his bloodstream. Even now he could feel his lower body tightening with memory and need for her.

Delia smarted beneath that hooded, hot gaze Jake

was turning on. He was still so sure of himself and his masculinity. Clearly, nothing had changed since she'd broken up with him. Six feet tall, he had a boxer's body without an inch of flab anywhere on it. Trying not to look at his long, well-shaped hands, or his callused palms, she found her nerves rippling in response. *Stop it!* she ordered herself sternly. *Stop it, stop it, stop it! What's past is past!*

Delia vaguely heard General Ashton and Professor Carswell bringing Jake up to speed on last-minute changes to the mission. Her heart wouldn't stop pounding. She kept her gaze pinned on the mission-brief pages, her hands flat on the table in front of her. It was common knowledge at Time Raiders that she and Jake had once been a red-hot item. Which was why she avoided him at every opportunity.

"We all know," General Ashton was saying, sending Delia a look across the table, "the reason Captain Tyler is on this mission is because he's able to mind read. Athena is going to jump you both to February 20, 44 B.C. We don't know where Servilia, Julius Caesar's mistress, is, exactly, but we know she is in Rome at this time. Argenta's journal cites Servilia as owning a piece of the Karanovo disc. Once you arrive, Captain Sebastian, you are officer in charge of this mission."

"Good," Delia said, giving Jake a glance that

spoke volumes. She could see his flat brows tightening over that order.

"We will need Captain Tyler's ability," Athena agreed. "Being able to mind read isn't straightforward, unfortunately, but requires sifting through a lot of mental garbage. Sometimes it's impossible, due to whatever else is going on at the time. That's where you come in," she said, turning to Delia. "Captain Tyler will need uninterrupted time to focus and try to search another person's mind. You will aid and abet him in this, Delia. He can't talk and mind read at the same time. You'll act as guide and guardian, giving him the space to do his job."

"Yes, ma'am," Delia murmured.

"We know that a lot of things will be happening," the general interjected. "Getting close to Servilia is prime—she is your target of opportunity. The more time you can spend with her, the easier it will be for Captain Tyler to dredge through the contents of her mind."

"And his ability to read minds has limits," Athena told Delia. "He has to be close to his subject, no more than twenty feet away, for optimum brainwave stimulation. Our brains have a great capacity for electrical activity, but there, too, one has limits."

"Okay, I can handle that," Delia assured them.

Once Servilia saw how drop-dead handsome Tyler was, Delia was sure she'd keep him close to her.

"My intent when I send you back is to make you a brother-and-sister mercenary team from Greece," Athena said. "This takes advantage of your heritage, Delia. You were born on the island of Delos, which the Romans believe is where their sun god, Apollo, was born. And you know I will send with you the ability to speak the dialects of Greece and the Latin of Rome. Your ability to see auras surrounding people will help, as well."

Relief flooded Delia. Brother and sister. Not lovers. *Good.* She'd dodged that bullet. Frowning, she said, "Athena, do you think that Romans of that time will accept a woman warrior, a mercenary?"

"We learned from the time jumps you made to Pompeii to retrieve Argenta's journal that women were depicted in frescoes fighting one another in the Circus Maximus. Granted, they were probably prisoners of war, but they were gladiator-trained women warriors. General Ashton and I feel that having you a freeborn woman from Delos and a warrior will intrigue Servilia, and not necessarily raise questions."

"We hope," the general said. "There's little history on Julius Caesar's longtime mistress. Servilia hung around him through several marriages, including the last one, to Calpurnia."

"To make things even messier," Athena warned them, "Queen Cleopatra from Egypt had Julius Caesar's son, Ptolemy Caesarion, a year earlier. She lives at the house of Marius, where Julius Caesar has residence. We can only guess how Servilia, who stuck with Caesar through thick and thin, might feel about this."

"Probably pretty unhappy," Delia mused.

"Jealous?" Jake suggested. "Angry enough to see him assassinated on the Ides of March?"

Shrugging, Athena said, "No one knows. But you two are being put into a period of tumult, conspiracy and secret machinations. You know that Marcus Brutus, son of Servilia, was part of a plot to assassinate Caesar, on March 15. As you get close to Servilia, you will automatically be putting yourselves on the firing line regarding this conspiracy, which will obviously be in play."

"That means you have to stay alert," Ashton warned them in a heavy tone. "Since Servilia's son, Brutus, is a part of this plot, then is she? If so, you must remain aloof, yet somehow find the fragment of the seal that is in her possession."

"A dicey proposition," Delia murmured. "Talk about landing in the eye of a tornado…"

"General Brutus," Jake said, "was the number-two man to Julius Caesar for nearly twenty years.

He was with Caesar as he conquered Europe and then Britain. I think we have to realize that Servilia's genes helped make Brutus the great general and warrior he was." Opening his hands, Jake conjectured, "Knowing Brutus was part of the plot, I think we ought to assume Servilia's in on it, too. She must be hurt that Caesar had a love affair with a twenty-one-year-old Egyptian queen, had a son by her, and even brought her to Rome. Servilia *has* to be angry."

"Enough to kill the man she loves?" Delia wondered aloud.

"The passions of people in power aren't necessarily controlled by morals," Athena warned. "Remember, Servilia likely enjoyed high status because of her relationship with Caesar. She may have been dethroned when Cleopatra bore his only son. Is this aristocratic woman capable of murder? No one knows. But that's something you should assume."

"Also," General Ashton said, "how does Caesar feel about Servilia now? Is it possible he wants her dead? Would he arrange somehow to get rid of her, the old mistress? And what about Cleopatra? Would she send someone into Servilia's villa in Rome to murder her? To get a possible rival out of the way?" The general shook her head. "History tells us that

Servilia survived her son, General Marcus Brutus. And after Caesar's assassination, Cleopatra fled Rome with Caesarion to protect him from the anarchy that erupted shortly after. Octavian, who eventually took over and became the emperor Augustus, had Cleopatra's son murdered in Egypt. Cleopatra, of course, committed suicide by having a poisonous asp bite her on the breast.

"Brutus met his end in the Battle of Philippi, years later. And Servilia outlived them all. This woman is a schemer of the finest order, and you two should not underestimate her. She's clearly a power to be reckoned with, a politician in her own right. After all, it is believed that she actually helped Julius Caesar with the strategy that brought him victory during his Gallic campaign. He gave her a priceless black pearl as thanks for her insight. She's not to be trifled with."

"The power behind the throne?" Delia murmured.

"Assume it," Ashton growled.

"We're going to time-jump in an hour," the professor announced. "My intent is to dress you as mercenaries, on horseback—Delia and Philip of Greece. You'll show up in that time with the correct clothing and weapons. And of course you will have full awareness of then and memory of the present day. You both have had ample experience living in two worlds at once because of the other missions you've accomplished."

Athena awarded them with a smile. "Just to go over some important fail-safe points…" She pulled out an armband from her lab coat pocket and handed it to Jake. "You can wear this on your arm or wrist, it doesn't matter which. What does matter is that as soon as you locate the target fragment and have it in your possession, you must press the quartz crystal. That sends a signal back to me. I'll be made aware of the transmission and come into the lab, don the headband and bring you home."

"These bracelets also protect us from possible injury," Delia said. She'd done the most time travel, and knew that from experience. "If one of us gets hurt and needs immediate first aid, we can press the crystal and be brought back."

"Absolutely," Ashton agreed. "Or if one of you loses an armband, you can hold on to one another, press the crystal of the remaining one, and both of you will return. But do not lose your armband. We can't afford to leave either of them in another time."

Delia took hers from her lab coat pocket. She could see the faint lavender light emanating from the oval crystal embedded in it. "Our lifeline to the present and to getting help," she murmured grimly.

"Never lose it or set it aside," the general warned. "Anyone getting ahold of that armband could press or touch the crystal, deliberately or by mistake, and they would be coming back to us."

Shaking her head, Delia muttered, "Can you imagine that? Some poor person from another time ending up in this lab?" She almost chuckled, though it wasn't funny.

"Not something we'll do," Jake said tensely. He ran his fingers across the smooth surface of the band. "I usually leave mine on my upper arm, covered by the clothes I'm wearing. It keeps curious people at bay. I almost had a woman touch it one day when I was back in Egypt in the time of Ramses, and had it on my wrist. Scared the hell out of me. If I hadn't jerked away, she'd have pressed that crystal and I would have disappeared right before her eyes."

Athena nodded. "Yes, the armbands garner a lot of attention. Hiding them is smart. I shudder to think of someone stealing the cuff, or you taking it off and someone toying with it. I don't want someone from the past showing up here." She gestured toward the room where the time jumps were initiated.

"We'll hide them well," Delia assured the worried professor.

Ashton stood. "All right, any questions?"

Jake shook his head. He saw Delia do the same.
As he stood to shake hands with the general, he slid
a glance down the table, to where Delia stood
chatting with the professor. How beautiful she
looked in that pink sweater outlining her curvy
body. Her black wool slacks only accentuated those
long, delicious thighs he'd explored so many times.
Every inch of her was burned into his brain and
body. Even now, despite the stress and pressure of
this mission, all he wanted to do was pull her into
his arms and go to bed with her. Sex with Delia was
mind-blowing. He had never forgotten it or her.

Jake savored this unexpected opportunity that had
thrown them together again. Maybe he could convince
her to pick up their relationship once more....

Chapter 3

"Captain Tyler?" Delia said as he walked down the hall toward the time jump lab. "I want a word with you."

Her heart pounded erratically as he turned, surprise written on his features. Why did he have to be so damn handsome? Tightening her mouth, Delia approached.

"Oh, it's 'Captain' now?" he teased, a grin creasing his face. He was still in the U.S. Army, on loan to General Ashton. She looked focused, her golden eyes narrowed on him as if he were her chosen prey.

"Cut the crap," she snapped as she halted in front of him. Jabbing him in the chest with her index finger, she rasped, "This isn't some fun play date we're going on. And that brings me to why I'm having this conversation with you, Captain." Her nostrils flared. "You are *second* in command. I'm the OIC—officer in charge. I've never worked in a team situation on a jump before, and neither has anyone else. You'd damn well better keep your eye on the prize and not start being a jerk like you were over in Afghanistan. Do you hear me?"

Jake felt the heat of her words. Still, his flesh riffled pleasantly from all that energy she was aiming at him, gruff though she was. "We're not enemies, Delia."

"The hell we aren't. I saw the smirk on your face in there during the mission briefing. You're looking at this like some kind of lark, and I'm damned if you will. *My* life will be on the line out there. If you want to screw things up because of your arrogance and overconfident ways, that's fine. But not on my watch, and not with me. Got it?"

The blazing gold of her eyes mesmerized Jake, as it always did. Memories, hot and evocative, came bubbling to the surface as he recalled their wild lovemaking in Afghanistan. There wasn't a moment he'd spent with this fiery, feisty woman warrior that he couldn't recall in detail. "Got it? Sure, babe, no problem."

Delia clenched her teeth, repressing the urge to slap his face. Jake was the ultimate cocky male, times ten. Nothing shook his masculine cool, not even her anger. "Cut the 'babe,' too. It has no place where we're going."

Shrugging, he managed a thin smile. "Hey, Del, I'll be a good boy. We'll get along fine on this mission. You just get me some space where I can try and read those Romans' minds. That's all I need from you."

Well, that was a lie, but Jake saw she meant business.

He needed *her*. His body ached to have her again. And even though Delia was no longer in the Marine Corps and had gone back to civilian life before being called up for the Time Raiders missions, she was still a military officer in bearing and stature. She had earned his respect in that regard from the moment he'd met her.

Backing off, Delia searched his glittering, sky-blue eyes. She felt anger right alongside passion. It had been two years since their split, but it seemed like yesterday. Unconsciously rubbing the area of her heart, she muttered, "Don't worry, I'll make sure you get mind-reading openings."

Jake grinned a little more widely. "Hey, I'm looking forward to this mission with you, Del."

"Well, I'm not! I fought it! I fought the fact it was you they'd chosen! You're the last man I'd ever want to time-jump with!"

"Ouch," he murmured, still smiling. "And you're the first woman I'd choose to be on a deserted island with. We're opposites, Del. But opposites attract."

"Damn you, Tyler!"

Chuckling, he wanted to reach out and touch her soft brown curls. Jake squelched the urge, seeing real anger in her eyes and hearing the desperation in her tone. "You hurt my feelings, Del."

"You are incorrigible, Tyler!" Delia planted her hands on her hips. "Your love for yourself, your total narcissism, is going to be your downfall someday. But not with me and not on this mission. All I care about is keeping my record clean and finding this fragment. And it had better be your focus, too."

Wiping the smile off his face, Jake realized he'd backed Del into a corner. He had no wish to make this time jump with her so upset. Holding up his hands, he murmured, "Okay, okay, time-out, boss. We'll make this work."

Not mollified, but seeing that he was struggling to toe the line, Delia said, "You've got the biggest swelled head I've ever seen, Tyler. And the moment you disobey my orders or think you are better than I am, I'm punching that cuff you're wearing and you're going *home*. I'll complete the mission on my own."

Jake frowned. "You wouldn't do that, would you?"

"In a heartbeat, Tyler." Again she waved her finger in his face. "Trust me when I say that I'd *much* rather perform this mission without you than with you. You step out of line one inch and you're gone."

Jake knew that Professor Carswell could send him back to that time once more, but he suspected Delia had already talked to her. And if he did return to the present midmission, they'd expect a very good explanation. More than anything, Jake realized, he wanted to keep Delia safe and alive on this very dangerous venture. "Listen to me, will you? You're famous for not listening and always interrupting when I talk, but hear me now." He leaned forward and pinned his gaze on her. "We're a team, Del. You and me. I'm not going to jeopardize either of our lives."

"Yeah, right," Delia muttered angrily. She didn't want her voice carrying down the hall for the others to hear. "Your need for controlling a situation and everyone involved had better remain underground. You never could work as a team, which is why I couldn't believe it when Ashton and Carswell chose you. Everything in your psychological profile shows you can't share power, and there's no way I'll believe that you've suddenly changed for this mission. I'll be watching you like a hawk. One screwup and you're gone."

Jake saw something different in Delia's eyes. Her words were cutting and sharp, but the hunger for him in her eyes was just as real. Reaching out before she had a chance to back off, Jake curled his hands around her shoulders and pulled her forward against him. He saw surprise flare in her eyes. Not one to be bossed around by an angry woman, Jake lowered his head. His lips sought and found hers.

Delia's anger exploded and dissolved as Jake's persuasive mouth fell upon her lips. Instantly, she tried to pull away from him. No good! Jake's hands were firm. He held her close. Oh, how she remembered his body and the way it curved and complemented her own! His mouth moved commandingly across hers. For just a moment Delia wanted to forget the hurt of their past and give in to the hunger that had always existed between them.

When Jake felt Delia stop fighting him, he smiled against her lips. It wasn't a victory. He wanted a win-win situation for them, as it used to be, as it could be again. Her lips were full and soft.

As he grazed them gently they parted. A groan rose in him as he felt her arms coming up across his shoulders. Yes, this was more like it. This is what they'd shared so hotly between them two years ago.

Moving one hand through her silky strands of hair, he tilted her head slightly and Delia leaned fully against him. The trust she gave him was incredible. Once more, she was vulnerable. It made kissing her, exploring her, even more wonderful. Jake knew if they were caught kissing, all hell would break loose. Reluctantly, he left her wet, gleaming mouth. As he did, he opened his eyes and drowned in the fire of hers.

"Like old times," he said, his voice rough with desire.

Delia wanted to fight back, but she couldn't. She did want to trust Jake once more. If only he would let her in, allow her a more intimate connection with him in other ways. That is what drove them apart. The wall he'd set up between them had never been dissolved. They were great in bed together, but that was all it was. Delia had craved the intimacy, but Jake had never been able to give it to her. Ultimately, it had driven Delia away from him.

"Damn you, Tyler."

He smiled a little as he released her. "It was good, Del. Just like before."

Pulling nervously at her sweater, she muttered,

"I know…." How would she make this work with him? How could she continue to resist his dancing eyes that told her he wanted her—physically if not emotionally. She wanted him, too. Somehow, Delia knew she had to suppress her personal urges and get on with this mission.

"Relax," Jake murmured. "We have each other's backs on this mission."

Nodding, she took in a ragged breath. Her lips tingled wildly. Looking up at Jake, Delia whispered, "Come on, we've got to get to the lab."

"Are you ready?" Athena called. She picked up the headband and gently settled it in place. Twenty feet away, encased in a glass cylinder, the two people she would send back to 44 B.C. sat relaxed in their chairs. They wore civilian clothes, but that would change once the process began.

"Ready," Delia called. Shaken by Jake's unexpected kiss, she could barely think.

"Ready," Jake echoed. He reached out and grasped Delia's hand. The love he held for this courageous woman was still there.

"Good," Athena murmured. She checked and made sure that the door to the small enclosure was locked. Outside, a bright red sign above the door said Do Not Enter.

She settled herself in the comfortable leather chair and put her feet up on the stool.

Athena had made sure that both of them had their armband on. As she sent them back, their clothes would automatically change to match that of the time period.

Glancing to the left, she noted General Ashton and her assistant standing at a console outside the area, both of them on alert. It was imperative that Athena not be jolted or her attention broken once she put on the headband. In order for the time jump to be successful, she could not be distracted. If that happened, the subject could end up in the wrong time or die in transit.

"Close your eyes," she told the team as she readjusted the headband. She could already feel the warmth of the stones and the powerful energy contained in them flowing into her brain like warm, comforting water. She closed her own eyes, confident that Ashton would be videotaping the entire jump session, the sensitive instruments on the console recording every brain wave and fluctuation. When the time travel process was complete, they would all know it. Athena always felt a tiny, painless jolt, heard a "ping" sound that alerted her that a successful jump had been accomplished. If the "ping" didn't occur, that meant her thoughts hadn't been totally focused. It was a fear that Athena lived with.

Leaning back in the chair, Athena drew several deep breaths, beginning to relax into a deep state of meditation. And then she felt herself opening up and connecting with the crystals. They were alive, it seemed to her—powerful, throbbing, sending tingling waves throughout her body.

Within seconds, she'd lost all sense of self and instead focused on seeing Delia and Jake moving back in time to 44 B.C., to meet Servilia, Julius Caesar's mistress. The more Athena honed in on that moment, mentally and emotionally, the more strongly the energy swirled through her. It was an organic process, a joining of her physical form and emotional intent with the laserlike power of the crystals, which now throbbed in unison with her brain waves.

Delia sat with her eyes closed, enjoying the sensation of warmth wrapping around her like a soft blanket. She knew it was due to the energy sent through Athena from the crystals. Since she'd made so many time jumps, Delia knew to relax fully into the building energy and surrender to it. Instantly, she felt a shift deep within her core. A sense of movement started, as if she were being physically sent through a tunnel, spiraling slowly. Logically, she knew that her physical body was changing state, becoming less dense, until she was nothing more than a cloud of energy particles. She felt neither hot nor cold, simply cocooned in warm energy as the transit continued.

Knowing she had to keep her mind blank and clear, so that no disturbing thoughts interfered with Athena's intense efforts to place them at the chosen time and place, Delia tried not to wonder about how they would appear in 44 B.C. Jake had a number of time jumps under his belt, so she felt confident he wouldn't interfere with this process, either. But it was always a possibility….

The spiraling was slowing down. Delia could feel a different kind of heaviness taking over, pouring through her, as she began to reassemble into a physical state in the targeted time frame. She gripped Jake's hand. It was an odd feeling. Odd, too, was the sensation of her mind expanding, as if her skull were too small for the amount of information downloading into it. She kept her eyes closed and tried to be receptive.

Next came the awareness of different clothing, a heaviness across her shoulders that had not been there before, and finally movement beneath her. It felt as if she was riding a horse, that was plodding along at a slow pace.

Sounds began to emerge from the depths of the silence. Horses hooves on cobblestones. The snort of one of the animals. And then the temperature changed—it was chilly. A cold gust of wind brushed Delia's face. She almost opened her eyes, but it wasn't time yet.

Remaining relaxed, she focused on the swaying movement of the horse between her legs, felt its thick winter fur against her calves. Finally, she heard the pinging sound that always happened when a transit was complete.

Instantly, Delia opened her eyes. It was important to orient immediately to her surroundings. Looking left, she saw Jake riding a black horse next to her. She was astride a bay gelding. They were no longer holding hands. A part of her cried out for the loss of contact.

The world opened up around them. They were on a thirteen-foot-wide road made of smooth black basalt cobblestones. The Via Appia, Delia realized, one of the main Roman roads that led southward from Rome, to the strategic port of Brundisium, on the "heel" of the boot of Italy. A massive stone aqueduct paralleled the road, transporting fresh water to Rome for the citizens' baths, gardens and fountains.

Looking at Jake, she saw he was dressed in a

leather helmet with a crest of horsehair, dyed blue, atop it like a brush. He wore, as she did, a hardened leather breastplate held in place with straps across the shoulders.

"Okay?" he asked as they guided their horses along the empty road. The Latin came easily to him, another sign that the jump had been completely successful. Delia silently blessed Athena and her laserlike ability to focus.

"Okay," she murmured in Latin. Looking at herself, Delia saw she wore a rough brown woolen tunic that fell to her knees. The long-sleeved garment kept her warm this cloudy, wintry day in southern Italy. Knee-high leather boots kept her lower legs and feet cozy. Glancing back, she saw a round shield of beaten bronze hanging at the rear of her saddle. It was important to know she was armed, and she reached to her waist in search of weapons. A sword and scabbard hung at the side, swinging with the gait of her horse. Good, she had protection.

Further investigation revealed a dagger in a small sheath tucked into her thin leather belt. Delia longed for a handgun, but knew it wasn't possible to bring one back in time without raising suspicions. Touching her head, she felt the clipped horse's mane on top of her own helmet, standard headgear for a Roman soldier.

"We're Greek mercenaries!" Jake stated, unable to keep a note of wonder from his voice. He looked around at the landscape—brown, desolate hills with naked trees standing starkly against a gray sky. The Via Appia curved ahead, disappearing around a bend. Looking behind, he saw no one coming. "We're thirty miles south of Rome," he noted, pointing to a small stone marker at the side of the road telling travelers how far they were from the city.

Delia nodded, continuing to take in her surroundings. It was midday, nearly noon. Her stomach grumbled and she felt hungry. In a cloth bag by her right knee was some food. "But where's Servilia? Why are we out here in the middle of nowhere?"

"Yeah, good question," Jake muttered, again searching the hills that rose on both sides of the highway. "Via Appia is a busy route. Why is this stretch empty? That doesn't make sense...." He knew the Appian Way was the oldest of many Roman roads. Appius Claudius had begun work on the famous highway in 312 B.C. "Hell, there should be foot traffic, chariots, wagons, Roman soldiers coming and going." Frowning, he halted his horse and studied the landscape. "Is it possible Athena screwed up in the transport? Wrong place and time to intercept Servilia?"

Shrugging, Delia halted her animal. It sawed

against the reins, trying to reach some sparse brown grass on the side of the road. "I heard the 'ping.' Did you?"

"Yeah," Jake said, adjusting his helmet. There was a strap to keep it in place. He wanted to remove the damn thing, but something cautioned him not to. "Pretty barren-looking, isn't it?"

"Not the Italy I know," Delia murmured, more in jest than anything else. "But it is winter. And Italy does get snow." She shivered and pulled her wool cloak tighter about her. The heaviness she'd felt on her shoulders was the weight of the cloak, she realized. It had been dyed marine-blue, the same color as the horsehair in their helmets. Jake had a shield that was similar to hers, almost a duplicate. Each one was hand beaten, obviously created by a smithy who knew weaponry.

A crow cawed in the distance. Jake looked toward a bunch of scraggly trees on a low hill to his left. "Well, we aren't in la-la land. There's another living beast," he said, gesturing to the noisy bird. It cawed again from its perch atop the hill, then flapped its wings.

"My gut tells me we're at the right place and time," Delia told him. She urged her horse to a faster walk. "Let's just keep going. Maybe we'll intercept Servilia on this road."

Jake nodded, and they rode side by side, their legs occasionally brushing. "Nice horses, huh?"

"Yeah. Well kept. Well fed. We must have some money."

"If we're mercenaries, we've been paid well," he said, pointing to a large leather bag of coins tied to his belt and hidden by his cloak. "At least we won't want for food and starve. That's a good thing." He grinned.

Laughing shortly, Delia muttered, "Always thinking of your stomach, Tyler." She was still thinking of that unexpected kiss Jake had initiated back at the lab. So was he, by the burning look he gave her each time their gazes met.

"Philip to you, dear Delia, my sister."

He was right, she had to get out of her twenty-first century way of thinking. "Okay, Philip. Funny, you don't remind me of a Philip."

Jake grinned. "Why, thank you, dear sister of mine."

"Oh, cut the crap, will you?"

He chortled quietly, then saw the ears on his gelding suddenly prick up. Both horses came to a halt, as if sensing something that was blocked from sight by the curve in the road. "Hey…" he called softly to Delia in warning.

"They're picking up on something," she whispered. And then she heard sounds of a battle, the scream of a woman. Automatically, Delia reached for her sword and drew it expertly out of the scabbard. Another benefit to this type of time travel was that Delia would already know how to wield a sword and fight with precision and skill.

"Servilia?" Jake asked as he gripped his own sword in his hand.

"I don't know!" Delia clapped the heels of her boots to the flanks of her gelding. "Let's find out!" The wind tore past her as the animal charged around the bend of the Appian Way.

Chapter 4

"Help me! Help me!" a gray-haired woman shrieked in Latin as she ran down the Via Appia away from a horse-drawn cart. Two men on foot chased after her.

Intuitively, Jake knew it was Servilia. The dark green muslin tunic she wore was nearly hidden by a cream-colored stola. The orange palla she had draped over her fashionable ensemble to ward off the winter chill flapped like wings around her as she tried to escape her pursuers.

"It's Servilia!" he shouted to Delia.

They rode side by side, the hooves of their

horses clattering sharply on the smooth stone road. A battle ensued around the rectangular wooden wagon drawn by two panicked gray horses. The driver was wounded and trying to keep the wild-eyed animals from running away. Jake counted six men attacking the wagon—well-outfitted robbers with plenty of weapons. All were on foot, but he suspected somewhere over the hill they had horses tied.

The patrician woman's small contingent of attendants were either dead, wounded or valiantly trying to fight in the melee. And now Servilia, who had escaped her fabric-draped cubicle in the wagon, was running for her life, the men closing in on her, swords raised.

Jake shouted to Delia, "Let's go! You get these guys, and I'll go after the woman."

"Right!" she replied.

Jake swerved his thundering gelding to the left. The tall, thin woman screamed again, her once-plaited hair streaming wildly around her face like Medusa herself as she fled. Abruptly, she stumbled, losing one jewel-encrusted leather sandal, but she kept on running.

The wind whipped by Jake as he raised his sword, heading toward the nearest robber, a thickset man with long, shiny black hair and an unkempt beard. His eyes narrowed, he was swinging his sword at Servilia, just as Jake reached him.

Leaning down, he engaged the robber, who stared up at him with a shocked expression on his face. Obviously, he hadn't expected Servilia's little band to have reinforcements.

Bringing down his arm with savagery, Jake struck at his opponent. The blade caught the man in the right shoulder, slicing through the thick black wolfskin cloak he wore. Jake heard him grunt. The weapon he carried clattered on the cobblestones, skidding away from his opened hand. He died where he fell.

One down and one to go. Jake yanked his gelding around, the horse skidding on the slippery surface of the road. Sparks flew from its iron shoes. The animal snorted, dug in with his hind legs and finally rebounded. Jake focused on the other robber, who had stopped, eyes bulging with surprise. Up ahead, Servilia continued to run, disappearing around the curve in the road and out of sight.

The second robber shouted a curse and ran in the opposite direction, leaping up a dirt slope covered with yellowed grass. He obviously wanted nothing to do with Jake and his charging horse.

Bringing his gelding to a sliding stop, he jerked his attention back toward the wagon. Delia had killed two of the ruffians, he noted, and the others were fleeing, scattering like startled crows up and over the hill. She was now riding swiftly to aid him.

Grinning triumphantly, Delia swung her mount around and galloped up the Via Appia after Servilia. She soon found the woman collapsed alongside the highway, her frizzled locks blowing in the wind like writhing snakes. Her face was chalk-white and her dark eyes huge and frightened after the trauma she'd just experienced.

Servilia was easily in her fifties, Delia guessed as she rode up and pulled her horse to a halt. Julius Caesar was probably around fifty-five, she recalled, though no one in modern times knew his exact birth date.

Delia sheathed her sword, slid off her panting horse and stretched her hand toward the woman, who was shaking badly. Jake dismounted and together they approached her. Servilia's head snapped up and she gripped the edges of her orange palla to her slim body. She had a beautiful gold-and-carnelian brooch pinned to the fabric to keep it around her shoulders.

"*Domina,* I am Delia of Delos in Greece. My brother, Philip, and I were riding together when we heard your screams. You are safe now. The robbers are either dead or fleeing. Are you all right?"

Delia removed her helmet, allowing the woman
to see that she was a female wearing a man's dress
and armor.

"By the goddess Diana," Servilia cried, looking
up at her, "you are a woman! This is extraordinary!
Apollo, who was born on the island of Delos, must
have sent you two to rescue me! This is truly a
miracle from Diana. Thank you, Delia and Philip of
Delos. You have saved my life." Servilia stood and
then drew herself up, her chin at an imperious angle.
"You do not know who I am?"

"No, *domina,*" Jake lied, "I do not. Whom do I
address?"

"I am the mistress of Julius Caesar. I am Servilia
Caepionis."

Her tone was haughty. Jake could see that even
though she'd narrowly escaped being hacked to
death by robbers, she was quickly gathering her
nobility around her once more. He admired the
heavy golden necklace Servilia wore, studded with
deep orange carnelian cabochons.

Playing along, he bowed deeply. "My sister and I
are honored by this chance meeting, my lady. We are
mercenaries looking for work as guards in Rome."

Wrapping the palla tightly around her, Servilia
studied them. "If you seek work, you are hired,
Delia and Philip of Delos. You have just saved my

life. Julius Caesar, Dictator of the Roman Republic, will be greatly indebted to you and your brother for doing so."

Jake nodded and stepped aside. He drew the reins over the head of his horse. "Shall we walk you back to your cart, my lady? Some of your men are wounded and we must tend to them."

"Yes, yes of course." Servilia quickly took the lead and walked rapidly around the bend of the Via Appia. "There is a rest station less than four miles back, only twenty miles from Rome. I was going to Pompeii, to my villa, but I won't now. I will return to my *domus* in Rome. We must get my personal physician alerted and bring my loyal slaves the medical help they deserve."

"As you wish, my lady."

Servilia glanced at them speculatively. "I am hiring both of you to guard me from now on. You will be well paid, I promise."

With a deep bow, Delia murmured, "We are indeed blessed by your bounty, *domina*. Thank you." As she straightened, she saw Jake's sword dripping with blood from the robbers, and with his features taut, his eyes narrowed, he looked every inch a warrior.

If only Servilia knew who they really were! How amazed she would be! Of course, that couldn't happen.

Servilia seemed to take a long time assessing Jake, but he was a damned handsome man no matter what era he was in or what costume he wore. Delia tried not to smile. Jake Tyler had charisma to burn, and the fact wasn't lost on the Roman matron.

Servilia walked to her wagon. Her Thracian driver had a sword wound on his thigh, but claimed he was capable of driving her back to Rome. In his forties, the man had wisely torn a strip from his dark brown tunic and wrapped the wound to stop the bleeding. Servilia slipped back into her imperious ways and ordered Philip to help her other two male slaves, who had more serious wounds, into her wagon.

Delia tied her horse to the rear of the cart, noting the expensive, dark green fabric stretched over the top and down one side. She helped Jake load the two men into the conveyance. The space was padded with thick blankets and a mattress filled with sheep's fleece. There were colorful silk pillows strewn about to make the ride as comfortable as possible for Servilia. The fact that this powerful and aristocratic woman would give up her quarters for her injured slaves said something good about her in Delia's estimation.

Jake was attending to the men, wrapping their bloody wounds with strips torn from one of the blankets in the cart. With all this commotion, he wouldn't have time to try to read anyone's thoughts, Delia knew. She watched Servilia climb gingerly up on the wagon and sit next to her driver.

"Delia," the woman called, "I want you to ride ahead to my house in Rome, as fast as you can." She slipped a ruby ring from her fourth finger and held it out. "Take this ring. My physician, Alkaios the Greek, is at my *domus*. Tell him what happened, and instruct him to prepare a room for my wounded slaves. He will know what to do. This ring will give you entrance through the nearest gate to the city, which is heavily guarded by Roman soldiers. It will help you in every way. Everyone recognizes the jewel Julius Caesar gave me on my birthday years ago."

Taking the ring, Delia tucked it carefully into a leather pouch tied to the belt at her waist. "I will, *domina*," she promised.

Delia saw the woman's gaze drift speculatively to Jake. Yes, she wanted the handsome soldier of fortune. Did this powerful woman have plans for him other than simply as an escort and bodyguard back to Rome? A feeling of jealousy niggled at Delia.

She was mounting her horse when Jake emerged from the cart a final time, done binding the wounds of the two slaves. As he approached his own horse, she rode up to him.

"You have an admirer," she whispered. "Servilia

is eyeing you like a hungry wolf." Settling the
helmet back on her head, she grinned as Jake's eyes
grew wide with surprise. "When in Rome, do as the
Romans do," she reminded him with a chuckle.
Then, growing serious, she told him about Servilia's
orders.

"As soon as I'm done in Rome," Delia added,
"I'll ride back out and meet you."

Jake nodded. "Good." He glanced to where
Servilia sat with her head held high, shoulders back,
her gray hair still hanging in a tangled mess around
her thin, aristocratic face. "So, I'm stud muffin
material, eh?"

Giggling softly, Delia said, "Yeah. They want
your body no matter what their age." Her smile
broadened. "Hey, she told me to take off for Rome."
Lifting her hand, Delia said, "I'll see you in a few
hours. We're hired by her, and now we're on track."

Gripping her wrist, Jake murmured. "You okay?"

His obvious concern shook Delia. Quickly, she
jerked her arm away. Trying to ignore the heat
flooding her body, the tingles his fingers had left,
she muttered, "Well, of course I am!"

An impish grin spread across his perspiring
features. "You fought well."

"As if I wouldn't?" Delia snorted. "Give me a
break!"

Laughing heartily, he shrugged. "Hey, you wielded that sword like a natural. I'm impressed."

"That would be a first." Yet Delia couldn't help but smile in return. She had always loved Jake's deep, rolling laughter. And the way his eyes often danced with merriment. She wondered if he would ever stop being a terrible tease, but knew the answer to that.

The tense, dangerous meeting with Servilia had them both on an adrenaline high. Professor Carswell had picked a helluva way for them to meet this woman.

"Well," Jake whispered, pulling his horse alongside Delia's, "I'll keep my hands off her. My target is *you.*"

Giving him a dirty look, Delia held her mount to a standstill. "Dream on, Tyler. It won't ever happen."

She saw his sensual mouth pull into a boyish grin, threatening to melt her pounding heart. Jake was well-meaning, but he always wanted to dominate her. And he had once more, at the lab. The look in his eyes told Delia he wasn't going to forget that kiss. Neither was she.

Turning her horse toward Rome, she said in Latin, "Later…"

As Delia and Jake approached with Servilia's cart the wooden gates of Servilia's home, she admired the six-foot-high brick wall around the property. Servilia lived on a crowded street lined with dwellings and shops for as far as the eye could see. Foot traffic, lumbering oxen carts, Roman cavalry and the occasional horse-drawn chariot speeding by all created a sense of vibrant life in this powerful city.

Delia stepped through the gates, which had carved upon them an effigy of the huntress Diana holding a bow and arrow. Beyond the vestibulum, or entrance, was an airy atrium. On one plastered wall was painted a garden scene of a white marble bird bath surrounded with flowers and greenery. The space was fragrant with the smell of bread baking in the kitchen at the rear of the house, and Delia realized how hungry she'd become.

Servilia left the cart once inside the gate. She walked up to them. "You will be given an *insula,* apartment, here in my town house," Servilia told them. She gestured around the atrium, which was covered by a red-tiled roof except for one rectangular area in the center. That opening allowed rainwater to collect below in the impluvium, a sunken stone basin that caught the precious liquid and channeled it to a cistern beneath the tiled floor.

Delia saw the house manager, a thin man in a dark blue tunic, come forward and bow deeply to his mistress. He had an olive complexion, black hair and brown eyes. Servilia quickly introduced the man, then ordered him to prepare a meal for them. Nepos murmured assent, bowed and quickly walked from the atrium to another part of the rambling, single-story home.

Servilia led them to a large main room, and almost at once Delia could feel a welcome warmth from the central heating she knew ran below the mosaic-tiled floor. Everywhere she looked were frescoes depicting the goddess Diana. One showed the huntress running with a stag, a dog at her heels. Another celebrated Diana with her women as they danced around a bush of holly with red berries.

Tucking their helmets beneath their left arms, Delia and Jake stood patiently and at relaxed attention in front of the powerful Roman woman.

"I cannot ever repay you two for saving my life, but I can give you the employment you seek," Servilia told them. "You did not have to rescue me. You could have sided with those thieves and robbed me." She held up her right arm, which was adorned with several thick gold bracelets. And the gleaming ruby ring was once more in place on her finger. "Instead, you protected me and helped my slaves. In Rome, we honor those who have honor. You are freemen from Greece.

And you are obviously well educated and can read and write in several languages."

Delia glanced at Jake. She had a feeling Servilia had questioned him on the way into Rome, finding out all sorts of things about them. She watched him smile and nod at the aristocrat, and Servilia gave him a look of raw longing that said plenty. Jealousy again rose up in Delia. How could Jake find anything appealing about this thin Roman matron whose hair was now fixed in a makeshift chignon at the nape of her neck?

Bowing, he murmured, "*Domina,* we live to serve you. We will die to keep you safe. Your generous allowance of one gold aureus a month is more than we ever dreamed of receiving for our services."

"Yes, well…" Servilia sniffed, taking a gold cup filled with red wine from a red-haired, white-skinned slave called Jura. "You will find me a generous patron, Philip. After all, it was you who saved my life." She took a sip of the warm mulled wine and lifted her hand to another slave standing near the doorway to the room. "Come, let us drink to this new alliance in the tablinum, the dining room."

Once there, Delia and Jake accepted silver goblets of wine from Jura, who nervously served them. Delia felt sorry for the young woman. She appeared to be of Britannic or Germanic origin, her red hair drawn into one long braid down her back. Delia saw several scars reminiscent of whiplashes across her lower arms, the only part of her not covered by her light blue tunic. What had this woman endured? Had Servilia had her whipped for some slight mistake? Delia didn't know, but thanked her for the wine. The slave looked shocked that she would even deign to speak to her.

Sipping the wine, Delia relished its fine quality, and enjoyed the herbal flavors it contained. The concoction warmed her, and Delia drank it fairly hastily. She was tired now, and dusk was darkening the sky above the atrium. Delia longed for a hot bath, clean clothes, food and sleep, in that order. After a time jump, she always needed more sleep for a day or two, to adjust to the energy transit.

Servilia sat at a long, rectangular cedar table, while they stood nearby. There was a silver dish with yellow cheese on it, and another holding fragrant, freshly baked bread. A knife lay nearby. Several more painted scenes on the plaster walls showed the huntress Diana, one with her horse and her dogs, one of her worshipping the full, silvery moon in an inky sky.

Servilia seemed pleased that her new guards quickly drank the mulled wine. "My physician prescribes this particular herbal wine to me when I'm under stress. It makes me sleepy and I always have pleasant dreams that night."

She looked toward the door, where an older woman stood waiting. "Geta is my head house-keeper. Geta, I want you to take my new guards to their apartments. See that they want for nothing. Alert Nepos to prepare baths for them. My best food from the kitchen is to be shared with them afterward. Nothing is too good for them, for they saved my life today. Take their clothes and have them washed and cleaned. Make sure they have fresh tunics and cloaks from my stores."

"Yes, *domina*," Geta said with a broad smile, "it shall be done."

Jake bowed to Servilia. "My lady, we thank you for your generosity. We never expected such gifts."

Servilia glowed, looking twenty years younger after hearing his gruffly spoken words. She obviously enjoyed such praise, and Jake resolved to use that fact to find out what made this woman tick.

"It is not out of generosity, Philip of Delos. It is that I owe you my life. What is a life worth?" She opened her hand and gestured around the room. "Caesar himself will hear from my own lips of your daring, your morals and courage. That I promise. He always rewards those who fight to protect the innocent.

"Tomorrow, you will sup with me here in the dining room. I bid both of you good-night."

Delia bowed and murmured a few words to Servilia, then followed Jake out of the room. The slave led them through the interior of the house, the peristylium, where bedrooms, a bath and a culina, or kitchen, were located. There was such beauty in the softly glowing walls where braziers strategically offered light as night fell, reflecting off the cheery yellow-painted plaster.

Their apartments were located on the left side of the peristylium, at the rear of the sprawling home. Servilia's rich abode sat below a hill where the temple of Diana stood. To the south was the Circus Maximus.

Delia always found that time jumping excited her as nothing else could. To ride past the vaunted arena and see it in its prime had stolen her breath. Truly, this particular building showed off Roman ingenuity and an understanding of engineering not matched in earlier ages.

Once they'd been shown their apartments, they quickly discovered that an inner door linked the two. Jake knocked on it and entered Delia's chamber. The portal was made of cedar, hand-smoothed and decorated with bronze figures of Greek athletes wrestling.

"Hey," he called softly. Delia was sitting on a couch that would double as her bed, removing her leather armor. Jake liked the way her coarse brown tunic bared her lower legs and showed off her breasts beneath it. His hands recalled holding her breasts, feeling their warmth, their incredible sensitivity, those nipples tightening beneath his thumbs.

Swallowing hard, he decided this wasn't the time or place to recall such things. Delia's brown hair shone in the light of a nearby brazier. Flickering shadows highlighted her beautiful face.

In front of the couch was a woven rug of burgundy and gold. Thick drapes in similar colors hung across one wall, and Jake suspected they held the warmth in the room. A tapestry hung on another wall, the scene extolling nature and wild animals. All helped to keep the space pleasantly comfortable.

Delia sat up and pushed her fingers through her hair after divesting herself of her armor. The curls bounced right back into place. "Hat hair," she griped. Jake looked too damn good in that brown wool tunic, girded with a thick leather belt studded with brass. His umber-colored hair was cut short, just as the Roman legions had theirs shorn.

Trying to ignore how her heart was pounding because of his unexpected entrance, she met his gaze. Did anything ever wipe that smile off his face? Delia thought not. Still, heat riffled through her body, especially her breasts, where his eyes had hotly lingered. Damn his masculinity. Why couldn't she remain immune to him?

"We're in," Jake said quietly. He switched to English, which wouldn't be understood by a slave who might be eavesdropping outside the door. Sitting down beside her, he ran his hand over the fabric. "Silk. Impressive. The rich lived well in Rome, didn't they?"

"Yes," Delia agreed, leaning against one curved side of the couch. She drew her legs up beneath her. "This *domus* is beautifully appointed and shows Servilia's power and wealth. But then, she's been Caesar's pet for how many decades? He was known to be generous to those loyal to him."

Nodding, Jake looked around the spacious apartment. There were ebony chairs upholstered with gold-and-burgundy fabric here and there. An ebony table had an exquisite mosaic of the head of the goddess Diana.

"I managed to get into Servilia's mind a little," he confided quietly.

"Really?" Delia sat up and curved her arms around her drawn-up legs. "What did you access?"

Grimacing, Jake said, "Nothing about the stamp. But she's angry as hell about that attack."

"How so?" Delia couldn't keep the surprise out of her voice. "I wonder if Servilia had a falling out with the dictator of Rome."

"Well," Jake offered, giving her a slight smile, "it's complicated. Servilia thinks Queen Cleopatra, who is here in Rome with Caesar's son, initiated and planned the actual attack against her. Servilia is green with jealousy toward the Egyptian queen, who is only twenty-one years old. Servilia wonders if Julius approved Cleopatra's sending brigands against her."

"Turf war," Delia murmured, nodding. "So, do you think the queen set Servilia up?"

Jake shrugged. "I don't know. But Servilia has demanded that Julius visit her tomorrow, to get answers."

Rubbing her hands, Delia said, "Wow, we get to meet *the* Julius Caesar! That's exciting!"

"Yes, it is." Jake continued to study her in the muted light, which accented her face lovingly. He ached to reach out and slide his hand across her high cheekbone, feel the warmth and firmness of her skin. Forcing himself to focus, he added, "I'm sure Servilia will give Caesar an earful tomorrow. Whether or not she'll accuse Cleopatra remains to be seen. Servilia has to be careful not to alienate the emperor. If she does, he might leave her and never return, and she couldn't stand that. She doesn't want to drive him completely into Cleopatra's arms."

"Yes, that's true." Delia shook her head and tried to ignore Jake's nearness, which was proving impossible. His face was cast in shadows, and his beard, which was starting to grow in, made him look dangerous and sexy. No wonder Servilia was drawn to him. Hell, Delia was, too, but knew better than to go there…or did she?

"I did get one piece of information from her thoughts, though," he said with a frown. "She's going to the temple of Diana tomorrow night. She wants you to go with her. There was something about a secret meeting of powerful and influential Roman women that would take place there."

Raising her brows, Delia said, "Could it have to do with the stamp, do you think?"

"Hard to tell. But I got the sense that this clandestine meeting is important. And that Servilia is the high priestess of whatever ritual is scheduled."

"That could be our clue. Maybe it does somehow involve the relic we're looking for."

The two of them gazed at each other thoughtfully.

"Are you okay?" Jake asked at last, studying Delia intently. Her gold eyes were bruised-looking and he knew she must be exhausted. He wanted to take her into his arms, but stopped himself.

"Tired. Hungry. Wanting that hot bath," she grumbled good-naturedly. "How about you?" Seeing the warmth in his blue eyes, Delia felt her heart expand with quiet joy. As much as she'd fought taking this mission with Jake, she found herself secretly glad he'd come along.

Good thing he wasn't reading her mind! Delia would know instantly if he tried such a thing, which would be beneath him, anyway.

"My hand is bruised from swinging that sword," he admitted, flexing his fingers. "I'm not used to that kind of workout."

"I dunno," Delia said, "you look in pretty good shape to me." Instantly, she regretted her throatily spoken words. Jake was clearly surprised by her compliment, and she saw a wicked gleam come into his eyes. "Now, don't even *think* that was an invite, Tyler, because it wasn't."

"No?"

"No."

"Damn, you are such a tease, Del."

"I didn't mean to be. The words just popped out of my mouth. I'll be more careful next time around."

"Don't be. I like that you still see me as sexy."

"That's in the past, playboy. It's been over between you and me for two years. Finished. Done. The end."

Chuckling darkly, Jake stood up and rested his

hands on his hips. "You're *such* a liar," he declared, gazing down at her blushing features. "But I like you despite that trait."

"Get out of here, Tyler. You're so full of yourself I can't believe it."

"Well," he sighed, a grin playing at the corners of his mouth, "Servilia certainly finds me manly." He flexed his biceps. "Reading her mind, I know she wants to invite me to her bed. But she's got other fish to fry, like Caesar and Cleopatra, first."

"Must make your ego feel good that you're right up there with a dictator and royalty," Delia mocked. Jake was a magnificent specimen of a man, no matter what age he hailed from. And he knew it. He also knew how to make a woman sing with utter bliss as his hands and lips ranged knowingly across her body....

Slamming the lid shut on the memory of the many times they'd made love, Delia gave him a fierce scowl. "Get the hell out of here, Tyler. I'll see you tomorrow morning."

"How about a little peck on the cheek? A good-night kiss?"

"I can't believe how brazen you are." Her voice rose a notch. "We're brother and sister, in case you forgot our cover story. What if a slave walks in unannounced and finds you kissing me?"

Laughing, Jake said, "Romans would think nothing of it. They had very pliable morals when it came to sex, in case you didn't know."

Her mouth flattening, Delia growled, "Leave. Now."

"Sure?"

"Tyler, you are pushing the limits."

"Okay, okay." He leaned over and caressed her jaw, so naturally Delia didn't even see it coming. They had been lovers for two years. The best years of Jake's life, if he wanted to admit it, but his ego wouldn't let him go that far. Fingers burning from contact with her soft flesh, he straightened and saw the shock flare to life in her gold eyes. "But you'll be in my dreams tonight, my Greek goddess…."

That did it. Delia found herself moving into his arms. There was no mockery in his eyes, just hunger—for her. She slid her arms around his waist.

"I'm jealous, Jake. I see how Servilia looks at you."

Thrilled with her response, Jake wrapped his arms around her shoulders. "The only woman I have eyes for is you. Didn't that kiss back at the lab tell you that? Two years might be between us, but what we have never died. You know that."

Shrugging, Delia murmured, "I seesaw back and forth with you, Jake. I want you, but I want the intimacy, too. All you want is the good sex we

share, but not the emotional sharing, the intimacy."
She saw his eyes darken. It was his past that had
made him wall up and never be available to her in
an emotional sense. Delia had held out hope for two
years that he'd eventually dissolve those walls and
let her in. But he never did. Would this mission
help him do that? She didn't know.

"Even if you see me as a goddess," she whispered,
reaching up and grazing his cheek that now needed
to be shaved, "I want to see the man you are. *All* of
you, Jake. Someday, I'd like to share what you hold
in your heart for me...." She pushed up on her toes
and connected with his mouth. Her world halted and
warmed beneath the strength of his arms as he crushed
her against him. The air rushed from her. His hand
moved through her hair in a gentle, searching motion.
How Delia ached to love him—all of him. The com-
manding strength of his mouth took hers. And she sur-
rendered to Jake just as she always had. The past was
now her present. As she kissed him eagerly, Delia
realized that what they shared in the past was back—
just as steamy, raw and intense as before.

As his hand moved down across her tunic to
caress her breast, she moaned. Tearing her mouth
from his, she stepped out of his arms. "Jake..."

Breathing raggedly, he rasped, "If we weren't
here..."

"I know," she said, her voice hauntingly low with desire.

Looking around, he wrestled with his desire. Mouth tingling, the taste of Delia on his lips, Jake gave her a long, intense look. "I'm not promising to keep my hands off you any chance I get on this mission, Del."

"We can't allow our feelings to compromise the mission. You know that."

Nodding, Jake forced himself to move away from her. If he didn't, he was going to lift Delia up into his arms, carry her over to that bed and keep her a prisoner within his arms all night long. "I know. And I agree. Mission first."

Chapter 5

Centaurian Constellation

"My lord Kentar," said a male voice from Centaurian Central Command, "we are picking up variations in the time sine waves in the fourth quadrant of our galaxy."

Kentar stood in front of his wall of computers with two male assistants. He scowled, his black brows dipping into a V of displeasure.

"I see," he murmured as he pressed the glistening screen, which popped and moved with images from around the galaxy where his constellation of

Sagittarius was located. Only his kind, the Centaurians, had the Navigator genes enabling them to wear the headband and journey back and forth in time. They could also fold time to allow instant movement of ships throughout the galaxy in the blink of a humanoid's eye. No one could time travel without a headband. And there were no authorized Navigators in that region. "Which system?"

"My lord, it is Section 504.2. A solar system with a small yellow sun surrounded by nine planets. The disturbance is coming from the third planet. According to my research data, it is inhabited by primitive humanoids."

Brows knitting even further, Kentar brought up the solar system on the wall screen. "They call it Earth."

"Yes, my lord."

Looking at the data quickly downloading onto the massive screen, Kentar groaned. "This is where we lost that Navigator headband, isn't it?"

"Yes, lost in a crash on a desert on one of their continents in 1947 A.D., by their time. There was a mission to capture fifty Earth women, but it failed due to the crash."

Rubbing his square chin, Kentar studied the time ripple information. "Someone is utilizing that headband without our approval."

"Yes, and it's not the first time, my lord. The other occurrences were so swift that we couldn't lock onto the energy of the headband to get real-time data. Since then, we've reset the sensitivity of our scanner, and caught him in the act."

"I see the thief sent a person or persons back to 44 B.C., to a place called Rome in their Earth history. They managed to be successful in doing it. Julius Caesar was an emperor at that time."

"Yes, my lord. It's our first real opportunity to follow the energy on this time jump."

Smiling slightly, Kentar nodded. "Indeed it is." He knew that whoever was using the headband had the rare Navigator DNA required to work with this prized and precious device. Few peoples and cultures outside the Centaurians had that gene, but sometimes one or two humanoids would show up with it dominant. Kentar, as band stallion of his culture, made sure one of two things happened. His DNA allowed him to be immortal. Only his genes allowed that possibility among the Centaurian civilization. One day, when he was ready to relinquish his leadership, he would will himself to die and one of his handpicked sons would take over. But that time wasn't now. Once found, such a humanoid either agreed to work for the Centaurian Federation, or was killed, to stop the potential passage of the special gene outside of Centaurian control.

"Do you want me to authorize a time jump to that planet by one of our Navigators? To have him go undercover and find out who has the missing headband, my lord?"

"Send Torbar Alhawa of the Desert Horse Clan. He's had Earth missions before. Get Torbar as close as possible to the alien time-jump target zone. We can communicate with him when he checks in with command. We'll identify the time jumper and trace him or her back to whoever has our lost headband." Rubbing his long fingers together, he said with pleasure, "And then, we can finally retrieve what is ours." It was to Kentar's undying shame that the device had been lost on a mission he'd initiated. No one wanted that black mark erased from his family's name more than he.

"Yes, my lord. I'll get the mission underway immediately."

Kentar went to his desk. His office was at the top of a thirty-story glass structure held aloft with gleaming silver metal from the mines of the Taurean constellation. The day was bright, the sun making the sky a kelly-green color. Two moons were slowly rising in the west above the Centaurian city of Pegasus.

On his desk computer he quickly sifted through information about Earth. Historically, a Navigator assigned to guide a Centaurian cruiser had chosen to get a closer look. He had taken one of the small saucer-shaped launches and entered the atmosphere of that planet, planning to check on female humanoids, who had strongly exhibited the genetics needed to operate the organic headband. The energy connection between it and the person became as one and therefore, organic. The Navigator was to steal fifty females and bring them here, to the Centaurian capitol, for testing.

"Didn't work back in 400 B.C.," Kentar muttered, checking the ancient mission notes. Centaurians were always looking for other species possessing paranormal genes to work with time travel. They had discovered in 10,000 B.C., on a routine mission to test humanoids in this quadrant of the galaxy, that females of Earth possessed such DNA. And in 400 B.C., a mission was launched to verify the fact. They had captured a hundred Earthlings and brought them back to Pegasus, to work with in their scientific laboratory.

"Bunch of animals," Kentar growled unhappily to himself. The females were wild, violent, ignorant, and fought the Centaurians. They refused to work with them or even allow the vaunted Navigator band to be placed on their heads for trials and scientific tests. In the end, they had to be slaughtered and burned.

Unfortunately, the Galactic Council got wind of the covert mission and Centaurians had been penalized as a result. According to the rules of the Galactic Council, no one could extract members of a species from their world for transport to another without approval.

Rubbing his chin, Kentar continued to frown as he reviewed other missions that had been initiated in order to keep tabs on Earth's evolving humanoids. His people kept secret why they'd kidnapped the Earthlings. The council thought they wanted them as slaves and nothing more. If word ever got out that Earth females possessed the Navigator gene, it could mean the end of Centaurian power.

Band stallion leaders through the centuries had carefully kept silent about their find to the Galactic Council, of which they were a powerful member. In order for them to remain the prime traders, the Navigator headband had to be zealously guarded, available only to their species. The potential of Earthling females was a dangerous secret they harbored; if word ever got out, their empire might crumble.

Oh, it was true, Kentar sourly acknowledged, that populations of one or two other constellations might possess a genetic anomaly, and a humanoid would sometimes be born with the DNA required to work with the headband. In those cases, Centaurian spies traveling throughout the galaxy found these rare beings and urged them to join and be trained by the Centaurians. Most did, because it meant high status in the federation, great wealth and a chance to operate an organic spaceship responsive only to a Navigator. Those who didn't died in mysterious circumstances, their killers never found.

These trading vessels plied the entire galaxy by warping in and out of the time sine waves, orchestrated by the Navigator wearing the headband. The ship, with the help of the headband, connected with the Navigator's mind and desire. The organic melding between metal and human could only occur because of the combination of the Centaurian's specialized DNA. That was why Kentar kept a sharp eye out for recessive gene anomalies becoming dominant among other species. The Centaurians maintained a stranglehold on the commodity market of inner and outer space travel. As a result, every constellation in the galaxy had to hire a Centaurian Navigator if they wanted to be in the galactic trade business. Journeys by obsolete spaceships plying outer space could take years or even centuries to complete. With a Centaurian Navigator wearing a headband, they plied inner space, taking only a matter of minutes to go from one point in the galaxy to another.

Kentar saw his second in command, Charl, a promising young stallion in his forties, approach his desk. Charl's clan was the draft horse breed and he had the body of one: short, stocky and heavily muscled. His ancient family line hailed from the Belgian breed and he had the flaxen hair and chestnut-colored skin to prove it. "Yes?"

"My lord, this is an exciting discovery regarding that missing headband. Are you satisfied with sending Torbar? Perhaps you should go there yourself?" Charl knew the shame Kentar carried, from losing the headband on a mission he'd initiated. Charl saw this as a ripe opportunity to have his beloved leader boost his image among the populace. Who better to retrieve it than the lord of the band?

Kentar rubbed the back of his neck, considering the request. There was a thick ridge of flesh running from his hairline over his skull and down his spine to his tailbone. At one time in Centaurian history, millions of years ago, their horse ancestors had evolved into centaurs, half horse and half humanoid. Eventually, they'd become bipedal, their mane and tail atrophying to the point where only a ridge of thick, hard flesh reminded them of their equine roots. Across the galaxy, the trait identified them immediately as a Centaurian, for no other humanoid species had a similar feature.

"Perhaps, Charl," Kentar said thoughtfully. "Follow the mission for now. Let's see what Torbar can turn up in 44 B.C. If he fails, then I will consider going."

Bowing briskly, his assistant turned and went back to work at the massive screen. The galactic business of the Centaurians flashed continuously across it, posting orders, updates, departures and arrivals in foreign star systems.

Kentar's mind ranged back to the rebel on Earth who possessed their valuable Navigator headband. Torbar should be in position there tomorrow. What would he find?

Torbar Alhawa snapped the neck of General Marcus Brutus's chief scribe, Seuso. The man, a Greek in his late fifties, uttered a sharp cry and sank like a bag of grain onto the blue-and-white mosaic floor. When Torbar had materialized, the scribe had looked up from his table, surprise and shock on his clean-shaven face. Possessing strength superior to any Earthling, Torbar had stepped forward and killed the scribe.

Thanks to Navigator technology and the thin gold band he wore around his head, Torbar knew all he needed to know. Stretching Seuso's body on the floor near his chair, he arranged the scene to look as if the old scribe had fallen and broken his scrawny neck, thereby dying of natural causes.

Feeling a rush of satisfaction, Torbar straightened. In time jumps like this, he would often possess the body of someone close to the center of the action. When a second scribe came into the room moments later, Torbar immediately did so.

Settling into his stolen persona, Torbar quickly absorbed all he needed to know. Kapaneas was a scribe in Seuso's employ—the number-two scribe to General Brutus, who had served Julius Caesar for decades.

Flexing his long, veined hands, Torbar quickly left the well-lit room and called out in Latin for help. Instantly, two Roman Praetorians, guards who protected Caesar and his staff, came clanking down the hall in their hobnail boots. Their armor was of hardened leather; the helmets were red horsehair crests. Each man had drawn his gladius, the short sword that was his main protection.

"He's dead!" Torbar cried, pointing at the opened door. "I walked in and found Seuso dead!"

The guards hustled past him. Torbar stood in the semidark hall and smiled. He knew the drill: the guards would call General Brutus's physician, also a Greek, and he would pronounce the scribe dead.

Pulling his black wool cloak closer to his body

against the chill, wintry draft in the hall, Torbar headed toward Kapaneus's own apartment, located in the peristylium. In the morning, he knew, General Brutus would declare him his chief scribe.

As he went, Torbar kept his mind open and receptive. A Navigator had many paranormal talents, one being an ability to read minds. Torbar felt the messy turmoil of the Roman guards finding the scribe lifeless on the floor. And he sensed the thoughts of several slaves lingering nearby in the passageways, nervously waiting to be called. So, he wondered, what did General Brutus have to do with Julius Caesar and this lost Navigator headband?

Telling himself to be patient, which was not his forte, Torbar remembered he was in the forty-year-old body of a Greek scribe. The man was too thin, and pathetically out of shape, but Torbar would have to deal with it for now. Another Navigator talent was the ability to subdue the spirit of a person possessed. Torbar could read the scribe's mind and know what he knew, information that would come in very handy. And when Torbar finished his assignment and left Earth, returning to headquarters in the Centaurian constellation, the spirit of the Greek would come back, and the scribe would continue to live. However, Kapaneus would have no memory of

Torbar's residency in his body, or what had happened; it would all be a blank to him.

Yes, "possessing" was a unique quality that allowed Centaurians to maintain superiority in the galaxy. No one but a genetically advanced Navigator could accomplish such a magnificent feat. Again Torbar smiled.

Pushing open the wooden door of the scribe's apartment, he entered the warm room, brightly lit with braziers. What would tomorrow bring? Who had the headband? And more importantly, what person had made the time jump back here, and why?

"By the gods," Brutus snarled, "this is a curse!" Upset to learn his chief scribe had died of a stupid accident, he sat in the dining room scowling at his breakfast of warm milk, olives, goat cheese and bread. His slave attendants winced at the angry tone in his deep, thunderous voice.

The physician, Eusebios, nodded his balding head sorrowfully. "Not a curse, General, but old age. Seuso had complained lately of feeling dizzy, of the room whirling around him. He must have had a spell, then fell and broke his neck. I am sorry, my lord."

Brutus, who was dressed in a wheat-colored wool tunic and thick yellow cloak, glared at the Greek.

"So be it, Doctor." He lifted his chin and glanced toward Torbar, who sat in a corner of the room, ready to record whatever the general wished him to.

"Kapaneus?"

"Yes, my lord?" Torbar said, keeping his head bent respectfully.

"You will now be my chief scribe."

"As you wish. I live only to do your bidding."

Grimacing, Brutus waved the physician and the slaves away. "Leave us!"

Torbar waited patiently, the tools of his trade nearby. Clay tablets, pens to impress words into the soft material, sheepskin parchment all lay ready for use when the general so ordered.

"Kapaneus? Send a tablet to my mother, Servilia. Tell her I will attend her banquet." In a low growl, he added, "I doubt it will be a happy affair. She is furious over Queen Cleopatra coming to Rome with Caesar's only son. I don't know why my mother is doing this. Caesar has always wanted a male heir, and neither she nor any other woman could give him one. You'd think Servilia would understand this and stop begging to get back into Caesar's good graces in the bedroom. He has eyes only for his son and that bitch of a foreign queen."

Shrugging, Torbar murmured, "General, who knows what goes on in the minds of women?"

Laughing sharply, Marcus ripped off a piece of the warm brown bread and placed several bits of cheese upon it. "Indeed, Kapaneus. Women! They are a necessity for a man to warm his loins in, but little else, in my experience. You marry one and she becomes a shrew, telling you what to do or not to do. My own mother was practically Caesar's top general in Spain during the Punic Wars. She told him how to run his army and campaigns! By the gods, women should be born with stitches through their lips, don't you think?"

Torbar grinned beneath Kapaneus's black mustache and beard. "Oh, General, I favor young men, so I do not know. I find beautiful male youths to be far more palatable to my temperament, while happily warming my loins."

Laughing again, Marcus swallowed his bread, then drank the warm goat's milk from his goblet. "I think I'm going to enjoy having you as chief scribe, Kapaneus. You have a far better sense of humor than Seuso ever did."

"Thank you, my general. I'll get this tablet off within the hour to your mother, Servilia."

"Good, good. I believe our emperor is going to see my mother this morning, is he not?"

Torbar reached for a parchment and consulted it. "Quite so, General. He is going to thank two Greek mercenaries who saved your mother's life from those robbers yesterday."

Frowning, Marcus wiped his mouth with the edge of his cloak. "That attack bothers me. Who put those ruffians up to such a thing? My mother's conveyance clearly carries the standard of Caesar. Why would they risk death by attacking?"

Shrugging, Torbar said, "Stupidity among the poor, I suppose."

"I don't know…" Brightening, Brutus sat up and ran his hands along his tunic, across his massive thighs. "I will see them at the banquet for the emperor tomorrow night. I'll give them my thanks at that time."

"May I go with you, my general?" Torbar gave him a slight, obsequious smile, while mentally ordering the officer to agree to his request.

"What?" Brutus shrugged. "I did not know scribes enjoyed such boring, political events. You need not go. I won't require your services."

"But I'd *like* to go," Torbar insisted. His mission was to find the time jumper. And a banquet would be just the place to gather clues on the identity of the interloper. At least, that was what Torbar's finely honed intuition told him.

"Of course." And then Brutus gave a wicked laugh. "I know. You are lonely, without a youth. At such a party there will be many youths parading their wares."

Torbar let the general think what he wanted. "My first duty, my only duty, sir, is to you. All else pales beside my loyalty to your household."

Pleased, Marcus stood up. He rearranged the thick leather belt he wore, adjusting the dagger that hung on his left side, the gladius on his right. "You are making the loss of my old friend and scribe easy on me, Kapaneus. Thank you. And yes, do come with me to my mother's house. I doubt I can bear being there for more than an hour as she hotly pursues Caesar around the *domus* like a mare in heat."

Chuckling darkly, Torbar dipped his head and began writing on the parchment, adding this activity to the general's very busy schedule. Maybe these Earthling males weren't so bad, after all.

As he worked, his mind ranged forward. Caesar was going to see two Greek mercenaries this morning. Who were they? How did they happen to be on the Via Appia when Servilia's wagon was attacked? Sensing that was something to be investigated, Torbar reined in his impatience. Today, he had to orient himself, becoming completely familiar with this time, place and all the players. He had plenty to do until the banquet commenced.

Chapter 6

Jake spotted Delia in the hall outside her apartment the next morning. She was dressed in a pale blue wool tunic that fell to just below her knees. Even though the garment wasn't the utmost in feminine fashion, it flowed deliciously across her breasts and gently flared hips. Just looking at her made him hungry to have her all over again. He'd had torrid dreams last night of making hot, wild love with this woman.

As Jake approached, Delia looked in his direction. He smiled, enjoying the way her shoulder-length hair drawn into a ponytail at the nape of her neck emphasized the delicate curves of her oval face. The morning light flowing in from the atrium showed off her patrician nose and soft, full mouth.

Jake was lifting his hand in a silent hello when he was suddenly bombarded with mental images from an approaching party. As he reached Delia, he took her by the shoulder and hauled her against him.

Without a word, he slid his hand behind her head, leaned down and urgently placed his mouth upon hers. Instantly she splayed her hands against his chest and tried to push him away, but he didn't let her. There wasn't time for explanations. Jake took her mouth uncompromisingly.

"Stop!" he rasped against her mouth, when she tried to wriggle out of his grasp. "Servilia is coming!" And then he brought her fully against him.

In shock, Delia felt Jake's arms clasp her solidly against his tall, powerful frame, his mouth wreaking havoc on hers. Breathing hard, she forced herself to relax against him when she heard his rasped words about Servilia. Mind spinning from his unexpected move, Delia felt her body respond automatically to his deepening kiss. What did Servilia have to do with this? Why had Jake suddenly reached out and grabbed her…? Then she heard the brush of sandals crossing the tiled floor.

"Oh!" Servilia said, halting.

Jake heard the woman's surprised exclamation but pretended not to have noticed her approach. He continued to kiss Delia as if it was the last embrace he'd ever share with her. And it would be for now, he knew. She'd be angrier than a cobra, spitting venom at him the minute he released her. But right now, Jake needed her as cover.

Servilia raised her brows as she watched the brother and sister kissing hungrily in the hall. With a slight, twisted smile, she murmured, "Ah, well…" and turned away.

Jake heard Servilia leave. As soon as her footfalls had faded he released Delia.

"Jake!" she growled, yanking herself out of his arms. She wiped her throbbing lips. "What was that all about?" Never mind that she was breathing raggedly and her nipples were pressing against the rough weave of the tunic she wore, begging to be teased by him. Glaring at him, she saw regret in his eyes, along with a burning desire. Wiping her mouth again, she backed off. "What did you do that for? I thought we agreed that the mission came first!" she demanded harshly.

Jake held up his hand, put a finger to his lips and walked to the end of the hall. No one was there, no slaves lingering nearby. Turning, he walked rapidly back to where Delia was standing, her face taut with anger. Gripping her shoulder, he drew her close, his lips near her ear.

"I'm sorry, but I had to do that, Del. As I was walking toward you this morning, I mentally felt Servilia coming. She wanted to go to bed with me."

Delia shot him a withering glance. "And that's why you kissed me? So you wouldn't have to 'bed' that woman?"

Giving her a dark look, Jake growled, "Listen, we're here to find that fragment. I knew she wanted me, but thought it would pass. However, I picked up her intentions so strongly just now, I know she wasn't going to take no for an answer." He searched Delia's upturned face and noted her cheeks were flushed a bright red. Smiling slightly, he murmured, "Hey, it wasn't all that bad, was it? I haven't lost my touch, have I?"

Nostrils flaring, Delia stepped out of his grasp, hating this reminder of the past, of the delicious sex they'd shared joyfully with one another. "You're such a Neanderthal, Tyler!" Delia's tone softened. "I couldn't care less if Servilia wants you! We're done, you and me. Finished!" She didn't believe her words and she saw Jake didn't, either. Looking around him and down the empty hall, Delia shook her head. "Now she's seen *us* kissing! What will she think? We're supposed to be brother and sister, in case you forgot your cover!"

What a spitfire, Jake mused. Delia was all of that and more when she was backed into a corner. He lifted his hands. "We're in Rome, sweetheart. I minored in this period of history at university. Love between a brother and sister was accepted for what it was. Incest was alive and well in the ancient world, in case you forgot. I knew Servilia wouldn't think a thing of the morals of us kissing. I just wanted her to believe *you* hold my amorous interest and no one else. I think she got the message. She'll stop stalking me, and that's one less thing we have to deal with while we hunt for this fragment. Now do I make sense?"

Fuming, Delia nodded. "I see your point. But damn it, Jake, we have to concentrate on the mission!"

He managed a boyish smile. "Oh, come on, Del. Was it *that* bad? I've seen the look you give me from time to time. You *want* me. I want you. I'm going to take every chance I get to remind you of the two good years we shared."

Delia groaned and rolled her eyes. "Jake, that *is* the past. Yes, I like what we had. What I didn't like is you're locked up tighter than Fort Knox in an emotional sense. I want intimacy, not just good sex."

Jabbing him in the chest with her index finger, she added, "Get it in your head, Tyler, that I want this mission our priority. What you and I shared years ago is over with."

Breathing hard, Delia stepped away and wiped her mouth to stop it from tingling. *Such a lie!* she thought, but Delia made sure her defenses were in place so he couldn't possibly access her mind. Not that Jake would do so without her permission. Still, Delia visualized thick white walls of energy around her head every morning when she woke up, and reinforced the image again before she fell asleep at night. She wanted no one penetrating her thoughts.

"Excuse me," a young male slave called from the end of the hall. "Lady Servilia asks your presence in the tablinum."

Groaning softly, Delia gave Jake a glance and then looked past him to the young African boy dressed in a dark green tunic. "We'll be there shortly. Thank you," she answered.

The lad bowed and hurried ran off.

"Great, Tyler. Now she wants to see both of us," Delia sniffed.

Stepping away, he grinned. "I wonder if she's going to slap our hands for kissing?"

"This isn't funny!" Delia seethed, smoothing her tunic and rearranging her thin leather belt, which held her sword and dagger. "She's a woman of immense power, Jake. She can do anything she damn well wants. What if she's jealous now? She could fire us, or worse...."

"We're freeborn," he reminded her lightly. "And Romans know the difference between us and the slaves they keep."

Shaking her head, Delia swung down the hall, Jake on her heels.

"Stop worrying," he told her.

"What if Servilia decides to get even with us because of your idiotic maneuver?"

"I thought about that, but I very much doubt she will."

"Right," Delia breathed angrily, trying to get herself back under control. Slowing her pace as they turned a corner to the peristylium, Delia took a deep breath to compose herself. "If you're wrong, we could be in hot water."

"Hey, I did the best I could at the time."

"Just don't let it happen again, because next time, Tyler, I won't go along with it." She gave him a withering glare. "Until you feel you can trust me, share yourself with me—and I don't mean sexually only—there is no future for us."

"Yes, I got it. Now let's take a few more calming, deep breaths and see what Servilia is up to." Jake knew he locked Delia out. Hell, he'd locked the world out. Yet, as he kept pace with her, Jake grappled with wanting to grant her request. Was it possible to unlock and share his vulnerability with her? Jake wanted to, but he didn't know how to do it.

"I'm having a banquet tomorrow night," Servilia informed them. She sat on a wooden chair covered with gold silk fabric in the dining room. Two attentive Nubian males, both in their late teens, were serving her.

Delia stood next to Jake, at relaxed attention in front of her. "And I'm assuming you want us to guard you, *domina?*" she asked.

The gold and silver bangles on her thin wrist jangled pleasantly as she waved her hand. "Just be around. I want some private time with Julius, which is why I've created this banquet in his honor."

"Do you expect any trouble, my lady?" Jake asked.

Shrugging a shoulder, Servilia said, "We've never had any. The walls around my *domus* provide security from the general populace of Rome. While I live on a busy street, with the temples of Minerva and Diana nearby, my guards ensure no strangers or possible enemies can enter."

Jake wasn't so sure, but said nothing. "Then

we'll blend in, take walks around the grounds near the walls from time to time during the event."

"Do what you need to do," Servilia said, dipping her hands in a silver bowl. The other slave handed her a towel and she daintily dried her fingers. "I've thrown many banquets over the years and the only problem we have is with drunken senators who chase my slave girls and boys around, wanting to rut with them." She chuckled indulgently.

"I see," Jake said, keeping his voice nonjudgmental. He felt sorry for the slaves, who had no way to turn down the advances of a powerful senator. If they didn't allow the deed, they could be killed. Which was worse?

Frowning, he studied Servilia, who had a smirk on her painted lips as she met his gaze. He could feel the woman's amusement over him having Delia as his chosen lover. That was okay with him; at least Servilia would find her pleasure elsewhere.

"You may leave us now, Philip," the aristocratic woman said. "I want to talk to your sister alone."

He bowed and left.

Servilia stated, "There is a meeting at the Temple of Diana tonight, and I want you to attend with me." She gave Delia a long, sharp look. "Although I pay you to be my bodyguard, you will fill another role tonight."

Nodding, Delia said, "My desire is to please you, my lady. I will gladly guard you with my life, no matter where you go."

"Come, sit at the table with me. We must talk," she told her.

Delia sat in a chair near the matron's elbow. Folding her hands, she waited patiently for the older woman to speak.

"Do you belong to any secret society, Delia?"

Thrown off guard by the whispered question, she felt her eyes widen. "No, my lady, I do not."

"Good, good. And what do you believe?"

Delia treaded carefully, knowing she had to answer diplomatically. "My lady, I was born on Delos, the birthplace of Apollo. My family honors him with a statue in our peristylium." She saw Servilia's face lose a bit of tension.

"Are you more partial to gods or to goddesses, warrior woman?"

Seeing the blue of Servilia's aura change to silver, Delia instantly knew how to interpret that question. Silver was the color of the feminine, gold indicative of males. "My prayers are spoken to Diana the huntress, my lady. She of all the goddesses is a warrior like myself." Shrugging, she added, "So is Minerva, but my heart belongs to Diana."

"Just so," Servilia replied, looking pleased. "This is a very good omen."

Pink colors swirled in Servilia's aura and Delia knew her answer had been correct. She was glad the Roman matron couldn't hear her heart pounding inside her tunic. The reason Delia had mentioned Diana was because Servilia's villa was just down the street from that goddess's impressive white marble temple, atop the Aventine Hill. It was a matter of deductive reasoning. A temple to Minerva also sat on the slope. Delia felt either answer would have sufficed.

"I'm relieved," Servilia murmured, her thinned lips relaxing into a smile. Gesturing to a young female slave who waited nearby, she ordered, "Murena, bring us two goblets of Setinum. Now."

The slave quickly bowed and dashed off to fulfill her order.

"Do you know of Setinum, Delia?"

"My lady, I hear it's the finest of all wines produced in Rome."

"That it is. A very strong, sweet winter wine that comes from the hills of Setia."

Hearing the matron's approving tone, Delia added, "It is a very expensive wine, *domina*. Certainly not to be wasted upon the likes of me."

Servilia looked very pleased with her answer.

"Indeed, it is." Reaching out, she patted Delia's clasped hands. "Obviously, you know of Setinum. If you were poor or your family mere plebeians, you would never know of its value to us."

"My family," Delia lied, "are merchants in olive oil, my lady."

"Ah, that explains it," Servilia declared. "Should I know of your family?"

"No, my lady, we supply olive oil to the region. None of it is shipped to Rome. We are a small agricultural family, but are well off."

"Just so," Servilia replied. She smiled as the slave brought a tray bearing two golden goblets filled with red wine. Servilia handed one to Delia, and after the servant left, held her own goblet up in a toast. "To strong, powerful women. We must always band together."

Surprised, Delia nodded, touched the woman's goblet and then sipped the wine. It tasted good.

Servilia's aura now swirled with pink, silver and blue tones, indicating she was past whatever had caused her upset. Trying not to sound too curious, Delia said, "My lady, is there a special holiday to the goddess Diana here in Rome that I do not know of? Is that why you want me to accompany you tonight to this ceremony?"

Sipping the wine with obvious pleasure, Servilia

smiled. "You have not forgotten any ceremonies to our beloved Diana. No, this is a meeting of the strong and powerful women of Rome." She raised her chin and gave Delia an imperious look. "Do you know of Diana's arrow?" she asked in a low voice. "Do you know the legend of this magical object?"

Stymied, Delia shook her head. "My lady, the goddess is famous as an archer. She brings down stags with just one well-placed arrow."

"True." Servilia laughed a bit giddily as she drained her goblet. Setting it on the table, she leaned forward and whispered, "What if I told you there is an arrowhead the goddess has given us, and it has magic? That if you are in the same room with it, you feel the magnificent power that radiates from it?"

"I—well, my lady, I would believe you. But I did not know such an object existed." Delia's mind spun. Was this the fragment from the Karanovo seal? Unsure, she searched Servilia's narrowed eyes. They gleamed with laughter and triumph.

"I came into possession of this magical arrowhead through a woman historian from Pompeii. Her name will remain secret. It is enough to know the Cult of Diana holds this magical weapon."

"I see…." Delia knew she was talking about Argenta, who had written the *Ad Astra* journal.

"You do not, but you will." Servilia sat up and patted Delia on the shoulder. "Tonight, shortly after dusk, as a high priestess of our secret cult I will bring it out of hiding, and you will see its power."

"I shall be happy to go to Diana's temple with you."

Servilia looked at Delia's soldier garb. "I want you to wear women's clothing, a tunic with a palla. See my head seamstress and tell her to create one for you this morning."

Nodding, Delia murmured, "As you wish, *domina*."

Chapter 7

The gathering of Roman matrons from all over the city occurred after night had fallen. Delia stood behind Servilia, who was dressed in a dark blue tunic topped by a light blue stola. An oval brooch of lapis lazuli set in gold held the stola in place over her shoulder. Her hair had been curled and set with plaits at the back, a fashionable arrangement for a female aristocrat of Rome.

Delia herself was dressed in a pale pink tunic that fell to her ankles, and a cream-colored palla. Beautiful as the garments were, she felt naked without her sword and dagger nearby. Her hair, naturally curly, fell around her shoulders instead of being pulled back and clasped at the nape of her neck. Servilia had approved of her feminine apparel.

Delia tried to look relaxed and nonchalant in the group of women. The jewelry and fine fabrics they wore were rich and beautiful, the colors reminding her of a rainbow.

They stood in a small alcove off the main temple of Diana. The thick oak door was shut and only women of high rank were allowed entrance. There were more than twenty present and the room was filled to capacity. In the center was a small marble altar. Spread across the flat white stone was a gray wolf pelt. And upon it, wrapped in red silk, was something small and rectangular.

From her position behind Servilia, who was welcoming everyone with a smile, Delia studied the object. Whatever was wrapped in that red cloth was powerful. She could feel ripples of energy emanating from it, like small tidal waves. A silvery radiance throbbed around it like a small sun.

Delia reined in her curiosity when she saw Servilia turn toward her. Each matron had introduced herself, and now it was her turn to be recognized by the group. Delia realized that the older women in the room were wives or daughters of senators, or from old Roman families. Though they ranged in age from thirty to sixty, they all looked to Servilia as if she were a goddess herself. Clearly, Julius Caesar's mistress enjoyed her exalted position.

"And now," Servilia was telling them as she wrapped her bejeweled hand around Delia's upper arm and drew her forward, "you have heard how this young woman and her brother saved my life recently. I have asked Delia of Delos, whose family is in the olive oil business, to join us. Her line descends from Apollo. And she has agreed to join our clandestine efforts to bring power back to women and wrest it from the men, who daily steal it away from us. Delia?"

Stepping forward, Delia bowed and murmured, "May the goddess Diana bless all of us, *domina.* I live to serve her and you."

Murmurs of approval rippled through the gathering. Delia returned to Servilia's side. "Thank you for allowing me to be among you. I am a woman warrior, and proud of it," she declared. "I take advantage of who and what I am. When I decide to marry, it will be on my terms and conditions."

Applause erupted.

"And if I decide to bear a child, I will pray to Diana that it be a girl."

The women shouted passionately.

Servilia smiled smugly as she turned to her friends. "Did I not tell you that Delia of Delos would be a fine addition to our society? Does she not come straight to the point, like the goddess Diana's arrowhead?" Servilia laughed with delight.

The women agreed, voicing their praise and approval.

For a moment, Delia felt the warm camaraderie of the matrons. Servilia had gathered the most powerful women in Rome into this small, cloistered room lit with four braziers. Too bad no one in history knew of her feminist movement or that she'd been leader of a matriarchal revolution.

Glancing at the altar, Delia saw the red-wrapped ceremonial item glowing more brightly. It had become ever more responsive to the women and their emotions. Now, it positively gleamed, shooting out rays of energy from the red silk fabric it was wrapped within. Whatever was in there was palpably felt by all the eager participants. Delia was absorbing waves of energy, and obviously so were all the others, for their collective gazes were locked on the small altar in the center of the room.

Servilia looked up. "Lock the door," she demanded throatily.

A younger priestess turned and shot the brass

bolt across the door. The sound reverberated throughout the room.

"Our ceremony has now begun," Servilia intoned, her voice cracking with emotion. "Let us women, who are the real power, touch the goddess Diana's arrowhead and allow it to imbue us with another month's blessing...."

The songs of the women gathered in the temple of Diana were low and passionate. The fragrances of rose and myrrh filled the dimly lit room.

When the singing stopped, all gazes traveled once more to the altar in the center of the room. "And now," Servilia said, "let us thank the goddess Diana for her arrow." She moved forward and removed the red silk wrapping. Delia saw the silver radiance suddenly flare as Servilia picked up the box beneath. Instantly, as the matron held it up, Delia saw incredible bliss come over her drawn, aging features.

"Ahh, the arrow of Diana once again works her magic," she murmured.

Delia heard all the women sigh. There was an incredible sense of excitement swirling within the warm room. What with the oil from the braziers and the myrrh and rose fragrances, it was hard to breathe.

The high priestess of the temple, Hermina, stood

next to Servilia as she opened the box. Her silver hair was caught up in a gold net at the nape of her neck. Her long tunic was pure white, woven of the finest of cotton. Her stola was a light blue and draped across her thin shoulders.

"Allow the goddess to fill you with purpose for all women," Servilia intoned, taking a small, wedge-shaped object from the box and holding it up for all to see. And then, with a flourish, she placed it in the hand of the high priestess.

Delia's eyes narrowed as she watched what happened next. The object was small and she couldn't see much about it, or tell if it was indeed a part of the Karanovo stamp. But she saw the silver emanations flash and change in brilliance as the high priestess held it in her left palm. As her fingers closed around it she pressed it to her heart, closed her eyes and uttered a sigh of absolute joy.

"Oh, I live for this night every month," Hermina whispered in a tremulous tone. "The light and energy of the goddess Diana is filling me once more...."

Delia could see that it was. The silver aura around the piece was flaring outward like the corona of a mighty sun. The radiance was so intense she could literally feel rivulets of energy pulsing rhythmically through the room and filling everyone's aura.

Stealing a look around, Delia saw that all the women had their eyes closed, their hands crossed over their hearts as they absorbed the profound warmth and energy. Following suit, she placed her hands across her heart.

Servilia stood next to the high priestess, wearing a smug look on her proud features, a smile that said the matron knew what she had in this "arrowhead." Delia had a hundred questions, but compressed her lips. Would she get to hold the piece, too? Was it really an arrowhead? She wasn't sure, because the room was so shadowy. The braziers gave off light, but not enough for her to see the object clearly. Not yet, at least.

"And now," Servilia announced, "I am going to gift our latest sister, Delia of Delos, with Diana's blessing to women who know we are powerful." Servilia stepped in front of her and said, "Our goal is to once more elevate women to our rightful status as equals to men. We are not beneath them, as they would like to think. Each woman here is charged with supporting our gender to attain all that has been taken away from us. By holding this arrowhead you are promising to aid all womankind in regaining our equality."

Delia nodded and opened her left hand. As Servilia pressed the metal piece into it, she got her first look at it. The object wasn't perfectly wedge-shaped, but had jagged edges. Seven dots were stamped into it, and a line scored into the metal beside them. Dark and old-looking, it appeared to be made of bronze, though she couldn't be certain.

The energy from the disc flooded her hand. Delia saw the silver radiance suddenly balloon, filling the entire room as never before.

"Wonderful!" Servilia cried, lifting her hands upward. "Do you feel that, my sisters? Do you see that Delia of Delos is indeed one of us?"

Cries and murmurs of appreciation echoed in the room. Delia stood there, rocked by the power of the fragment. Surely this was a piece of the stamp! She found it nearly impossible to think, for the energy flooding her body sent wild, warm tingles down to her feet and then upward like Fourth of July sparks throughout her whole being. Delia sagged against the wall of the temple, the sensation was so overwhelming.

Laughing, Servilia said, "Look! Diana's arrow has claimed Delia as her own!"

Feeling almost faint, Delia curled her fingers around the metal. Her heart was pounding, but it wasn't out of fear—it was joy. Her happiness was so intense she felt she might explode. Gasping for breath, she clung to the fragment as visions started to come to her. What she saw stunned her. And scared her.

"It is time," Servilia murmured, gently opening Delia's hand. "You have just married the goddess Diana and you are one of us. You are now Sister Delia of the Cult of Diana...." And she removed the object from Delia's sweaty palm.

Moving back to the altar, Servilia took her place next to the high priestess. She closed her eyes and pressed the metal fragment against her heart.

Delia fought the faintness and turned her attention to Servilia as she held the vaunted object. The matron's face, usually drawn and tense, was now glowing with a youthful radiance that belied her age. The silver emanations still pulsed like broad beams of sunlight throughout the room, clear through the matron's swaying form. Delia heard Servilia moaning with pleasure, her body rocking back and forth in rhythm with the fragment. She saw the high priestess gently place her hand on Servilia's shoulder to help her remain upright.

Yes, there was no question that this metal object was powerful. Every woman in the room had a glowing face, eyes bright and glistening with happiness. Clearly, the circular pattern of dots emblazoned on the piece meant something.

Unable to think clearly, Delia finally pushed

away from the wall and straightened. Though she still felt wobbly, her knees weak, there was such a profound sense of peace and love flowing through her that she hardly noticed. She brushed the curls off her brow, feeling shaky and tearful.

Every woman present still had her hands clasped over her heart, and now Delia understood why. Pressing her palms to her own thudding heart, she could no longer escape reality. Whatever the small fragment of metal was, it had forced her to confront what she did and did not love in her life. The magical object had made her see all her heartbreak and heart triumphs, as if there were a movie in her head showing her the whole of her life up to this point. Jake played a part in the movie, maybe one of the most important roles.

Pursing her lips, Delia closed her eyes and pressed her hands tighter to her thudding heart. Her love for Jake was overwhelming. He was a control freak, and couldn't open up emotionally, but despite those things, she continued to love him. Up until the moment she'd held the fragment, Delia had lied to herself. The stamp stopped the lie and made her face the truth.

Opening her eyes, Delia swung her attention to Servilia, who was now placing the metal in the next woman's outstretched hand. Each woman would be able to hold the sacred object and, Delia was sure, receive some kind of healing.

Gulping, she tried to reconcile all that had happened to her. After they returned to Servilia's home, what was she going to tell Jake?

"What did you find out?" Jake purposely spoke in a low tone, in English. He sat expectantly on Delia's couch. She had just closed the door after coming back from the ceremony. Two braziers were lit, chasing the gloom from the apartment, and though her face was in shadow as she turned and walked toward him, he saw a strange look in her eyes.

"Plenty." Delia reached for a leather pouch at her waist and opened it. Pulling out a paper, she spread it flat and handed it to him. It held a drawing of the complete Karanovo stamp. Digging again into the pouch, she withdrew a small but powerful lithium flashlight and snapped it on. One of the things Professor Carswell had developed for a time jump was a special pouch for the mission specialist to carry. It contained many useful twenty-first-century items that would never be found back in the era they were visiting.

Settling next to Jake, Delia narrowed her eyes as she studied the paper. "Bingo!" She placed her index finger on the drawing. "This is what I saw. Those seven dots in the shape of a circle. That's what was on the object they all referred to as an 'arrowhead.'"

Jake enjoyed having Delia so close to him. The fact that her arm brushed his, that her hip and thigh were so near, robbed him of his focus. Her cheeks were ruddy from the walk back to the house, and he could smell the cold air still trapped in her tunic and hair. "You found it! Great job!"

Feeling pleasure over his compliment, Delia secretly enjoyed the contact with Jake—way too much. Taking the paper, she refolded it, put it back into the pouch and got to her feet. Standing in front of him, she kept her voice soft so only he could hear. "It's the real McCoy, Jake." And she told him about the ceremony.

Jake listened intently for the next ten minutes. When Delia finished she ran her fingers through her dark, curly hair, pushing it away from her face.

She was so beautiful his heart ached. Sizzling heat purled through his lower body. There was no question he wanted her but he knew Delia didn't feel the same about him. Rubbing his stubbled jaw, he asked, "Where do you think they keep the fragment?"

"I don't know. The high priestess put it back into a small wooden box stamped with gold. She was the first to leave and Servilia the last. I couldn't run out and follow the high priestess to see where she took it."

"Could you see emanations from the box, though? Wouldn't that help us in the search?"

Snapping her fingers, Delia said, "Yes! I saw silver rays shooting out all around the box as she held it. Why didn't I think of that?"

"You look a little dazed," Jake observed drily. "Even now, your eyes have a faraway look in them, as if you're not really all here yet after the experience of holding the fragment."

Nodding, Delia went to the table and poured some water into a wooden cup. "You're right. I feel like I'm in two different places at once. I know I'm *here,* but damned if I know where else I feel a part of right now. I just feel…as if someone cut me in half." After drinking deeply, she set the cup back on the table. Giving Jake a searching look, she said, "A good night's sleep will help, so wipe the worry off your face, okay?"

"Concern, not worry," Jake corrected with a slight grin. "But your spacey feeling is understandable. You held something that none of us knows anything about. You're a psychic bloodhound and that fragment has a powerful energy, judging from the way it affected you."

Delia nodded, feeling exhaustion creeping up on her. She sat down in a chair, folded her hands in her lap and propped her feet up on the couch near where

Jake sat. "All the women were glowing after holding that fragment." She rubbed her face. "I wonder if it affected us all the same way? Or differently?"

"Servilia hinted that it would give you energy of some kind for the coming month?"

"Yes. Right now, I feel wiped, and parceled out to who knows where. That's not a great sensation, let me tell you."

"Maybe the fragment interacted with you differently? As a time traveler?"

Delia shrugged. "I don't know. We'll just have to see what influence it has on me."

"More mystery. We have more questions than answers," he rumbled, propping his elbows on his thighs. "So how do we get to this object and steal it?"

"We need time," Delia muttered, looking around the shadowy room. "We can't do anything tomorrow because of the banquet Servilia is throwing for Julius Caesar. We have security detail all day and then we're escorting her tomorrow night. That leaves us no time to reconnoiter the temple and find out where that fragment is kept."

Delia felt badly about taking the fragment from the women. She had grown fond of Servilia. Guilt ate at her. She was going to betray the woman's trust. Damn it.

"Are males allowed into the temple of Diana?"

"Yes. I saw men making offerings at the main altar. It appears to be gender neutral, welcoming all who want to worship the goddess."

"Servilia and her group of women remind me of a band of feminists living long before the word was coined."

"Yes," Delia said. "I really respect her for what she's trying to achieve in bringing equality to women. If she'd been successful, would we have avoided some of the darkest moments in history? I wonder…." Was it possible because she and Jake were going to take the fragment that the women's attempt to equalize the genders was unsuccessful? Delia knew it was possible and it left a bad taste in her mouth.

"Servilia sees the damage of inequality," Jake said quietly, holding Delia's gaze. "That alone makes her a very important woman in *her*story, not *his*tory." He smiled gently. "I'm glad we were able to save her life."

"That's for sure."

"We need to scout out that temple," he stated, getting back to business. "When's the best time for you to see auras? Dawn or dusk?"

"Either is fine. But we'd probably draw less attention if we go wandering around at dusk. Romans work all day and usually go to the temple to give their offerings before heading home at night to their families."

"Okay, then the day after tomorrow, why don't you and I go individually to the temple? I can map out one half of it and you the other. We can meet back here and put the blueprint together. And while you're there, if you pick up any energy from that fragment, you can note the vicinity and check out who is guarding it."

Delia gazed at him quizzically. "You read minds, Jake. I wonder if you can get close enough to the high priestess to read hers?"

Chapter 8

"I have to get within twenty feet of that priestess." Jake frowned. "They aren't stupid. Many were considered clairvoyant or supersensitive. If the woman feels me trying to get inside her head, that could hurt our chances of retrieving the object."

"Mmm, you're probably right." Looking up at the low ceiling, Delia said, "I'll do some investigating, Jake."

"What if we don't find anything?"

"Then somehow, with you at my side, I'll have to distract the high priestess so you can try and read her mind."

Shaking his head, Jake said, "Everyone thinks mind reading is easy, but it's not. Do you know how much mental garbage I have to sort through in order to find the one thing that will lead us to what we're looking for?"

Delia nodded sympathetically, feeling for him. She saw the concern on his face. The shadows in the room only made Jake look more ruggedly handsome. Her gaze came to rest on his pursed lips. *That mouth...* Sighing inwardly, she tried to ignore the sensations and memories that arose from simply focusing on his mouth.

Sitting up, Jake muttered, "We're tired. Let's hit the rack and get a good night's sleep. I've got a feeling it's going to be a tough day tomorrow."

He wanted to stay, to ask her to share his bed but he saw confusion in her eyes. The fragment had done something to Del and he knew sleep, not love-making, was the required Rx here.

Withdrawing her legs so he could pass by, Delia said, "Yeah. I'm just wondering how to approach Servilia about this ceremony tonight. Will she discuss it? Will she get angry if I try to talk about a topic that's taboo outside the temple? I don't know the protocol and it's driving me crazy. I've got a million questions for her, Jake. And we need every bit of info at our disposal before we try and take that fragment from the temple."

Leaning down, Jake rested his hand on Delia's slumped shoulder and pressed a chaste kiss on her forehead. Her soft curls tickled his nose. "Get some sleep, sweetheart. We can't solve a puzzle like this when we're so tired. Good night…"

Before she could respond to his impulsive act, he was gone. She heard the door between their rooms open and then quietly close. Frowning, she rubbed the spot tingling wildly in response to his kiss. Delia hungered to follow Jake, but under the circumstances, she had to get sleep. Maybe then, Delia would feel more like herself in the morning. If she slept with Jake, she'd get no sleep.

Mouth quirking, Delia got up, went over to the table and poured water into a bronze basin. Removing her tunic, she stood naked in the warm room. Grabbing a cloth, she quickly washed up as best she could. There was herbal soap in a dish nearby and soon the scent of lavender was floating around her like a fragrant cloud. Lavender could mask a lot of body odor, Delia was discovering. What she needed to do was visit the baths at the rear of the house and really get clean, but time wasn't on her side right now.

Her mind spongy, she patted herself dry with a

towel made of soft woven cotton. After shimmying into a long muslin gown, she stretched out on the couch and pulled a heavy wool blanket across herself. Two gold silk cushions became a pillow for her head. The braziers sputtered out, the last of the oil finally consumed by the flames.

As the room fell into darkness, Delia sighed and closed her eyes. The fragrance of lavender rose from her body, heavenly to inhale. It masked the olive-oil scent that always hung in the apartment. Burning oil was the main way to create light in the ancient world. Delia longed for electricity.

As she lay there, feeling sleep slowly descend, she longed to have Jake at her side. The room was warm due to the heating conduit below the floor, but the February night outside was cold, with ice covering puddles on the cobblestone street in front of Servilia's home.

Jake was like a big, warm bear, and Delia smiled softly at the thought. The only times he'd really held her were after they had made love. The warmth and intimacy he shared with her after the fireworks were over had been Delia's favorite moments. He would talk of his dreams, of her, of their future. It was the only time Jake ever opened up.

Delia had needed more than that fleeting connection and intimacy. If having sex was the only way they could communicate, she knew their relationship had been doomed before it ever got off the ground.

Jake would always revert to his bossy, arrogant, superconfident self shortly afterward, putting on that mask he usually wore. It was as if he were emotionally dressed in armor.

Frowning, Delia snuggled into the golden cushions. Why couldn't he open up? She'd shown him for two years that she was trustworthy. But in the end, Delia had discovered, Jake trusted no one but himself. It had shattered her love and ruined their relationship.

As sleep pulled her over the edge into oblivion, Delia ached to love Jake once again. It was a special hell being around him all day. How thrilling it would be to reach up and touch his wonderful male lips. Feel the warmth of his hard muscles beneath her grazing fingertips!

Once more, Delia wished she'd never been forced to take this mission with him. It was like being tempted over and over again with the one thing she'd always wanted and never could truly have—Jake.

"I meant to ask you if you enjoyed my impromptu kiss the other morning," Jake teased as they walked around the rear of Servilia's home the day of the banquet. They wanted to make sure everything would be secure. The February morning was frosty, the limbs of many of the bushes growing up against the pink stucco wall covered in a thin sheet of ice from the rain and snow of last night's storm.

Delia's breath came out in a misty white cloud as she laughed. She had pulled the hood of her cloak over her head for warmth, and wrapped her arms around her torso as they walked the perimeter. "I like kissing you. I always have." Shooting him a glance, her mouth twisting in a wry smile, she added, "Our problem isn't physical and you know that, Jake. That's what stops me: you refuse to open up and be intimate with me."

Jake absorbed her teasing smile and the dancing light in her golden eyes. Black curls peeked out from beneath her dark brown hood, emphasizing her ruddy features. "You're right," he said contritely. And then he grinned. "Must be the times we're in?"

Delia's laugh was explosive and echoed against the wall. "You'll use *any* excuse, Tyler, for your closed up ways of looking at the world. No matter what era you're in, you're never going to change. Which is a pity."

"Hmm." He caught up with her, his gaze ranging

across the wall, seeking possible places where bandits might breach it in order to get inside. "And if I could change?"

Shaking her head, Delia muttered under her breath, "Listen, Jake, you've had two years to change and I don't see that having happened." She swung toward him. "You haven't changed. You're too closed up, too protective, for whatever reason, and you'll never trust anyone outside yourself. That's what I see." She halted, resting her hands on her hips, the handle of her sword brushing her fingertips. "You don't see it, but I do. And we've had a lot of heated discussions over this very thing—communication, trust, intimacy. You just refuse to hear me, because I think inside you're scared, and that fear is greater than any desire you have toward me."

Jake slowed and glanced toward Delia. He saw her golden eyes turn dark and passionate to match her softly spoken words. Smarting, he lost his smile. "Maybe you're right," he murmured. "But I want you, Del. I've never stopped wanting you, even after you walked out of my life in Afghanistan."

Frustration thrummed through Delia as she searched his now serious-looking features. Jake had his cloak wrapped around himself, but his head was bared to the cold. Unable to ignore how handsome he was or the shape of that wonderful mouth, she felt her anger cool. "Well, if you want me, you're going to have to change. I don't want to be around a man who's so controlling he can't open up to me and be vulnerable. For whatever reason, Jake, your past made you that way. And you won't even talk about your growing-up years, so I might try and understand why you are the way you are. You trust no one but yourself. In the two years we were together, I showed you I was trustworthy, yet you refused to let down your walls and let me know the man inside."

He kept his voice low as he said, "And if I did that, would you give me another chance, Del?"

Jake had often baited her like this in their two-year affair, and she'd get suckered in by the ploy. Later she'd find out he was manipulating her.

That blew Delia's mind. Things had to be his way or no way, and she wasn't about to become a slave to him. She thinned her lips. "Listen, Jake, we've been here before. And every time you tantalize me with something about your secretive past, it's like a game you're playing. I'm not going to get pulled in like I did before. I can't. Don't you understand how much it hurts me?"

Holding up his hands, he said, "We're both hurting. No, no game this time, Delia."

Eyeing him skeptically, she muttered, "Well,

you're going to have to prove it, Jake, because I'm not going there with you." She turned and continued her appraisal of the wall, checking the many olive trees with gnarled and scrawny limbs reaching toward the rain-swollen sky.

"How about after we get done with our security check, we go back to my apartment and enjoy some warm wine?"

"It's only 8:00 a.m., Jake. I don't drink wine in the morning." Delia sighed. "What I'd give to have a mocha latte right now. Romans didn't have coffee in this era and I'm suffering caffeine withdrawal."

"Yeah, you are snarly and irritable," Jake agreed with a chuckle.

As they rounded the front of Servilia's home he noted the guards at the entrance. They looked cold, and he felt sorry for them. Their cloaks obviously weren't made of the heavyweight wool fabric Jake and Delia's were. The guards leaned their rectangular shields, made of leather and metal, against the wall near the gate. Each carried a spear and wore a gladius tucked in a scabbard in his belt.

Delia gave Jake an evil smile as they finished their circuit and headed into the beautiful dwelling. She said in a low tone only he could hear, "*You* make me snarly, Jake. And you can't blame my coffee-withdrawal symptoms on that."

Taking it all in good humor, he eyed the slaves going about their duties. The atrium was beautiful, the impluvium full because of the rain last night. The water magnified the mosaic on the bottom, of dolphins cresting blue-green waves. "Can we continue our talk in my apartment? Wine or no wine?"

Delia wanted to say no, but she remembered the power of Jake's unexpected kiss the other day. She wasn't about to tell him how much she'd enjoyed it; that would only make him bolder. If he had any inkling, he'd be preening like the cock of the walk. "I've got a few minutes," she mumbled.

Brightening, Jake said, "Great!" and rubbed his hands together as they moved into the warm part of the *domus*. In the basement, slaves kept a fire going twenty-four hours a day. The heat moved through clay pipes, warming the floors of all the rooms.

Shaking her head, Delia pushed her hood back and quickly dragged her fingers through her curls. She shouldn't care about Jake, but she did. That fact hit her hard, because she had worked for two years to get him out of her mind and heart. It hadn't worked, she was realizing with panic. The awareness had been sharpened by holding that powerful talisman in the ceremony last night. It wouldn't allow her to lie to herself about her feelings for him.

Jake opened his apartment with a flourish and

bowed as she walked in. As he shut the wooden
door, he said, "See? I can act like a gentleman and
not the Neanderthal you accuse me of being." He
pulled off his cloak and tossed it over the arm of the
red silk couch. Helping Delia off with hers, he
admired her firm, womanly form beneath the pale
blue tunic she wore. It wasn't high fashion, but it
didn't have to be to look good on her.

He poured water from a clay pitcher and offered
it to Delia, but she shook her head. Jake drank deeply
from the wooden cup. Watching her over the rim, he
saw that her features were set, her mouth thinned as
she sat down on the couch and waited, hands folded
tensely in her lap. Finished drinking, he set the cup
next to the pitcher and turned toward her.

"I realize I haven't been the most forthcoming
guy on the planet," he began, opening his hands.
"And I know I avoided all your questions about my
family when we were over in Afghanistan."

"That's an understatement," Delia said, watching
the mask Jake usually wore fall into place. "You
acted as if your childhood years were for Q clear-
ance only." That was the top security level authorized by the government.

"I'm uncomfortable discussing personal things,"
he muttered.

"Jake, that's not normal. When two people meet,

they explore one another, talk of their families, their brothers and sisters, their growing-up years. It's a natural part of becoming intimate and establishing a connection."

Jake had heard this argument from Delia many times before. "Men aren't open books by nature," he argued.

"Give me a break. That's society hammering that little mantra into your brain. And it's wrong."

Chuckling briefly, he saw Delia's mouth hitch into a slight grin. "One of the many things I like about you is your honesty."

"Yes, well, it hasn't gotten me anywhere with you, Jake. You prefer that icy tower you choose to live in. You wore me down emotionally with your lack of intimacy. The only times you were open and available to me were after we made love." Delia gave him a flat stare. "And I had to have more than that."

Jake stood with his hands behind his back, in the typical "at ease" posture of a soldier. She could see fleeting emotions in his eyes, but his face remained unreadable.

Delia frowned, then stood up and shook her head as she paced across the room. "Jake, this is getting us nowhere! I remember having this very same discussion when we were together. You're a closed book that will never open up to me or anyone else."

She stopped and said, "Something awful happened to you when you were little. I just know it in my heart and my gut. But damned if you'll share it with me. You don't trust me enough to do that."

Shrugging, Jake stared at the travertine marble floor tiles with their pink, brown and cream striations. "I can't remember anything awful happening to me, Delia."

"Then tell me about your childhood, Jake." Why did she even care at this point? Delia felt suffocated by the past coming back to haunt her all over again. Jake was a good man, and no question, he was very intelligent and attractive. Any woman would love to have him in bed with her. Delia wanted more, however. Much more. And she wasn't about to settle for what he thought was the right amount of intimacy between them. Outside the bedroom, he closed up like Fort Knox and was completely unavailable to her emotionally.

"Well," he murmured, "I was an only child, but I don't think that was bad."

"If I recall, your mother was a professor of history and your father a professor of medicine at Cornell. Is that right?"

Nodding, Jake sauntered toward Delia. She moved away from him, distrust clearly written in her eyes.

Turning instead to the couch, he sat down and

rested his elbows on his knees, hands clasped between his thighs. The tunic's rough wool weave felt like sandpaper. "That's right, they were."

Delia crossed her arms. "Jake, what one memory stands out in your childhood?" She'd asked this question several times before. And he would never answer her.

"Well," he said, studying his clasped hands, "probably my most vivid memory from being a kid is of my father. He was a tough man. He was never pleased, and crying or any sort of emotion always set him off. If I showed any feelings, he'd make fun of me. I was a sissy or a little girl. Eventually, I just closed up, Del."

Delia saw a wisp of pink color swirl through his aura, briefly lightening the darkness around him. He was telling the truth! With her heart thudding in response to his quietly spoken admission, Delia tried to put on hold her impatience and distrust of where this chat might lead them.

For once, Jake was confiding in her. What had changed? Her mind whirled with questions.

"Okay, you were being verbally abused by your father. How often?"

Looking up, Jake met and held her gaze. "I remember it happening a lot until I was around ten years old. I couldn't take his embarrassing me, so I stopped talking about anything that would make me a target."

"I understand," Delia murmured. "He shamed you into not acknowledging your real feelings. So you closed down."

"Hey, what did I know? I was just a kid," he confessed, straightening and running his hands down his thighs. He hoped Delia realized how personal this conversation was becoming. Searching her pensive features, Jake wondered what she was thinking. Even though he could read minds, he would never try to penetrate Delia's thoughts without her permission. Clearly, she was struggling to understand. He could see wariness in her golden eyes.

"My parents never shut me down like your father did you."

"Maybe I wasn't like most kids, Delia. Maybe all parents tell their kid to stop crying or feeling bad."

"No, good parents want their children to own their feelings. That is positive. You can share your emotions, be vulnerable and not be afraid of intimacy, then."

"I don't know that…"

"What did you do when he made fun of you?"

"I had books to read or a computer to play with. My parents were well off as professors. I didn't want for anything material."

Unfolding her arms, Delia allowed them to fall to her sides as she walked closer. "No child does well when they can't be themselves, Jake," she said. "I don't pretend to be a psychotherapist, but clearly, his constant tirades caused you to lock yourself up."

"I never thought about it," he grumbled. "Millions of kids get parents who yell at them."

"Well," Delia said a little more softly, "children respond differently given their personality and circumstances, Jake. Maybe you're really a marshmallow inside and that experience devastated you."

"I've never been a marshmallow!" he retorted. "My father wanted me to be a real man."

She saw surprise mirrored on his face. "I wasn't criticizing you, Jake. Relax. It was a compliment." Now she understood and the anger she felt toward Jake's father was red-hot. He harmed his son with verbal abuse. The professor might not have laid a hand on his son, but the damage was the same.

"Men aren't built that way."

"You have a heart just like I do. And you have the *right* to feel all your emotions!" She gave him a tender look.

Watching him frown, Delia saw his aura begin to swirl with reddish-brown ribbons of color. That meant he was getting angry and defensive. Well, what was new? Why wasn't she learning the lesson in all of this—that Jake would never go there. His father had done a good job.

Scowling, Jake rubbed his chest. His heart was pounding hard and he tried to remain immune to Delia's impassioned argument. Women never played fair; they always tried to hook you with their emotional ploys, which had nothing to do with logic and reason. So why was he feeling as if his heart was being squeezed in his chest? Why did he feel such desperation?

Watching Delia pace the room again, Jake hated admitting he didn't want to keep pushing her away. But he was doing so, as always. Her expression was one of sympathy mixed with frustration.

Heading for the door to her own room, she picked up her cloak from the couch, where he was sitting. "I've got things to do," she muttered, "before tonight's event. I'm leaving, Jake."

"Wait!" He stood up as she reached the doorway.

"What?" Delia said, holding his confused gaze. She saw the colors in his aura changing, the angry red hue dissipating. In its place, fuchsia tones began swirling around his heart. She'd never seen that before. Usually, when she noted that in people's auras, it meant they were falling in love.

Discounting that thought immediately, Delia

tried to harden her resolve. She saw Jake rub his strong chin with impatience.

"Doesn't—" He stopped abruptly and frowned. Looking down at his boots, which were damp with melted frost after their walk around the grounds, he tried to think. Damn it, when Delia was near, his well-constructed, logical world shattered. All he could ever do around this woman warrior was become an over-emotional fool whose words always seemed to come flying out of his mouth the wrong way. "Doesn't the fact that I opened up to you just now mean anything? I was trying, Del."

"Yes, you did open up for a split second," she breathed gently. "And when we tried to talk about it, you just got defensive like you always do. I'm tired of that game, Jake. Tired to my soul. Right now, I don't have the emotional energy to put up with it."

His heart contracted with pain. Jake felt as if Delia had just pierced him in the chest with the blade she carried at her side. Searching her stubborn features, he rasped, "Well, it was a start, Del." Why the hell was he trying to convince her to stay? Obviously, she didn't want anything to do with him, whether he opened up or not.

"I'm older and wiser, Jake. It took me two years to figure out that you wanted me only on your terms.

That's not a relationship. I want a man who I can open up to, spill my heart to if I feel like it. Someone who will listen without interrupting me. Just listen, and not immediately try to fix whatever problem I'm telling him about." She saw Jake give her a helpless look, one of the few she'd ever seen from him. It touched her as nothing else had except that hot, seductive kiss out in the hall yesterday.

"I don't need a fix-it guy," Delia whispered, her voice off-key. "I need a man who loves me, wants to listen to me, cares enough to sit, hold me and just let me get something out of my system. I don't need a civil engineer coming in with a blueprint, to fix how I'm feeling at that moment. Many times we have to just muddle through an emotion, Jake. You seem so unwilling to even admit to feelings, or to go where another person needs you to be for them. In the past, when I would open up, cry or tell you how I felt, you always withdrew from me emotionally. When I wanted you to hold me, you didn't seem to have a clue what I needed. Ever. I had to *ask* you to put your arms around me and hold me. And even then, you weren't relaxed. You were stiff and uncomfortable, as if you didn't know how to hold someone who was hurting."

Standing, Jake felt her heated words slam into him, like one blow after another. His brows dipped and he felt anger along with desperation. His heart ached. He was hurting from Delia's emotional plea. Again, automatically, he rubbed his chest, unable to look at her for a moment as he scrambled through the haze of his roiling feelings.

"Maybe, Del, I don't recognize how or when to hold you when you're hurting."

Shock rooted her to the spot as Delia heard Jake's low, emotional admission. Her heart contracted with pain—for both of them. It made sense. If Jake had been shot down as a child, he wouldn't know.

"I need to remember what happened to you."

"What do you mean?" Jake winced inwardly. He'd sounded defensive, and saw Delia's reaction to his growling tone. She'd instantly retreated, but then, stopped and looked thoughtful, not angry.

"There's two people involved here, Jake. Now that I know why you closed up I have to stop reacting to the 'old' you. I can see you're trying. And I'm going to try to change my old habit patterns toward you."

Rubbing his jaw, Jake met her searching gaze filled with sincerity. He saw the set of her mouth soften. That take-no-prisoners look in her shadowed eyes disappeared. The sense of being trapped by her reaction dissolved. "We're a good team, you and I," he began in a hoarse, emotional voice. "If we can both try…"

Nodding, Delia whispered, "Then there's hope, Jake."

"It's not going to be easy," he warned.

"Anything worth having is always challenging," she said. Reaching out, she touched his jaw. "We've made progress. It's enough for tonight. We need to get to sleep."

As the door shut quietly behind her, Jake realized he'd made important progress. Turning away, he ran his fingers through his hair and cursed. Opening up to Del had somehow worked. Jake felt good and hope filled his heart. He picked up his cloak, wanting to go outside to feel his way through this amazing development. He would head out and tour the grounds again. He needed fresh air to think.

As Jake drew on the cloak and fastened it with a brass pin, what he felt in his heart for Delia nearly overwhelmed him.

No longer trapped or confused, he pulled open the door and walked out. He was drawn to a woman who refused to give up on him. If that wasn't love, what was?

Hours later, Delia once again walked the perimeter of the property with Jake. They had to finish their assessment for security purposes. Here, they were free to talk quietly, for there were no slaves around to listen.

"Are Cleopatra and her son invited to this party?" Jake asked, hoping to find a safe topic with her.

Delia said, "No, not a chance."

"Servilia is like a green-eyed monster about Caesar bringing his son here to Rome," Jake murmured. They halted beside the seven-foot-high wall. Jake could hear the creak of wagons going by on the street outside, the clip-clop of horses as they passed, as well as the chatter of people going about their errands.

Looking up, Delia saw the February sky was a pale blue now, with a few clouds floating past. The temperature had finally risen above freezing, but she was still glad for the cape wrapped around her body, and for the rabbit-fur lining in her boots that kept her feet warm. "Can we judge whether Caesar is friend or foe to Servilia, then?"

"Not yet," Jake muttered. As they walked down the gravel path parallel to the street, he looked at all the thick bushes and olive trees growing near the wall. "This is a great place for robbers to hide," he noted, pointing at the greenery.

"Yeah, lots of hidey-holes," Delia agreed. She surveyed the area, finding plenty of such spots. "Do you think Romans ever had a problem with robbers or groups of men scaling such walls and hiding inside to rob homeowners?"

"I don't think it was a huge problem," Jake murmured, eyeing the thick vegetation. "But the possibility makes our job harder. Everyone who is anyone in Rome will be at this shindig tonight."

"And what if Cleopatra was behind that attack on Servilia?" Delia said under her breath as they rounded the corner. There was about eight feet of space between the *domus* and the stucco wall. A narrow path had been worn by the gardeners over the years through the thick greenery. It was an ideal place for an attack.

"Wish I could remain close to Servilia during the party," Jake said, critically examining the situation. He halted about halfway to the rear of the house, checking to make sure they were alone. "It would be a perfect time to try and read her mind."

Delia turned and gazed up at him. How handsome Jake was as a Greek mercenary. Her body responded heatedly to the smoldering look he was giving her. But their earlier discussion made her tentative and she stepped back. "Do you think Caesar will buy Servilia's argument about the attack? That Cleopatra designed it?"

Shaking his head, Jake said, "Why would he?

He's in love with that woman." And then his smile grew. "Love makes us blind."

That smoky smile reminded Delia that Jake had romance on his mind. He wasn't trying to penetrate her thoughts, but she could see the change in his aura, from blue tones to rosy ones. Anytime someone had amorous thoughts or feelings, their aura turned beautiful shades of pink. As his gaze dropped to her lips, she felt them tingle. Unhappy with her body's response, Delia turned and walked to the rear of the property.

Jake followed. If Delia only realized that her gorgeous golden eyes gave her away, so he knew she was still drawn to him, she'd probably shriek in disgust. Hands clasped behind his back, he dutifully followed her, enjoying the feminine sway of her hips despite the bulky cloak she wore. He told himself to be patient, that he would eventually get Delia back into his arms—and his bed. But first, they had a banquet to get through, and they had to be on guard.

His intuition told him that things would go wrong tonight.

Chapter 9

Torbar scowled as he walked behind General Marcus Brutus at Servilia's *domus*. The place was crowded with powerful citizens of Rome, most gathered in the atrium and tablinum, where food, wine and conversation were ongoing. What he saw he didn't like. As a Navigator and Centaurian, he possessed powerful clairvoyant skills, among them the ability to see auras. So what was he seeing now?

Standing attentively near General Brutus, who was talking to Senator Cato, Torbar maintained his obsequious demeanor, yet raised his head just enough to study the two mercenary soldiers on either side of Servilia, who was chatting animatedly with Julius Caesar. For whatever reason, their auras were much different in color, strength and content than those of the rest of the humanoids. Keeping in check his disgust over their primitive level of development, Torbar switched completely to his clairvoyant facilities.

The woman dressed in Greek armor was alert, her face emotionless, her gaze constantly roving about the huge atrium. Neither the occasion nor the February dusk could hide the fact she was a warrior in all respects. What attracted Torbar was her aura. The egg-shaped cloud of energy around her had silver shining in the outer layers. No one else present, with the exception of the other Greek soldier, exhibited this phenomenon. Silver indicated advancement. Brows dipping, Torbar tried to penetrate the contents of her mind to find out just who she was.

Instantly, his efforts were rebuffed. The energy probe he'd sent slammed back at him with the same power he'd sent it out with. Rubbing his brow where an ache began, Torbar cursed silently. Yes, it was obvious she had walls up to protect herself from anyone telepathically trying to read her mind. And she was strong enough to stop a Navigator.

That wasn't good at all.

Torbar was shocked by her resistance to his probe. Since when could a mere Earthling stop a mighty Navigator in any way?

Switching his attention to the male soldier, whose aura also shone with silver, he sent another mental probe. The pain in Torbar's head increased substantially. Rejected again.

He had to be careful, Torbar decided. The silver indicated that both Greeks had psychic capabilities, but he didn't know what skills they had. And stupidly, he hadn't cloaked his aura. Instantly, he did so, but maybe it was too late. He saw the Greek woman soldier studying him intently from across the atrium, her gaze narrowed speculatively, then Torbar felt the energy of her assessment.

Cursing softly, he moved to the other side of General Brutus to get out of her sight. What had she seen? Did she know he was a Navigator? Torbar had to maintain his disguise so he could track down the time jumper and hopefully retrieve the missing headband.

Rubbing his brow and hovering behind the short, powerful general, who was dressed in a white toga with purple edging, Torbar concealed himself from the Greeks' gaze. His mind whirled with possibilities. He knew Kentar suspected that the Galactic Council sent emissaries to Earth from time to time. So had the Centaurians, though now they were barred from doing so by law. They had been caught stealing those female Earthlings long ago and were still paying a heavy price for it. They had to be sneaky during their illicit activities.

Pleiadians had been allowed to come to Earth as punishment for Centaurians breaking the galactic noninterference directive. He was sure the Pleiadians came joyously, for the females of this species possessed Navigator genes and were fully capable, if trained properly, of running the organic spaceships that previously only Centaurians could operate.

Racking his brain, Torbar systematically reviewed all the aura types known in the galaxy. None exactly matched the two Greeks standing in the atrium with him. So who were they? If they were alien, which he felt they were, were they a new, unknown species? The woman soldier was looking around the room once more. Torbar could detect the golden threads of energy she was sending out as she scanned the group. She obviously had felt his intrusion into her mind. Did she know what he'd done?

Cloaked as he was now, she would never find him. He would appear to be a lowly scribe to an important Roman general, nothing more. Smiling secretively, Torbar felt smug that no one in this gathering had the inherited powers and skills that a Centaurian Navigator possessed.

But who were these two?

Keeping her panic deep inside her, Delia felt the assault upon her thoughts by someone who knew what he was doing. And instinctively, she followed the energy pulse back to the person who'd tried to read her mind without her permission. She saw a dark-haired, brown-eyed male, very thin and holding tablets in one hand. He was standing beside General Brutus. Delia didn't know what to make of the attempted intrusion, so she checked his aura. That's when she was truly shocked. The scribe's energy field possessed a lot of bright red hues, more than anyone else at the banquet. She'd never seen an aura with so many different tones of red.

Unable to snag Jake's attention and alert him, since he was on the other side of Servilia as she chatted with Julius Caesar, Delia again scanned the mind prober.

And then, suddenly, his aura was gone! Swallowing, she tried to locate the scribe's aura once more, to no avail. It was as if he were walled up and hiding from her. Stunned, she watched him move unobtrusively to the other side of the Roman general.

This man wasn't like the rest of the people

here. Frowning uneasily, Delia turned and tried to catch Jake's attention. He was on the alert and looking around. Delia watched as he quickly scanned the room. Had the scribe tried to enter his mind, too? Why?

Frustrated, Delia knew she had to remain on guard and do her duty as a sentry for Servilia. And so did Jake. Were they under some kind of psychic attack? By whom?

Servilia grabbed Julius by the hand. "Come, my love, come out to the garden with me where we can talk privately."

Julius nodded, though he pulled his hand away.

Servilia would not be deterred. She gave him a flirtatious smile and drew him along, threading her way through the reveling senators and their paramours for the evening.

Delia fell into step behind the pair, but slowed her pace.

"Jake," she whispered in English, low enough that only he could hear her. "What just happened? Someone tried to probe my mind."

"Yeah," he said grimly, continuing to look around at the crowd. "Me, too. Did you see anyone?"

"Yes, for a split second, and then he cloaked and I couldn't see his aura anymore. That scribe over there near General Brutus is the man I'm talking about."

Jake swung his gaze in that direction for just a moment. "Yes, I see him."

"He's trouble, Jake. His aura was bright red. I've *never* seen an aura like that."

"I didn't get a good feeling from him, either," Jake growled. They were moving toward a small alcove with a marble balcony that overlooked the western side of the vestibulum. It was a secluded, quiet spot, away from all the festivities. Jake slowed his pace even more, leaving about twenty feet between them and the pair they were guarding. Obviously, Servilia wanted to talk to Caesar in private.

It was dark in the corridor, except for strategically placed braziers that provided just enough light for them to see into the grayness. "What do you make of it?" Delia asked.

"Damned if I know who or *what* he is."

"I sense he's a fox in the henhouse, Jake."

He pressed his mouth into a grim line, unable to disagree. Keeping an eye on the twosome, he saw Servilia wrapping her arms around Julius's shoulders, and wondered if she was trying to win him back from Queen Cleopatra. Tearing his gaze from that scene, Jake looked over at Delia. She was tense, her eyes darting and watchful. "A fox from *where,* though?" he murmured.

Shrugging, she rested her hand on the butt of her sword. "I don't have a clue."

"He stood out like a sore thumb."

"Yes. I didn't really notice him until the mind probe. And then I automatically followed the hit back to who'd sent it. And it was him, Jake. I don't think he expected me to be aware of his assault."

"He hit me, too. Only I didn't have the skills to trace the probe back to him. If he can read minds, that's not good."

"No," Delia breathed unhappily, "it isn't. Could he be another time traveler?"

"From where? And who sent him?"

"Beats me. This is more Professor Carswell's territory, not ours."

"Maybe I should go over to the scribe and find out."

Grimacing, Delia said, "Let's not stir up things we don't have a clue about, Jake. I think we'd better stick to our plan to steal that fragment from the temple and get the hell out of Dodge."

Moving his shoulders to rid himself of the accumulating tension, Jake saw Servilia try to kiss Caesar. When he gently separated himself from her, the Roman matron looked hurt and angry. "No matter the age, love is hell," he whispered to Delia.

Giving a sigh, she said, "There's nothing easy about love. Servilia had been so looking forward to seeing Caesar tonight. I know she wanted to try and patch things up between them." She felt badly for the older woman.

"Impossible, when a beautiful twenty-one-year-old Egyptian queen has given him something he's wanted forever—a son," Jake said drily. "There's no way he's going to trade his young mistress for this fifty-year-old woman."

"Love can happen no matter *what* your age," Delia said, giving him a dirty look. "Older women are too often discarded in favor of younger flesh. Maybe they don't possess the physical beauty they once had, but they have maturity, wisdom and an internal beauty that makes their auras shine."

"Your argument isn't lost on me," Jake answered in a seductive whisper. "Look at you. You're not an eighteen-year-old. You're reaching the end of your twenties, and you're still beautiful and powerful."

Swayed by his teasing, Delia tried to ignore the heat that smoldered in Jake's eyes for her. "Just another of your lines. I'm twenty-eight and I've earned every bit of smarts and maturity I have. I don't want a man who's always pining over young bodies, like Caesar here."

Jake wanted to reach out and touch Delia's

shoulder, but couldn't. They were on detail as sentinels. Any fond or personal gestures would not be appropriate. "I happen to pine for just one woman."

Again Delia snorted. "Give me a break. You'd say anything to get me into bed again."

Jake sighed. "That's not always true, but we can't really discuss it now. How about later when the banquet ends? You and me in your apartment with a glass of wine?"

"I'll think about it."

Undeterred, Jake laughed softly, being careful not to interrupt the escalating drama out on the balcony. "You're right, we need to focus on our mission."

Just then, Delia heard a rustle and saw a movement beyond the balcony, in the darkness beyond the braziers. Jake noticed them, too. Both stepped forward, raising their shields and drawing their swords.

Julius Caesar was talking passionately with Servilia, who was standing at arm's length from him, sobbing. He was so deeply engrossed in speaking to his mistress that he didn't notice anything else.

Jake moved to the curved marble balcony and confronted the two of them. "There's someone out there, Emperor. We suggest you retire within while we find out what is going on."

Servilia blinked, and he could see the kohl around her eyes had run as a result of her tears. Julius gripped her arm, spun her around and quickly led her inside. "I'll send my Praetorians," he snapped over his shoulder.

Delia and Jake were already over the balcony and landing on the soft soil. The rustling continued, coming closer. Delia's heart pounded with sudden terror as she saw five men appear out of the darkness, from behind the thick shrubbery. They were dressed like the robbers who'd attacked Servilia on the Via Appia. Who was sending these men to assault Servilia? Cleopatra? Caesar himself?

"Jake?" Delia whispered, lifting her sword and pointing to the right, where three of the five men were closing in, their swords drawn.

"Got it," he rasped.

Instantly, both she and Jake moved, keeping a few feet apart as they rushed toward the enemy. Delia saw that the two men on her left were well-equipped mercenaries. There was nothing ragtag about this group of interlopers. Their armor was unfamiliar, but well-maintained. What mattered most was that they were running toward them, swords uplifted, with the intent to kill.

As she anchored herself to take a blow from a short man with fierce black eyes and a beard, she realized that the man wanted to dispense with them quickly. *They were here to kill Caesar!* That thought slammed into her psychic senses as sharply as the blow to her shield.

Thrusting forward with her sword, Delia forced the soldier to yelp and leap aside. Holding the round shield in place on her left arm, she struck out with her blade again and again, deflecting the hacking blows the thug rained down upon her. Then Delia caught his incoming blade and, with a twist of her wrist, knocked it from his grasp. Lunging forward, she jammed her own sword home. The point of her blade found a slit in his metal armor across his chest. She felt it sinking deep until her forward motion was stopped as her metal struck bone.

With a cry, the man staggered back, his eyes wide with surprise. Delia jerked her sword free.

To her right, Jake had taken on three men. The fifth, the companion to the one she'd just taken down, gave a cry of rage and charged her.

She had no time to think, only react. Lifting her shield as he hurtled at her, Delia was thrown off her feet. The man was like a small bear, his weight superior to hers. Slamming into the ground, her breath knocked out of her, she smelled his garlic-laden breath, looked into his narrowed, murderous eyes and saw him lift his sword to cut off her head.

Twisting aside, Delia rolled, then jumped to her feet without her shield. The man howled in rage and followed her. Their swords clanged together. He charged her again. Delia stepped aside and again twisted her wrist. The man had seen what happened to his friend when she'd initiated that maneuver, and he leaped back so she couldn't impale him, too.

Her opponent was a skilled swordsman. Delia was breathing heavily, but so was he. She heard a scream of pain to her right. Shooting a quick glance in that direction, she saw Jake kill the second of the three men who had attacked him. It was at that moment her enemy struck. Delia felt the hot, stinging slice of his blade across her right thigh. Blood ran from the opened wound. *Damn!* She lunged once more, knowing if she didn't finish off her attacker quickly, she would weaken and he'd kill her.

With a feinting action, Delia sent her blade low, toward the man's abdomen. He parried it. As he did so, she shifted her sword beneath his and thrust it into his left shoulder. The man gave a startled cry and fell backward, arms flailing.

Yanking her weapon free, Delia turned swiftly to see Jake dispatching his third attacker. She was breathing hard, explosive gasps that turned to clouds of white mist in the cold evening air as she quickly backed off. Staring fixedly at the wounded man who lay on the ground groaning, his hand pressed to his bleeding shoulder, Delia heard Praetorian guards, the elite of the Roman army, whose only job was to protect Caesar, come running into the garden. They would take care of those who survived.

Grimly, Delia allowed the captain of the guard, a grizzled veteran of many campaigns, to take over. She saw Jake's eyes widen as he looked at her.

"I'm okay," she told him as he reached her side. She sheathed the blade in the scabbard at her side. "It's a flesh wound."

Gripping Delia's arm, he supported her, helping her to keep her weight off that bleeding leg. "Let me get you back to your apartment. We can take care of it there and see how bad it really is."

Unable to fight the concern in his voice, she allowed him to wrap his arm around her waist, then leaned on him for support as she limped down the hall. Behind them, she could hear the uproar from the guards, the excited hubbub the attack had created.

Turning her focus on her leg as they approached their apartments, Delia rasped, "Damn, I hope this isn't anything to write home about, Jake." All she needed right now was a serious injury. If it was bad, she'd have to press her armband and have Professor Carswell transport her back to the present to be operated on.

Keeping his panic under control, Jake shoved open Delia's apartment door and quickly helped her to a nearby chair. Closing the door, he discarded his armor and then leaned down and pushed back her bloodied tunic. The light from the braziers wasn't great, but it was all they had.

Kneeling down, his hands settling gently upon her wounded leg, Jake studied the bleeding cut. It was a clean, ten-inch-long slice and his heart thundered with fear.

Fear that Delia could die.

Chapter 10

"Lucky for us that we've got this pouchful of twenty-first century goodies," Delia muttered as Jake quickly cleaned the blood from the cut on her thigh.

Leaning down, he took soap and washed the area thoroughly. They put on latex gloves to prevent further infection. "Get the needle and thread out of the pouch, and start popping antibiotics."

"Right," Delia said, feeling the burning sensation as he cleaned her wound. She was aware that before penicillin was discovered, most soldiers would have died of infection after being wounded in a sword fight. It was almost a guarantee. She opened the packet of antibiotics and gratefully swallowed one. Jake handed her a wooden cup with water so she could wash it down.

They worked quietly, like the good team they were. "Glad that slash is horizontal across my thigh," Delia murmured at last.

Nodding, Jake washed his hands with soap and water. "Yeah, it will be easier to heal up. If it was vertical, even with stitches, it might rip open when you did any kind of even moderate exercise."

"I should have seen that bastard's ploy," she muttered, realizing with regret that she was now a liability to the mission.

Jake dried his hands and knelt in front of her. "Stop being hard on yourself. Considering the odds, we did damn good."

She handed him the surgical needle and sterile thread. One of the many things Professor Carswell had discovered on these time jumps was how essential it was to have a few first-aid items sent along. That way, if an individual got injured or sick, he or she could remain in place and not have to return for medical treatment, thereby scrubbing the mission. And there was no way Delia wanted to leave this mission now. Jake needed her.

But she couldn't become a liability, either.

"Give me the lidocaine," he told her. The packet's

contents would be drizzled into the wound to numb it so that Delia wouldn't feel anything as he sewed it up. Jake guessed it would take at least fifteen stitches to close it, and that would be no fun for her without the painkiller.

"Thanks," he said, and quickly applied the anesthetic. The bleeding had stopped, leaving an ugly-looking cut.

"How bad do you think it is?" Delia asked, eyeing her thigh. Jake was a paramedic and had more advanced medical training than she did.

"The blade didn't reach your muscles," he told her, threading the needle and then placing his hand on her bare thigh. "Once I get this sewed up and you're on antibiotics, we'll have to make sure we keep a tight dressing around your leg. That will allow it to close up and prevent it from splitting open again."

Pursing her lips, Delia felt the warmth of his hand on her thigh. He was all business, his dark brows drawn down in a V, his mouth thinned as he focused. All the same, she couldn't help being aware of his nearness, his touch. She remembered being explored by Jake. An incredible lover, he had made her body sing with pleasure so excruciatingly beautiful that Delia had sometimes felt faint from it. Drawing in a deep breath now, she closed her eyes.

"This might hurt a little," he murmured apologetically as he began to stitch the wound. "That lidocaine will take the pain away, but there's still going to be some sensation."

Without thinking, Delia placed her hand on his broad shoulder. She felt the tension of his muscles beneath her palm. The realization that they could have died minutes ago in the melee was just now beginning to dawn upon her. Contact with Jake comforted her and she started to calm down. She knew she must be in a mild state of shock.

"Good, just hold on to me," he murmured, bending close to her thigh in order to see what he was doing.

"You were always good to cling to in a storm," Delia admitted with a sigh. She wasn't going to tell Jake just how good it felt to touch him now.

He laughed softly as he continued stitching. "And you aren't? Do you know how many times, after coming off a bad mission in Afghanistan, I looked forward to being with you? I needed you, Delia. It meant so much to feel your arms around me...."

Shocked at the reply, Delia frowned. "Why didn't you ever tell me that, Jake?"

He gave a careful shrug. "I don't know. Maybe because I'm not an open book like you yet."

"Why now?" she asked in a low voice. Delia saw

the expression on his face, the way he narrowed his eyes as he methodically continued his doctoring.

"I thought you were dying out there. I thought…" he looked up and met her gaze "…I'd never see you again. I just couldn't…wouldn't…let that happen. It scared the hell out of me, Del."

Nodding, she watched as he dipped his head again and finished up sewing. "I see…." Well, did she really? Her heart was in turmoil. On top of that, Delia was having an adrenaline letdown from nearly dying in a sword fight.

Struggling to gather her thoughts, she said, "By any chance did you get to read the minds of any of those attackers? Who were they? Who sent them?"

Jake placed a dressing across the finely stitched wound, pleased with his efforts. Once that was in place, he dug into his pouch and retrieved a roll of gauze and some tape. Carefully, he wrapped the gauze around Delia's firm thigh four times before knotting it, then taping it in place. "Yes, I got some stuff," he admitted. At one time he would have slid his hand up her long, curved leg and begun to arouse Delia. To hear her moan and sigh with pleasure sent him spiraling on a high that made him feel as if he were in Nirvana. Instead, he pulled her bunched tunic down and gently smoothed the fabric.

Delia removed her hand from his shoulder. He

rose in one fluid motion, his face once more encased in shadows because of the poor lighting in the room. "What did you get?"

Washing his hands in a fresh bowl of cool water, he said, "Queen Cleopatra hired them. The last thoughts one guy I killed had was that the gold she'd paid him was on its way to his family in Greece."

Whistling softly, Delia slowly stood up and tested her leg. It felt solid and there was little pain. Jake had done a good job. She knew she'd have to be careful the next several days or the wound *could* split open again. But they didn't have days. "Wow, that's explosive. I wonder if Caesar will have the survivor tortured enough that he'll squeal?"

Drying his hands, Jake said, "I don't know. If they were the queen's guards, they won't fess up no matter what's done to them."

Shivering, Delia walked slowly and gingerly, continuing to test her leg. The lidocaine was still at work. When the anesthetic wore off, there would be pain and she'd take some of the aspirin to offset it. "But what if he does talk, Jake? That will sure put Caesar at odds with Cleopatra, won't it?"

Jake watched her slowly move around the apartment. There was more color in her cheeks than before. Was it because they'd been touching? Jake didn't know, but wished it was the reason. "Yes, it would. But we can't be a part of that drama. We need to get to the temple, find that fragment and get the hell out of this time zone."

"No disagreement there," she said drily, glancing at him from across the room. Jake had taken off his armor, and his dark brown tunic stretched across his magnificent chest. A chest she was so familiar with. Delia didn't try to stop the memories of grazing his taut flesh with her fingertips, or the soft, curly hair that grew there. He was incredibly masculine in all the right ways.

Jake walked toward the door. "I'm going to find out what's going on. See if that Egyptian guard talked under torture yet or not. You stay here and rest, okay?"

Nodding, Delia said, "I'll be all right, Jake. Just go do your duty. When you get back, we need to plot how to get into that temple. Things are escalating around here and I'm not ready for another attack on Servilia or her household." Delia patted her wounded leg. "Not now."

Grimly, Jake looked into her golden eyes. "No more fighting for you, sweetheart. You're officially on the disabled list. Got it?"

For once, Delia didn't contradict his gruffly spoken words. "Yes, sir." She saw care in Jake's eyes, and desire burning there as well. Her skin reacted with a hot flush from the top of her head to her toes. His fervent gaze, the huskiness of his voice were the responses of a lover. Did he know that? No, he couldn't. She trembled inwardly, knowing that right now she needed whatever Jake could give her.

The door closed quietly and Delia was alone. Frowning, she rubbed her arms, feeling the chill in the room. Exhaustion was avalanching down upon her as the adrenaline burned out of her system.

Limping to the couch, she stretched out on it, careful not to bump her sore leg. As she drew the blanket across her shoulders, she worried about Jake.

And what about that scribe with the red aura? She sensed he was dangerous to them. Was he still in the house? she wondered groggily.

Moments later, Delia was asleep.

Torbar knew that Kentar was going to appear shortly in his apartment at General Brutus's home. He'd received word telepathically an hour ago of his leader's wish for a mission status report. Torbar sensed a rippling effect in the apartment. Looking toward the door, he saw his leader slowly congeal before him.

"Welcome, my lord," Torbar murmured in their language. Kentar stood before him in the guise of a rich shipping merchant. Not only could a Navigator possess a body, he could appear and disappear at will.

Kentar swept in and waited impatiently as Torbar closed the door and leaned against it. "What is going on?"

Torbar told him quickly. Once finished, he waited, watching Kentar's scowl deepen as he thought.

"I was disturbed by your report on these two Greek soldiers with silver in their auras. You can't get any information from these two Greek mercenaries protecting Servilia?"

The lord of the Centaurian system sat down at a marble table and poured himself a cup of red wine. Torbar cringed inwardly at the scathing tone in his voice.

"My lord, they seem impervious to anything I can do to get a read on their auras or their minds."

"Humph. What do you make of this silver lining in their auras?"

"I've never seen it in an Earthling before. Does anything in our historical archives speak to this?"

Shaking his head, Kentar finished the wine and wiped his mouth. "No. It's an anomaly as far as I'm concerned."

"But something is causing it," Torbar said, spreading his hands. "I can't find what. Is it within them? Is it something they are wearing? I just don't know."

"All right," Kentar growled, "then do it another way. Hire one of the best prostitutes in Rome and send her to lower that soldier's guard." The Centaurian snorted. "Tell the woman to seduce him, undress him, and see if he wears a piece of jewelry or a pouch with a fetish in it...whatever...and have her report back to you."

"A good tactic," Torbar mused, then he shook his head. "I'm very frustrated, my lord. My abilities are unquestionable."

Waving his hand impatiently, Kentar stood up and strode to the door. "They may be from another galaxy, Torbar. Had you considered that?"

Stunned, he stared at his leader. "Er...no, I had not, my lord."

"For all we know this could be their first foray into our galaxy and they're snooping around. If it is, we need to know where they are from and what they want." Rubbing his bearded chin, he added, "What I do not like about this is the fact that this alien race has chosen Earth, of all places. These interlopers may know about Navigator genetics here and may be on a research mission."

Torbar's mouth dropped open. "That cannot happen, my lord! If anyone in this galaxy or any other gets their hands on Earthling females and engages their talents, our empire will collapse. We will lose our power."

Glaring at him, Kentar snarled, "That fact is not lost on me, Torbar. Don't get dramatic. That's *my* job." He jabbed his finger into the scribe's chest. "Get the best prostitute to approach the male mercenary. Let's see if she can melt his barriers."

Torbar bowed deeply to Kentar. "It shall be as you instruct, my lord. As soon as I hear back from her, I will contact you."

"Good," Kentar huffed. Turning, he pinned Torbar with a lethal look. "And I do not want to have to come back to this primitive planet ever again. Do you hear me?"

Tullia strolled through Servilia's atrium, a bouquet of spring flowers in her hand. The mid-morning sun shone brightly in a blue sky that was rare at this time in February. The guards at the gate had allowed her immediate entrance because they recognized her as one of the most skilled women in the arts of love in the city. Tullia was greatly admired and said to be the goddess Venus come to Earth.

Smiling inwardly, she glowed over the fact that Kapaneus, the scribe, had given her a gold aureus to come here and subdue Philip of Delos. She was to mold him into pliable clay with her soft, creative fingers. Tullia could not discern why it was so important to know what jewelry the mercenary wore. A silly request, she thought, but shrugged it off as a slave brought her to the soldier's apartment.

Jake had just returned from the baths, and was standing naked by the table when the door opened. Turning, he scowled. No one was to enter his apartment without knocking first. His brows flew upward when a tall, lithe young woman entered. She was dressed in a pale pink wool tunic and white palla, her black hair brought up on top of her head and anchored in place with a gleaming gold circlet. Her sultry gaze moved from Jake's feet up to his crotch, where it remained. A very pleased look came to her face.

"Ah, Philip of Delos," she whispered, "my name is Tullia and I am a gift for you." She opened her hands and floated across the room toward the man with the powerful build.

Swallowing shock, Jake didn't feel at all concerned about his nakedness. This young woman, whoever she was, had an inviting, husky tone. Her green eyes were huge and outlined with kohl. Her lips were painted a bright red and her cheeks were pink.

"A gift?" he demanded, ruthlessly probing her mind. Jake instantly saw Tullia wince. She stopped, a confused expression on her smooth, velvety face.

"I—I was sent here to please you, my lord," Tullia stammered.

He easily sifted through the contents of her mind. He saw that the scribe, Kapaneus, was behind this plot. *Why?* Finding no reason, Jake abruptly withdrew. Doing so would cause her an awful headache, he knew. Almost regretfully he watched Tullia's face drain of color. Raising her long, graceful hand to her flawless brow, she swayed in the aftermath of his mind probe.

Before he could order her out of his apartment, the inner door swung open. Delia limped in, dressed in a soft yellow tunic. Sleepy-looking, Jake realized she must have just awakened.

Delia halted abruptly, her eyes flying wide with surprise.

"Leave us," Jake ordered Tullia. "I want nothing you offer." The young woman gave him a doe-eyed look, but then her gaze cut to where Delia stood just inside the door, staring at them.

"Ah, my lord, I see," Tullia murmured, trying to speak through the pain in her head. "This gift is not meant for you, after all." She bowed to both of them, turned and quickly left.

Delia waited until Jake closed the door. "What was that all about?"

"Not what you think," he growled unhappily. He

was still naked, and now, beneath Delia's approving gaze, felt himself responding. There was nothing he could do about it. Grabbing a nearby black wool tunic, Jake quickly threw it over his head, jammed his arms through the openings and tugged it down over his awakened body. When he looked up, he saw a smile on Delia's face. Feeling heat sweep up his neck into his face, he couldn't believe he was blushing. Him, of all people! And in front of Delia, who had seen him naked plenty of times in the past.

"I hope you enjoyed the joke," he growled, swirling his cloak about his shoulders and pinning it in place.

"Hey, you look good naked," she murmured, limping to the couch and sitting down. "And obviously, that young woman thought so, too. Who was she, Jake?"

Frustrated by her teasing, he sat down next to her and pulled on his leather boots. "Kapaneus, that scribe we saw last night at the party, sent her here. Her name is Tullia. She's a prostitute."

"I didn't know you were paying for sex, Jake. That isn't at all like you."

Seeing the laughter in her gold eyes, Jake swore softly. "I did not pay for anything. Listen to me, will you? I read her mind and found that Kapaneus had paid her to undress me and make love to me. Why, I don't know. All I could get out of her was that she was supposed to look for any jewelry I might be wearing." He put on his second boot and then ran his fingers through his drying hair.

"Jewelry?" Delia glanced around. "Was Kapaneus paying her to come here to steal from you? Does this scribe think you're rich?"

"That seems a stupid assumption for him to make," Jake muttered. He took a deep breath, starting to relax. "You don't really think I would do anything with Tullia, do you?"

Shrugging, Delia said lightly, "Hey, we're not a couple anymore, Jake. What you do isn't my business any longer." That was a lie, but she couldn't admit it.

Giving her a grim look, Jake stood up. He reached for his belt and scabbard and settled them around his waist. "I have never had to pay any woman to go to bed with me and you know it."

Laughing, Delia enjoyed Jake's discomfort. The belt cinching his tunic made his broad, deep chest seem even more pronounced. A beautiful male chest that held a massive heart she used to listen to after making love with him, a drum that had lulled her to sleep.

Pulling herself out of the past, she said teasingly, "I'm sure this gift hurt your male feelings."

"It was a shock," Jake admitted. He picked up his sword from atop the dresser and slid it into the scabbard. "She just waltzed in here without knocking."

"What a trauma!"

"Stop laughing, Del...."

Covering her grin with her hand, Delia tried to comply, but it was impossible. "I'm sure under any other circumstances you'd have jumped her, Jake."

"Give me a break!"

"She's very beautiful."

"So what?"

"You like good-looking women."

He gave her a flat, harried glance. "I like *some* good-looking women. Not *all* of them. You are the one I like."

Chapter 11

"What did you find out about the survivor of that attack last night?" Delia asked as Jake entered her apartment later. She was still exhausted, and needed more sleep. But first she wanted to know if the enemy had revealed that Queen Cleopatra had hired assassins to attack Servilia's home during the party.

Shutting the door, Jake gave Delia a grim look. She'd bathed while he was gone and slipped into a soft green cotton tunic that brushed her feet. Thinking she looked pale due to the wound she'd endured, he tried to focus on responding to her questions. "He didn't talk, Del. Didn't speak a word. Needless to say, Servilia and the entire household are upset by the attack last night. Everyone is edgy and tense."

Watching as he took off his heavy woolen cloak and dropped it on the couch, Delia asked, "Did the prisoner confess to anything?"

"No. And these people aren't reticent about cutting up a person to get what they want. He didn't reveal anything, which has really infuriated Julius Caesar. A slave overheard the emperor talking to one of his guards, and he wasn't happy."

Watching Jake unbuckle his sword belt and set it on top of his cloak, Delia studied his drawn features. She had no idea what time it was; perhaps around noon. The attack last night had left them both feeling an adrenaline letdown that wasn't at all unexpected. She patted the couch. "Come, sit down for a moment. Are you thirsty?" She pointed to a cup and pitcher on the table nearby.

Shaking his head, Jake ran his fingers through his hair as he settled beside her. There was no way he wanted Delia to find out about the gory torture their attacker had experienced before dying. Jake could see the translucent quality to her flesh, the shadows beneath her eyes. As he sat back, he gripped Delia's hand momentarily and gave it a gentle squeeze. He didn't want to release it, but knew he had to. "No, not thirsty. Helluva day so far."

"That's very true," she whispered, searching his blue eyes, which were murky with worry. Her hand tingled where he'd gripped it for a moment. Secretly, she loved his touch. It made her feel so much better.

"You're right about things being in chaos," Delia said. "I'm afraid to ask what else can happen in a twenty-four-hour period around here. Who ever said Rome was a dull place to live?" She smiled wryly.

His mouth flexed. "It's been hectic, that's for sure." Jake leaned back on the curved end of the couch and simply observed Delia's softness. There was no question she was the ultimate woman warrior—fearless, smart and quick-thinking. As he gazed at her full lips, noting the way they curved upward at the corners, he found himself wanting to simply hold her. He needed Delia now as never before. What had happened to that attacker could happen to them if they were ever discovered.

Jake couldn't bear the possibility of them losing their ESC armbands or being separated from one another on this mission. Of Delia being tortured…

"Are you all right, Jake? You look…upset."

He gave her a teasing glance and deliberately lied. "I'm still in shock over Tullia's arrival. Who really sent her?"

Shaking her head, Delia looked mystified. "And why *did* they send her?"

"I don't know, but I intend to do a little questioning of the household slaves later today, when things settle down around here." He gave Delia an oblique look. "Despite Tullia showing up, you still love me just the same, right?"

Delia rolled her eyes. "I'll plead the Fifth on that one."

"But we aren't in the twenty-first century U.S.A. The Fifth Amendment didn't exist in this era." Jake grinned at her.

Holding up her hand, Delia insisted, "I'll still take the Fifth."

Okay, he could handle that. "At least you didn't say no," he stated.

"Don't read anything into that," Delia warned. When she saw his wonderful mouth lift, she couldn't help but laugh. "You have a nice way of making things light when the situation is heavy, Jake." Reaching out, she grazed his hand, which was resting on his large, strong thigh. "Thank you."

"Anytime," he answered, his voice rough with emotion. Jake would give anything for Delia to continue running her fingers over his body. Her touch ignited an instant fire, an ache in his lower body. "How is your leg doing?"

Delia shrugged. "It's aching a little, but that's to be expected. I'm taking antibiotics faithfully, so don't worry. Plus I got a good night's sleep. But I'm still tired, and I want to nap off and on today, to lessen the shock of the incident."

"No more bleeding?" he asked, peering down at where her tunic covered her thighs.

She shook her head. "No, it's fine. I checked the dressing and it's clean."

"We should change the bandage daily, add more antibiotic to the area, to keep it that way."

Delia nodded. "Not a bad idea." Then she frowned. "Jake, do you think Caesar suspects Cleopatra of planning that attack last night?"

"No. I was reading his mind yesterday after I left you. He's baffled. He still loves Servilia, although much less than he does the Egyptian queen. He thinks a small group of senators who don't want him as dictator and emperor of Rome might be behind that attack."

"Politics."

"When isn't it?"

"Historically, it was Brutus along with a group of other senators who stabbed him to death on March 15. And Marcus Brutus was here at the banquet."

"But Caesar does not suspect his old friend."

"Isn't that amazing, Jake? A few years ago, Brutus left Caesar and teamed up with Senator Pompey to fight Caesar in Greece, hoping to get the republic back. He was accused by Caesar's other generals of being a traitor."

"Yes," Jake murmured, "that's all historically true. And when Caesar gathered his legions, sailed to Greece and met with Pompey in battle at Pharsalus, it was Julius who won."

"I don't know how he could take Brutus back as a friend after he'd betrayed him," Delia said, shaking her head. Giving Jake a searching look, she said, "Do you have any idea how he could do that? Forgive a lifelong friend for turning traitor, joining the enemy and going to war against him?"

"I watched Brutus last night," Jake told her, "and there is an obvious connection between them. The general loves Julius, and at the same time I felt his concern that Rome needed a republic, not an emperor. I could feel Brutus being torn by these two things."

"Could it be that Julius forgave Brutus because of his own long liaison with Servilia? Could that be why he forgave the general for deserting him and fighting a war against him over in Greece? Brutus is, after all, her son."

Shrugging, Jake said, "We'll never really know,

Delia. Last night, Brutus appeared very concerned over the attack. When I scanned his mind, I discovered he had nothing to do with it. Brutus is like a younger brother to Julius in some ways. Maybe that's what explains their closeness. Does Julius see Brutus as family instead of just a fellow soldier?" Jake gave her a searching look. "I can't answer that."

"Historians couldn't answer that, either," she said, frowning. "And yet we know it will be Brutus who works with certain senators to set up Caesar's death, returning Rome to a republic instead of a dictatorship."

Jake gave her a slight smile. "Don't we all become traitors to one another in some shape or form, Del?"

Giving it some thought, Delia saw how in their own relationship that applied, up to a point. "You're talking about us, right?"

"I am." He spread his hands. "You walked out of my life because I couldn't be who you needed me to be. In a way, I was a traitor to you. I'm not assigning a right or wrong, Del. It just is what it is. No human is perfect. We're all flawed to a degree. Brutus had an ideological and philosophical disagreement with Julius about Rome—whether it should be a dictatorship or the democracy it once was. Brutus wanted the latter. Julius felt he'd earned the title of dictator and emperor of Rome because of conquering the rest of Europe, Britain and Spain for his people. So who is right?"

Nodding, Delia said, "Jake, I left you because you couldn't open up to me. I don't see that as being a traitor as much as not trying harder to learn to trust another person."

Jake held up his hands. "Fair enough, Del. But I'd like to think I'm trying to change. On this mission I've been trying to trust you. Was there ever a time when I didn't treat you as an equal?"

Giving him a sour look, she muttered, "I wasn't going to take the mission without those tenets in place. I was tired of how you'd treated me the two years we spent in Afghanistan together."

"I agree," he said, "and looking back on that time, I see it was immature of me, Del. Our talk has helped me." He raised his brows. "Don't you think I'm trying now?"

"Yes," she hesitantly admitted, "you are. But you know what, Jake? It'll take more than a couple of days to make me believe the changes are for real. Time will out."

"Okay," he murmured, "fair enough." Rising, he walked over and collected his gear and cloak. Heading for the door to his room, he said, "I'm going to go ask the staff about Tullia. If you need anything, I won't be far away. I'll change your dressing later."

"Okay, Jake." Delia watched him disappear.

Her heart had been pounding with fear. Why? Why did she fear Jake was really making changes to be more in line with what she needed him to be? Rubbing her face, she watched the brazier in the corner sputter nastily and go out, leaving the room in darkness. Pulling up her covers, she carefully lay down and drew the blanket up to her shoulders. Nestling her head on the golden cushions, she sighed deeply.

As she closed her eyes, Delia tried to stop the replay of her conversation with Jake. She'd seen the earnest expression in his eyes. All he had to do was look at her and she felt mesmerized by his masculine authority and sensuality. There was no mistaking the smoldering message in his gaze. Jake wasn't trying to hide the fact he wanted her sexually—again.

Pursing her lips, Delia tried to push the entire dilemma from her mind so she could sleep once more. Her thigh ached and so she honed in on that. The anguish she felt in her heart was even worse than the pain throbbing in her thigh. Pressing her face into the cushion, Delia forced herself to relax. When she awoke, Jake would change her dressing....

Her last thoughts were of the scribe, Kapaneus, and the red aura she'd seen around him. Now *there* was an anomaly.

"Tullia, what did you find out?" Torbar demanded as she floated gracefully into his small office at General Brutus's home near lunchtime. The prostitute was beautiful, no question. Stained with red pomegranate juice, her full, bow-shaped lips became the focal point of her glowing face. Black kohl only emphasized her exotic-looking eyes.

Shutting the door, Tullia turned and smiled coyly. "Ah, my lord Kapaneus, it was an interesting meeting late this morning with Philip."

Torbar tried to ignore the scent of cinnamon around her smooth, gleaming body. Tullia wore a modest pink tunic with a red stola, her hair piled high and held in place by a thin circlet of gold. Her delicate gold earrings were long and dangling. The fact that she dressed like a married Roman woman amused Torbar. Tullia seemed to have the talents of a chameleon. Smiling to himself, he admired the prostitute's canny ability to change facades. Perhaps that came from assuming different guises for her wealthy customers. Some wanted a willowy slave girl scantily clad in see-through gowns and others wanted a Roman matron who lacked sensuality until the garments were shed. Yes, Tullia was certainly a consummate actress, and Torbar kept that in mind as she approached him.

Lifting her hand in a graceful manner, Tullia laughed throatily. "My lord, I caught Philip of Delos completely naked in his apartment this morning."

"Ah," Torbar said with interest. He inhaled her spicy perfume along with the womanly scent that was making him grow hard with need of her. The prospect of taking Tullia after he heard her report made his blood run hot. Giving her a heated look she could not miss, he growled, "So tell me, beautiful and willful Tullia, what did you find out?"

She tittered and, reaching forward, slid her hand suggestively across Kapaneus's narrow cheek, then entangled her fingers in his neatly kept black beard. "I found out enough." Tullia wasn't about to tell the scribe that Philip had kicked her out of his apartment without sexually jousting with her. Flashing a sultry smile, she allowed her hand to drift to the scribe's thin shoulder. Stroking her fingertips across the fabric of his tunic, she said, "I saw a piece of jewelry upon him, my lord."

"Ah?"

"Yes." She removed her hand and pushed up her sleeve. "Here, on his upper arm, was a thin silver band. What was most intriguing was the large, oval stone embedded within it."

Torbar instantly tamped down his growing arousal. Tullia was interested in him or she wouldn't be touching him so suggestively. Of course, she'd want a gold aureus for any sexual favors and he was more than willing to pay it—but not right now. "Tell me about this stone."

"It was clear and flat, and highly polished, my lord."

"How close did you get to it?"

"Close enough," she replied with a pouty smile.

"Did he take it off?"

"No, he stood naked, except for that armband. He had just came from the baths when I entered his room."

"Hmm," Torbar said thoughtfully. "What kind of metal was it?"

Tullia shrugged. "It was silvery looking."

"Thin or thick?"

"Very thin, my lord." She held up her thumb and index finger to demonstrate.

Grunting, Torbar got up and began to pace. "And did he remove it when you made love with him?"

Tullia smiled coyly as the scribe strode back and forth in front of a large woven tapestry of Greeks fighting Roman soldiers. "He did not, my lord."

"Did he allow you to touch it?"

"No."

"I see… Afterward, did you ask him about it?"

Tullia continued to smile. "I did, but he refused to speak of it."

"Did the stone change color?"

"No."

"Did you see such an armband on the other Greek mercenary, Delia of Delos?"

"No." The harlot's eyes gleamed. "But you did not suggest I go to her, my lord. I am often sent to women to…make use of my talents, but that was not what you asked me to do. Perhaps, if you are curious, you will pay me to find out? I will be more than happy to discover if she wears a similar armband—or any other item of interest."

"Philip is my target for now," Torbar said curtly.

Something told him instinctively that the armband had to do with time travel. Since the woman had a similar aura, she must be wearing an armband, too. The fact that the lost Navigator headband was silver and held two quartz crystal cabochons was too much of a coincidence. He would contact Kentar….

Tullia walked toward the scribe, hips swaying seductively. "I expect full payment now, my lord."

"Of course." Torbar took two gold coins from

the purse hanging at his side. "This first aureus is for the information you just gave me." He dropped it on her palm. "And this one is for the pleasure you will now accord me in my apartment…."

Chapter 12

"Delia!" Servilia called, walking in without knocking on the apartment door. "How are you this morning?"

Groggy and just awakening from sleep, Delia pushed the hair away from her eyes. Servilia was dressed in a pale peach tunic, with a burnt-orange stola across her proud shoulders. "Uhh..."

"Oh, I'm sorry, I didn't mean to wake you," the matron said, coming over to the couch. "Philip told me he dressed your wound last night." She eyed Delia closely. "Do you need a physician? I have one of the finest in Rome."

Sitting up and trying to pull herself from the deep sleep she'd been in, Delia rasped, "No, *domina*. I'm fine."

"Philip said it was a leg wound?" the woman pressed.

With a groan, Delia straightened. Her thigh smarted as she moved it a little too quickly.

"You poor dear," Servilia murmured. Reaching out, she gripped Delia's shoulder. "You are truly heroic. You and your brother broke up an attack against my beloved Julius. You saved his life and goddess knows how many others by your swift actions." She dropped her hands on her hips. "Are you in pain?"

Delia ran her fingers through her hair, trying to get it into some semblance of order. "It's nothing, *domina*."

"Can you walk?"

"With a limp. I'm afraid I won't be of much service to you for the next several weeks."

"I'm not concerned about that," Servilia exclaimed worriedly. "So many die from such cuts."

"Yes," Delia murmured, "they do."

Looking around, the matron made sure there were no slaves present. Then she whispered, "Delia, the arrow of Diana can heal you. Did you know that?"

Staring up at the woman, whose hair was loose

about her shoulders today, Delia said, "Why...no. I didn't know."

"Yes," Servilia said with authority, "it can. One member of our group discovered this by accident, at one of our monthly meetings at the temple. Lollia had suffered a miscarriage. She was still not healed from it, but came to the next meeting. None of us knew about her pain or injury from losing the child. As you know, each of us holds the arrowhead. And when it was her turn, she said she felt this incredible wave of heat flow up her hand and to the region where she was in pain. When she passed the arrowhead to the next woman, her pain was gone, and she has felt fine ever since."

"A miracle," Delia said, feeling her pulse begin to race.

"Indeed it was. And I can tell you of other miracles Diana's arrowhead has performed. But I do not want to tarry. You need to hold it." She pointed a finger at Delia's wounded leg. "It will heal you."

"I can't walk to the temple, my lady. I must rest for several days while the gash closes."

Servilia smiled. "Your brother, Philip?"

"Yes?"

"Is he someone you would trust to go with me to retrieve the arrowhead and bring it back here? To you?"

Delia tried to cover her surprise and delight. "Why, *domina,* my brother worships at the temple of Diana. She is the patron goddess of our family."

Delia saw Servilia's brown eyes sparkle. The woman's thin lips lifted in a triumphant smile. "Then it is done! I'll have my servant fetch Philip. We will go to the high priestess at the temple of Diana and retrieve the sacred object. Philip will accompany me as my bodyguard. I'm not feeling safe since the attack last night."

Delia nodded. "Of course, *domina.*" She wondered if Jake would be shown where the relic was kept. That would be a wonderful and unexpected coup. Under the circumstances, with the wound she'd incurred, Delia knew they couldn't steal it as soon as they wanted. Her leg would take at least two weeks to heal before they could attempt the heist. However, if Servilia allowed Jake into the inner sanctum where the fragment was probably stored— and if Delia's wound *was* healed, which the Roman woman seemed to think possible—that could change their plans.

Patting Delia's shoulder as a mother might her daughter's, Servilia said, "You are too valuable to me, Delia. As a bodyguard you have no equal. I want your leg healed quickly so that you may continue to protect me."

"Thank you, *domina*," Delia murmured. She watched the woman turn gracefully, her leather sandals slapping softly against the marble floor as she exited, shutting the door behind her.

Not knowing what time it was, Delia got up and limped to the dresser that held the water pitcher and basin. It was time to get up, get washed, don clean clothes and then wait for Jake.

Jake knocked on Delia's door. It was midday and the winter sunlight was dazzling as it flowed down the hall.

"Come in…."

Delia's voice floated through the finely crafted wooden panel. Opening it, Jake found her in a fresh white wool tunic that fell almost to her ankles. Her hair was combed, and on the dresser was a basin full of soapy water.

"Just get up?" he teased, shutting the door behind him. "It's past noon. You must have slept late this morning?"

Delia tried to suppress her joy at seeing Jake. Maybe it was a reaction to last night's attack. "Yes. Servilia dropped by to see how I was doing. She woke me up." Maybe Servilia would see Jake later about going to the temple, Delia surmised.

Jake watched as Delia limped slowly to the

couch. She sat down and began the process of pulling on her knee-high leather boots. Striding forward, he knelt in front of her. "Let me help. How's your leg?"

Her flesh tingled as he eased the tunic up to view the dressing. "Painful but okay."

Jake gently placed his hand across her thigh in a protective gesture. It was a delicious piece of thievery on his part. "Any heat? Swelling?"

Swallowing a gasp of pleasure as his large palm carefully touched the bandaged area of her wounded leg, Delia managed to answer, "No, it's okay."

"Let me look…." He began to gingerly unknot the gauze and unroll it from around her thigh. "Did you know," he began in a conspiratorial tone, "you have the best-damn-looking legs I've ever seen on a woman? The curve of your thighs is sweet."

The feel of his roughened fingertips grazing her flesh sent wild prickles of heat surging into her core. "Thanks, but this is the wrong time and place," she retorted, gripping his thick wrist and halting his movements. Drilling him with a chastising look, Delia almost lost herself in his blue eyes. Jake had not yet shaved and the dark shadow of his beard, combined with the tousled strands of hair falling across his broad brow, made her want him even more. He made her ache for his touch, damn him.

The corners of Jake's mouth curved faintly with a wicked smile. "Now, darling Delia, you must let me look at the wound and check my handiwork. Are you sure you don't want to stop holding my wrist, and move your long, beautiful fingers elsewhere?"

With a grunt of frustration, she let go as if she'd been scalded. "You are incorrigible."

"Thank you," he said wryly, leaning over her thigh and examining his suturing work after he'd removed the dressing. "Hey, this looks very good," he murmured, congratulating himself. Glancing up, he saw the turmoil in her narrowed green eyes. And her soft, full lips were pursed. Jake knew he'd gotten to Delia with just his touch. That did his battered ego good. "Have you taken your antibiotic today like a good girl?"

"Of course I have."

He set the dressing aside and stood up. Going to the washbasin, he scrubbed his hands vigorously with soap and then rinsed them off. He dug into his leather pouch and brought out another packet of antibiotic ointment. Opening it, he knelt down and said, "We need to do this twice a day to keep infection at bay."

Sucking in a soft breath, Delia watched, mesmerized, as Jake leaned over, cupped her thigh with his left hand and then gently spread the ointment across the wound. Fiery geysers of heat flowed up her leg, and again it felt as if her womanly core were melting with need to be one with Jake.

Delia forced herself to calm down. He really didn't trust any woman, and Delia couldn't allow herself to fall in love with him a second time, knowing that.

"Feel good?" he asked, finishing up his work.

Delia clamped her lips together, unwilling to give him the satisfaction of knowing how easily he inflamed her. She watched as he rose and walked back to the dresser, opening a drawer and pulling out a long piece of cotton fabric. Taking his knife from its sheath, he quickly cut the cloth into strips. Rolling them up, he placed all but one back in the drawer.

"We'll change your bandage daily," he informed her as he came back and knelt in front of her.

"So you didn't run into Servilia?" Delia asked, trying to deflect her reactions to him. Maybe by talking about something else she could keep the breathless quality out of her tone.

Jake was an expert at field medicine, there was no doubt. With brisk efficiency, he had her wound wrapped and knotted off once more. "No, why?" he asked, looking up after finishing his work.

Delia quickly pulled the tunic back down and

told him what had happened. She saw Jake's eyes go wide with surprise, and then that boyish smile crossed his handsome features.

"This is a hell of an opportunity for us," he said in a low voice.

"It is," she agreed. Now that her wound was attended to, she noticed how hungry she was. A slave had brought her a plate of bread and some lamb soup earlier. "Would you get me my breakfast?" she asked, pointing to it.

"Sure."

Jake reached for the wooden tray and set it across her lap, then sat down next to her. "So, Servilia is going to take me to the temple of Diana? Maybe I'll get to see where they keep the relic."

Nodding, Delia dunked the thick, brown bread into the broth, which smelled of fresh rosemary. "I hope so. She's feeling vulnerable because of the attacks. She wants me back at work as her bodyguard."

"So, this fragment heals?" Jake murmured pensively. "That's a nuance we didn't know about."

"I'll believe it when I see it work," Delia said, wiping her mouth with a cloth that had been folded on the tray.

"Well, if it does, Delia, then that's a plus." Jake took a piece of bread from the tray and munched on it. "Does that mean the other segments of the stamp have the same ability?"

"I don't know. Maybe each one has a different skill attached or another piece of information. Maybe this seal we're searching for is magical beyond our imaginations."

Just being with Delia, sitting this close, was all the magic Jake ever needed or wanted. But he didn't dare reveal his thoughts to her. When she gave him that warm look, it made him hopeful that something might work between them. Their talk had shown him how to leap the hurdles that stood between them. He gave her a slight grin. "If that metal object does heal you, that's great news for us. It means we can leave here sooner rather than later. I don't know about you, but this conspiracy swirling around Caesar, and knowing he meets his maker on the Ides of March.... It's all getting too close for comfort."

"Yes," Delia agreed grimly. "I feel off balance here, Jake. It's an energy thing I'm picking up on. Ever since we saw Kapaneus at the party, I've had an awful feeling...." She pressed her hand against her stomach.

"The red color you saw in his aura?"

"Yes. That's not natural. A human's aura is composed of many colors, because we're emotional creatures by nature. And yes, we have red show up in our aura from time to time, especially if we're angry. Or—" she gave him a dark look "—feeling amorous."

"Hey, I like red. Is there any in your aura right now?" He craned his neck, teasing her. When he saw her cheeks flush pink he knew he'd gotten to her.

"Only you would ask something like that," she chuckled. "And I don't go around seeing auras all day long. I have to switch internally in order to see them. It takes energy and concentration."

"Oh," he said, feigning disappointment.

"Besides, with you, I don't need to see your aura to know you're a man on the hunt for any woman willing to throw herself into your arms—and your bed. Like Tullia."

"Ouch…! Hey, that's not fair."

Delia finished off the last of her delicious soup. "What in life *is* fair?"

"You've got a point there," Jake agreed with a lopsided smile. What he'd give to touch her lips with his fingers, to trace them and feel their soft texture once more.

There was a faint knock on the door. When Delia called, "Enter!" a woman slave, Spanish in origin, came hesitantly into the room. She wore a long green tunic, with her shining black hair piled up on her head.

"Mistress Servilia would see you, Philip of Delos. She is waiting in the tablinum for you."

Jake rose, then covertly winked at Delia. "Of course. I'll be there shortly. Thank you."

Delia waited until the shy slave quietly closed the door. She watched as Jake smoothed his tunic and rearranged his sword belt. "Good luck. I hope she takes you to where the relic is located."

"So do I," Jake said. He blew her a kiss. "See you later, sweetheart."

Delia watched him walk confidently out of her apartment. Suddenly, the room seemed barren. Delia grimaced, not wanting to admit that Jake was like sunlight to her heart, her life. His presence filled the apartment with an energy that made her feel good. But if he knew that, he'd use it against her.

"Better to say nothing," she warned herself. Setting the tray aside, Delia wondered if Servilia would show Jake the relic. Mentally crossing her fingers, Delia wondered if the "arrowhead of Diana" would indeed heal her leg wound.

The more they found out about this ancient object, the more fascinating it became.

Torbar felt his loins rejoice and he smiled in satisfaction. Tullia was dressing, after spending a delicious hour with him in his quarters. He saw the bruises already marking her golden flesh. Centaurians were always rough and primal with their females.

"I need your services today," he told her as he watched her smooth the folds of her pale pink tunic into place. Sitting up, he poured water into a silver goblet that sat next to the bed. He saw Tullia smile as she combed her long dark hair, then piled it atop her head again. Her lower lip was swollen from him biting it in the midst of their sex play.

Prostitution was an Earthling's concept. Her kind would be instantly killed on his constellation, where females were kept under lock and key. But here, she served a higher purpose for Torbar.

"Are you interested in working for me this afternoon, Tullia?" he asked.

"Of course, my dear scribe," she murmured, cinching her belt around her waist. "It will cost you."

He reached for his pouch and flipped her another aureus. She caught it gracefully. "You will come with me. We're going over to Servilia's *domus*. I'd like you to take the silver band you saw on Philip of Delos's arm. I *want* it."

Pouting playfully, Tullia came over after depositing the gold coin in the leather pouch at her waist. "He would not let me near it."

"He will this time," Torbar promised grimly. "He won't have a choice."

She gave him a confused look, and Torbar laughed deeply. Foolish Earth female. She had no idea of the power he had as a Centaurian. But she would find out shortly, and so would Philip of Delos. Both would become instant slaves to his will.

Chapter 13

"Here," Servilia said excitedly as she entered Delia's apartment, with Jake following behind. "The high priestess of the temple has approved your holding the sacred arrowhead."

Delia was sitting on the couch, having recently awakened from her nap. She watched as Jake closed the door behind him. Servilia seemed so proud of herself as she gave Delia the small wooden box embellished with gold.

"Thank you, *domina*. I'm forever indebted to you and the high priestess for your trust in me." Delia's fingertips tingled wildly as she took the box and set it beside her on the couch.

Servilia sat down next to her. "The priestess said to press the arrowhead onto the dressing where you were wounded. She said it might take a few minutes, but that you *will* be healed."

"This is amazing," Delia confided to the Roman matron, who sat expectantly, hands in her lap. Looking up, she saw Jake hovering near the door. Wishing she had the ability to telepathically communicate with him, to find out what he'd seen at the temple, she focused on the box.

"Open it. I told the priestess I would bring it back to her right away. We must not tarry."

Delia nodded. She knew it had taken an hour for them to climb the hill to the temple, retrieve the sacred relic and come back to the house.

Opening the wooden container, she ran her fingers over the fabric. Instantly, Delia could see that incredible silvery light shooting out like rays of the sun. Her hand began to feel tingles of electricity, as if touching a low-voltage live wire. Pulling up her tunic to expose the dressing on her thigh, she carefully placed the object, still wrapped in the cloth, upon it.

She closed her eyes, wanting to see psychically whatever was going to happen. Instantly, a bolt of heat, much like lightning, flashed into her leg. She jerked in response. Surprised, Delia kept a firm hand over the relic.

In her mind's eye, she suddenly saw the universe open up before her. A spiral-armed galaxy came into view. It was beautiful, with millions of stars making up the slowly moving mass. And then she felt as if she were being sucked into a vortex of spinning energy. Delia felt dizzy. Fighting the sensation, she honed in on the center of the vortex, like the very core of a whirling tornado.

Gasping inwardly, Delia felt heat flow through her thigh and surround the wound. At the same time she saw a constellation come into view: the same cluster of stars stamped upon the metal object she now held beneath her palm. As she spun dizzily around the vortex, the seven stars took on different forms and shapes, depending upon the direction she viewed from. From one angle, they looked like a crown. From another, a cluster of grapes hanging brightly in the sky.

It struck Delia, as she saw the grape cluster, that the constellation was one she recognized. This was the Pleiades, the Seven Sisters from Greek myth! Abruptly she saw a flock of seven white doves flying in front of her as she was drawn into the constellation at a dizzying speed. Delia felt they were a symbol. But of what?

Her leg felt as if it were on fire, but she ignored the pain, focusing completely on the vision unfolding. As she flew into the grape cluster constellation she felt drawn to one of the stars in particular. When she approached that particular glowing ball of white light, a huge yellow eruption occurred in front of her eyes. It felt as if she had broken some kind of energetic barrier, only there was no sound, just a sense of tremors rippling through her body, wave after wave.

Trying to breathe slowly and calmly, Delia realized the relic held an energy pattern. Was it trying to show her something? Tell her something of its origin? Unsure, she kept her concentration on the yellow light surrounding her. And then a new scene appeared. Delia felt herself slowing down, as if about to land. Feeling her feet settle on solid ground, she saw the hazy light change and begin to take shape in front of her.

Like fog dissolving in hot sunlight, the mists withdrew and a beautiful temple appeared, just like the one to Diana here in Rome. Delia's mind became confused. Was she in the stars? Or in Rome in 44 B.C., looking at that temple?

As if in answer to her question, she found herself standing on a grassy knoll next to a large rectangular pool of calm sapphire water. Lilies of different colors grew in profusion. Birds were flitting about. The sky was filled with fluffy white clouds.

"Welcome, Delia," a voice called.

Turning, she saw a woman wearing a radiant

white robe that hung to her ankles. Whatever the
material was, it gleamed with gold and white light.
Looking into the woman's gray eyes, Delia felt
herself filling with happiness. Just as she seemed to
be drawn by the stranger's eyes, she also felt as if she
was being pulled into the spinning vortex yet again.
Forcing herself to stop, she used all her strength to
stay where she was and focus on the woman.

"Who are you?" Delia asked.

"I am Adonia of the Pleiadian Council. Welcome, Delia. We have long anticipated your kind
finding our bread crumbs and then being sent to us
as a sign."

"A sign?" she responded. Looking around, she
saw that the marble temple stood on a slight rise.
People of all colors, ages and sizes were walking up
and down the long, wide steps. All were dressed
similarly to Adonia.

Smiling gently, the woman gestured for Delia to
sit down on a stone bench that faced the water.
"Your women of Earth possess special DNA. There
is only one other species in our galaxy that has a
unique gene that you do—people from the Centaur
constellation."

Delia sat down, feeling warmth emanating from
Adonia. Her oval face was calm, her eyes large and
wide spaced. Her dark brown hair was twined into

a braid that hung down the center of her back. "You aren't of Earth. Where am I?"

"You are here in the Pleiades, although we refer to ourselves as the Seven Doves of Peace Constellation." Adonia folded her slim hands in her lap as she faced Delia on the bench. "You are in the star system known to your kind as Merope, one of the stars that comprise the Pleiades as seen from your place in our galaxy."

"Ah," Delia nodded, remembering that seven stars comprised that constellation. "Did the relic bring me here?"

"Yes," Adonia said. "And your time with us is not long, so allow me to quickly give you important information you must have. The stamp that you now are aware of, and actively searching for, was planted by our Galactic Council many thousands of years ago in your time span. We cut up the seal into twelve different parts. And there is a special constellation connection, and information, implanted into each of those segments. Our council placed them in different civilizations and different ages in hopes that someday humans would evolve and begin to find them. Whoever finds all twelve pieces and puts them together into a disk once more will ensure that your world and people are ready to enter our galactic federation. Until that time, you'll be considered a backward and primitive planet." She gestured toward the temple. "In order to join the Galactic Council, a planet and its citizens must show heart and compassion. Without these qualities in place, you remain warlike and selfish, possessing energy that is destructive to our galaxy. We will not work with a solar system until its inhabitants demonstrate a genuine desire for peace and a capacity for compassion."

"And so," Delia said, rapidly trying to put it all together, "Earth has reached that fulcrum point? We've advanced far enough to earn the right to find the stamp and discover its pieces? So that we can join you in peaceful and compassionate efforts for everyone in our galaxy?"

Adonia smiled, clearly pleased. "You are truly the right emissary to have found the first piece of the seal. Yes. However, you must understand there are no guarantees, Delia."

Frowning, Adonia explained, "The Centaurian people possess a trait referred to as the Navigator gene. This special DNA strain allows a male of the Centaur species to organically move a spaceship through the veils and folds of time. Voyages that would normally take hundreds of years by ancient cruiser travel take only minutes. The Centaurians are zealous about keeping their genes to themselves, however. They will not share with anyone else, and so remain the most powerful traders in our galaxy. All star systems are forced to hire a Centaurian Navigator to guide their spaceships if they wish to do any interconstellation business."

Adonia paused, then added, "The Centaurians are very suppressive toward their women, who also possess this gene. They are brainwashed from birth onward and kept from assuming their equal rights in that society. No Centaurian female is ever a Navigator. Only the males are."

"You said Earth women possess this gene?"

"You do. The Centaurians discovered that fact eons ago, when you were in what you call your cave period. They ran blood tests on both humanoid genders and discovered their gene in Earth females. Now, you must understand, Centaurians weren't happy about this. We found out a long time ago that they illegally kidnapped a hundred women from Earth and brought them home. They tried to manipulate and force them into service, but the women revolted. In the end, they were all destroyed. The Centaurians kept quiet about the genocide incident. They did not want anyone in the council to know they'd discovered another humanoid species that possessed this gene, or that they'd broken our law of noninterference."

"Because," Delia surmised, her mind running quickly over the information, "if Earth women have the Navigator gene and it became common knowledge, then any star system could come to Earth and steal a woman to power a spaceship?"

"Yes and no.... We found documents in computers that the Centaurians had thought were destroyed. The information on their testing of the cave women from Earth was all there. They deduced at that time that the females were too primitive in spiritual evolvement and psychic maturity to do anything with them. So they left them alone, stopped the experiments and buried the data. Or so they thought. When the information came to light, our Council voted that since the Centaurians had broken a major rule of noninterference, special compensation should occur."

"What compensation?"

Adonia smiled slightly. "We were allowed to create a disk with twelve parts to it and drop it into various Earth civilizations throughout a five-thousand-year period. And if Earthlings ever evolved to the point of discovering the stamp and, secondly, realizing that the parts were seeded on their planet, it would break the Centaurian hold over galactic trading and transport."

Adonia gazed into Delia's eyes. "It meant that if

your kind ever began to discover the pieces, and if you put the entire stamp together, that would signal your readiness to join the council. If that event occurred, then all the star systems of the galaxy could come to you, train those females who volunteered to become spaceship Navigators, and thereby break the monopoly held by the Centaurians. We would not be forced to employ their Navigators anymore, but would have a choice. And the Centaurians charge very high prices. The council star systems could then enter into separate contracts with Earth women Navigators and the prices would stabilize."

"And if we wanted to learn to be Navigators, you would school us?"

"Yes, we have the knowledge and technology to do that. The Centaurian grip on the galaxy will disappear. It means, Delia, that economically poor star systems could enter into trade with larger and richer ones. Right now, over eighty percent of our star systems cannot afford to hire a Navigator. In essence, the Centaurians have strangled economic development in our galaxy, which is not a compassionate stance to take. We had no way to change the status quo—until now." She smiled broadly. "The Centaurians didn't want this secret to come to light, but it did. And the council elders allowed us the right to give you clues in the guise of the stamp. And now you are here. You are the first." She spread her hands and sighed. "We did not know if Earth would ever reach the necessary plateau of caring and compassion."

"We still have wars on our planet," Delia warned. "Even today, in the twenty-first century, which is where I came from."

"Yes, we continue to monitor you from afar, since we're not allowed to interfere. A part of your Earth population is definitely moving into their hearts and consistently practicing peace and compassion. We are all joyous over this development."

"But you can't help us?"

Shaking her head, Adonia murmured, "To interfere is to break the galactic law, and we will not do it. The Centaurians did, and now they risk losing their dominance of space transport and trade. It has been a long time in coming, but we have patience."

"The Centaurians know what's happening?"

"Oh, yes. The council gives updates on Earth to everyone on a regular basis." She frowned. "They, too, must not interfere in your progress, but no one trusts them. Some of us feel that they will send Navigators to Earth to stop you from fulfilling your mission. They know that if the stamp is found and reassembled, their control will be over for good. They don't want to see that happen. Although we monitor their activity, they are skilled in many ways. I personally believe they are sending spies among you. Be aware that a Centaurian in disguise may try to steal all you seek."

"You lack the ability to know if they are there on Earth, following us around?"

"That is correct. Remember, their Navigator gene allows them to move through space and time with just a thought. None of us," Adonia said, "possess such skills. So we are unable to monitor such activity. Many members of the council believe this is happening, but we cannot prove it."

Frowning, Delia asked, "Is there any way to identify a Centaurian spy?"

"No. That is why I am telling you this." Adonia sighed. "You must find out on your own, by being alert. We feel Centaurians are already among you. You must protect the fragment you have found. When you take it back to your own century, you must hide it so it cannot be found by them. Centaurians can read thoughts, see auras, mind-blast and make another species do things that they may not want to do. Because of this powerful psychic ability, they can control others' minds and emotions. They can also possess a body and operate out of it, as well."

"That sounds pretty dangerous."

"It is." Adonia looked at Delia and grasped her hands. "Be careful, my daughter. Take this information back to your own kind who hunt for the other pieces of the seal. I cannot divulge where they are or what times they are in. As I've explained, to do so would be to break galactic laws."

"Yet you suspect the Centaurians of cheating, of trying to stop humans from becoming who and what we really are."

"That's true. But we are working hard to develop instruments that can track these Centaurian spies. Until then, it is up to you." She squeezed Delia's hands gently. "And we feel Earth Navigators will be far superior to those we have currently. Right now, however, you are in for the fight of your lives. Just know that Centaurians lurk and wait and watch. They will steal the stamp pieces if given a chance. And will kill to do so."

Delia felt a warm flow of energy moving up her hands and arms and encircling her heart as Adonia held her gaze. There was something so ethereal and beautiful about her. "I wish we had more time to talk together…."

"But we do not. The council is allowed to speak with an Earthling who's holding a piece of the seal. I've broken no laws in discussing the facts with you. As your world says, forewarned is forearmed."

Delia released her hands and stood up. She felt the tugging, whirling sensation again. "I feel like I'm being pulled back, Adonia. Goodbye. I hope we meet again."

And then the scene began to dissolve and brilliant yellow light surrounded Delia once more. She had the sensation of moving through energy veils or walls, one after another. And then felt herself come back into her physical body. The heaviness, the grounding, occurred immediately.

As Delia opened her eyes, she heard Servilia say, "Now don't you feel better?"

Chapter 14

Delia withheld a gasp of disbelief as Jake carefully unwrapped the dressing from around her leg. Servilia stood off to one side, arms across her chest, the picture of confidence. As the last of the fabric fell away it revealed a long pink scar in lieu of the gash that had been stitched closed so recently.

Running her fingers cautiously across her flesh, Delia felt stunned. She was still caught up in the memory of her conversation with the Galactic councillor. Servilia's excited voice helped to focus her.

The Roman matron leaned over and smoothed

her hand across Delia's healed wound. "Oh! This is just as it was with so many other injuries," she breathed reverently. Looking at Delia, she smiled in triumph. "If you ever doubted the power of the goddess Diana, you will not now."

"I never did, my lady," Delia managed to reply in a strangled tone. How she wished she and Jake were alone! Desperate to impart all she had seen and heard, she said, *"Domina?* I feel tired now. I'd like to lie down and sleep."

Servilia continued to smile. "Of course, Delia. I'll give you the rest of the day off. By tomorrow you should be able to resume your full guarding abilities along with your brother." She took the relic enclosed in the cloth and replaced it gently into the wooden box. "Come, Philip. Escort me to the temple. The high priestess wants this back as soon as possible."

Wanting to stay, but knowing he couldn't, Jake rose. He gave Delia an apologetic glance that he knew she'd understand. She seemed woozy and her eyes had a faraway look, as if she were ungrounded and adrift. Reaching out, he touched her shoulder briefly and said, "I'll be back to check on you later."

"Yes, drop by when you return from the temple," Delia told him.

After watching the two of them leave, Delia got up off the couch, weaving dizzily. Right now, she needed to splash water on her face to try and regroup.

* * *

"How are you feeling?" Jake asked as he entered her apartment after returning from the temple.

Delia sat up on the couch and took a deep breath as he walked over and sat next to her. He laid his hand on hers, and she found his touch grounding. The swirling started to settle as he brushed his fingertips across her hand.

Closing her eyes, she muttered, "Lay your hand on my leg, okay? It's helping to bring me back. That relic really threw me out of my body, and I'm having a hard time trying to get back…."

Raising his eyebrows in surprise, Jake watched her take long, slow breaths. "Sure, I'd like to touch you whenever I get a chance," he teased. "That was a hell of an example of what that fragment can do. Did you feel the power amp up in here when you placed it against your leg?"

"Umm." Delia was focusing on the feel of his hand. He had grounding energy and she needed it. The relic had hurled her through currents of time to a far constellation. Opening her eyes moments later, she saw Jake giving her a concerned look. Without thinking, she placed her hand over his and patted it.

"Don't look so worried. I'm fine." Jake's care and concern for her were visible in his narrowed blue eyes. Delia was deeply touched. Giving his hand a squeeze, she added, "You can let go now. I'm all right."

Reluctantly, Jake did as she requested. Delia pulled her tunic down, stood and smoothed the fabric, then turned and looked at him. Seeing her serious expression, he sensed something profound had occurred during the healing. "What *else* happened?" he demanded in a low tone.

"A lot." She sat and faced him again. "Listen to this," she murmured, and launched into the story of her journey to the Pleiades.

After relating all she'd experienced, Delia sat back and gazed at him. There was shock in Jake's rugged features, and a long silence stretched as he sat there digesting the information. Finally, he pushed his fingers through his dark hair and gave her an intent look. "This changes everything."

"Doesn't it though?" Delia murmured wryly. "Does it mean we have Centaurians among us? Is there a spy here in Rome? Did they somehow follow us to this time and place?"

Shaking his head, Jake said, "I sure wish the Galactic Council would get involved. They've got a hands-off policy even though they suspect Centaurians of being down here messing with the situation, doing anything they can think of to keep their lock on travel in the galaxy. But if they know the

Centaurians play dirty, why won't they send help to counterbalance an unfair situation?"

"Remember, Jake," Delia said, "the Centaurians hold all the cards. Only they have Navigator genes. And over the millennia, they've developed instruments that are far beyond the technology of the other star systems in our galaxy."

"Because of this gene?"

"Yes. Adonia said other groups are trying to catch up, but simply don't have the capability to track them through time and space."

"The Centaurians have already shown their true character by kidnapping Earth women. Isn't that enough reason to have the council intercede? To protect the people of our planet?"

"The impression I received was that until they had the technology to track Centaurian whereabouts through time currents, they weren't going to do anything," Delia replied.

"You mean, proof beyond a shadow of a doubt," Jake growled. "And that leaves us wide open to attack by the Centaurians. Whoever the hell they are."

"From what Adonia said about them, they sound like the worst sort of society."

Jake sat back, deep in thought. Finally he said, "Isn't it interesting how archaeological history tells us that five thousand years before the Roman Empire, we had a matriarchal society, where the great mother goddess was worshipped. Men and women were considered equals. But then, everything changed, and many cultures became maledominated. I wonder if the Centaurians sent spies to Earth to tear down the great mother goddess and replace her with a male god like Zeus instead? Could they have done that?"

Delia shook her head. "I don't know, Jake, but it sure sounds reasonable, given their aggressive tactics. I wonder how they could do that? I mean, wouldn't it take thousands upon thousands of Centaurians coming down to Earth in disguise? They'd have to infiltrate an entire age in history, turning a whole culture against women. How…?"

"That's the question." Jake frowned. "Clearly, from what Adonia inferred, Earth is a tipping point in this galaxy because our females carry this critical gene."

"And maybe that's why Professor Carswell is able to use the headband and send us back in history! Her abilities are so powerful because she has the Navigator gene."

"That would explain it." Jake gave Delia a warm look. "And that would also explain why so many Earth women have this phenomenal sixth sense. In reality, it is their Navigator gene that makes them superintuitive, psychic, with a great ability to heal others."

"Then why do *you* have the Navigator gene, Jake? Obviously, you must. You possess powerful telepathic skills."

"I don't know." He gave her a teasing smile. "Maybe some Earth women can pass on their genetic heritage to their sons? Maybe my parents had it, and passed on a double dose to me? That might explain why I can do what I do. Some men may have just as strong a sixth sense as most women do. The Centaurians may not realize some men here have the gene, too."

Shaking her head again, Delia muttered, "Sounds reasonable. But Adonia didn't have time to explain it all to me. Damn, I wish I could go back and see her again. But I don't have a concept of her time period. If I did, Professor Carswell might be able to send me there."

"The relic sent you there," Jake mused. "Maybe someday it will again. For now, let's review what information we've gathered from Adonia."

"We know the seal was created by the council," Delia stated. "And we know the constellations carved on it are from the galaxy. It would make sense to me that each piece is encoded with information. I think once we get this fragment to Professor Carswell, she may be able to unravel the code and find out even more."

"Maybe even reestablish contact with Adonia," Jake said, a note of hope in his voice. "Professor Carswell is the person for this job. Her skills are so finely tuned that I'll bet she can crack the code and come up with tons of information." He scowled. "I'm worried that we have Centaurian spies around, though. They know that the council planted this stamp down here. And they've got special instruments to keep tabs on Earth. I wonder if they know we've found one of the twelve pieces."

"I think we need to assume that they do," Delia warned. "But how the hell do you tell a Centaurian down here from everyone else?"

"Adonia gave you no hints? Do they look different?"

She shook her head yet again.

"Wait!" Jake snapped his fingers, a triumphant look in his eyes. "Remember what you saw at the banquet? That scribe, Kapaneus, with General Brutus? You said he had a completely red aura, and you'd never seen one like it before?"

Eyes widening, Delia said, "You're right!" Standing, she began to pace. Her wounded leg felt fine now and she automatically touched it. "The red aura! I wonder if Kapaneus is a Centaurian in disguise! Did some spy possess his body?"

Rubbing his chin, Jake sat back and enjoyed Delia's graceful stride as she walked around the apartment, deep in thought. "I don't know. There's something else that happened at that party. Remember we both felt someone trying to get into our minds? Good thing we had our protection up and nothing happened."

Turning, Delia stared at Jake. "You're right! And it came from Kapaneus! Was this scribe who sent the mind probe at us really an alien in disguise?"

"If he is, the fact that it was repulsed probably surprised the hell out of him." Jake chuckled. "It sounds like Centaurians keep the whole galaxy under their control because of their highly developed psychic skills."

"Here on Earth, paranormal skills are just being recognized," Delia said. She rubbed her brow. "We have different basic skills. I can see auras. You can mind read. Some of the other Time Raiders can heal, others possess telekinetic ability to transport objects, or psychometry, to read anything they touch. No one person has *all* these skills in place."

"Yes, but if you were known to possess the Navigator gene, and were trained from birth onward to utilize all these skills, then your arsenal could be staggering. As any Centaurian's must be. What if Kapaneus can not only read minds, but do other things?"

"He would be pretty damned powerful if that's true. And if he can do all those things, and maybe others we're not even aware of, that makes him far more dangerous than we ever thought."

Holding up his hand, Jake said, "Whoa. Remember that if Kapaneus is in truth an alien, and he tried to get into our minds but our energy wall repulsed him, that means we're equal to him. Maybe even better."

"Oh, I wouldn't go there," Delia warned grimly. She pursed her lips, deep in thought. "If Kapaneus is a Centaurian alien and his aura is red, then we know something about the species. But it doesn't mean all Centaurians have red auras. Kapaneus might be an alien spy, but how many others are down here? Do they all have the ability to assume a shape and fit into a culture, like a wolf in sheep's clothing?"

Frustrated, Jake nodded. "It's a can of worms. All we can do is keep our eye on the prize, Delia. With your leg healed, we can move forward with our plans to steal the fragment out of the temple."

She returned to the couch and sat down, careful to keep space between them. "When you went with

Servilia, did they allow you into the place where the relic is kept?"

Jake smiled. "I got close enough. It's in a small room in the center of the temple, just behind the altar where people come to pray. I wasn't allowed in—there was a Roman soldier guarding the door. They change guards every six hours, and the room is locked. The high priestess has the key, which she keeps in a pouch on a jeweled belt around her waist. I waited outside while she and Servilia went in to retrieve the relic, then later to replace it."

"So we have to get rid of a Roman guard and break down a door?"

"That's about it. The door is on leather hinges. A couple of good blows with my knife—" he touched the scabbard on his waist belt "—and we'll be into the room. All we have to do is grab the box, put it in a sack and run like hell for a quiet area where we can hit our ESC armband and time-jump."

Delia knew they'd have to find a safe spot to pause with their stolen prize, press the quartz cabochon on their ESC armbands, and, within seconds, dematerialize, to be brought from this time back to the present. They would find themselves once more in the large glass cylinder in Athena's lab, prize in hand. "That sounds like a plan," she agreed.

Jake stood up. "You're looking tired, Delia. Why don't you lie down and rest? We can do some planning later today. And if we're lucky, maybe we can take that piece tonight, if you feel up to it."

She sighed. "You're right, I'm feeling wiped out. Helluva trip to the Pleiades, you know?" Her heart warmed when he smiled at her. Jake always had the ability to make her feel she was the center of his universe. Resisting his charm, she nodded. "I'll use the connecting door to come see you after I take another nap."

Giving her a thumbs-up, Jake walked to the door. "I'm going to go snoop around the villa some more. I'm still on duty and I've got to start making my rounds. See you later, sweetheart."

The door closed and Delia lay down. She drew up the blanket and dropped her head on the cushions. Tiredness overwhelmed her. Maybe due to the healing energy from the relic? The transit to that seven-star constellation? Unsure, Delia released the questions and let sleep claim her.

Jake was prowling about the atrium on his rounds. The afternoon was gray and chilly, and looking up at the dark, swollen clouds, he was sure it would rain shortly. Servilia was entertaining a group of women friends in the warm tablinum. They were dining on plates of vegetables, cheese and cold lamb cut into bite-size chunks, along with some ruby-red wine. Jake felt his stomach growl. After he finished this last round, he'd go to the kitchen at the rear and get the cooks to make him up a plate of food, he decided. As a hired mercenary, he didn't mingle with Servilia's many and powerful guests, but ate in the kitchen along with other hired staff. The slaves ate in cramped and crowded quarters in another part of the huge house.

Jake saw the two Roman guards at the main entrance come to attention. To his surprise, the scribe Kapaneus, along with Tullia, the prostitute, walked through the partially opened gates. The long, lean man was dressed in a tan tunic that almost grazed his sandaled feet. His dark hair was loose and flowed across the blue cloak wrapped around his thin form. Was he really a Centaurian who'd possessed a human body? Jake halted, his hands on his belt. Damned if he could see anything to make Kapaneus stand out from any other Roman.

Tullia charmed the two guards, giving them warm smiles and batting her thick black lashes. Jake admired her grace. Her black hair was elegantly piled on her head and captured with a gold circlet, just as it had been this morning. Her gown was a pale pink, with a wool cloak of white drawn about her body to ward off the February chill and dampness. He glanced at her small, dainty hands and admired how well kept they were. Clearly, Tullia did no physical work—unlike the slaves at this villa, whose hands were callused and chapped.

Torbar sensed his quarry as he led Tullia up the redbrick walk toward the entry. Even before he saw Philip of Delos, he felt his presence. With his hand on her elbow, Torbar guided the young woman into the atrium. To his left, the Greek mercenary was watching them with a distrustful scowl.

"Ah," Torbar said, giving him a smile, "there you are." He pulled Tullia along with him. Laughing inwardly, Torbar quickly marshaled his mental energy. Centaurian Navigators had many weapons at their disposal, having been trained from babyhood to utilize their full paranormal capabilities. One such skill was referred to as a mind blast, where a victim's mind was infiltrated and his desires controlled. As Torbar gathered energy for the onslaught, he injected the intention that Philip would be filled with lust for Tullia.

Jake started to open his mouth to speak when he saw the scribe's eyes narrow to slits. In the next second, he felt as if he'd been physically struck. Reeling from the wave of energy that slammed into him, he couldn't speak.

As the Greek mercenary staggered back a step, Torbar snickered softly. Leaning over, he whispered to Tullia, "You know where his apartment is. Take him by the hand and lead him to it. Get that band off his right arm. Once you have it, get out of there and bring it to me. Understood?"

She nodded. "Of course I understand." She wrested her arm from his grasp.

Torbar straightened. He sensed and saw the lust suddenly burning in the Greek's eyes. *Good.* The mind blast had worked. Watching Tullia sway her hips in a provocative manner as she approached the mercenary, Torbar noted how Philip had eyes only for the prostitute. He would be putty in her expert hands....

Tullia smiled up into Philip's blue eyes. "I bid you good afternoon, my lord. I am a gift from Kapaneus to you." She eased her scented, soft hand into his battle-hardened one. "I am to please you in all ways that you desire, Philip of Delos. General Brutus also sends his regards to you for protecting his mother, Servilia. He thanks you for saving her life last night. Come, let me take you to your apartment...."

Chapter 15

Tullia laughed throatily as Philip ran his large, roughened palm across her waist to capture her hip. She fell into his arms and slid her hands around his neck. Pushing the door to his apartment closed, she stretched up and slid her tongue across her lower lip. With a growl, he took her mouth with savage intensity. After moving her hands across his broad shoulders, she trailed them down his upper arms. Her fingertips felt a ridge of metal. Beneath the sleeve of his tunic was the armband Kapaneus wanted so badly.

Pulling away, she laughed gaily and led Philip

to the couch. "Come, my dear Greek soldier, let us tarry over a bit of wine first?"

She dodged his groping hand, twirled out of his grasp and walked over to the table. Earlier, Kapaneus had had a slave bring wine laced with herbs designed to knock a horse unconscious.

"I don't want wine," Jake protested, beginning to unlace his boots after sitting down.

Giving him a teasing look, Tullia turned with two silver goblets in hand. "Ah, but when I explore your mouth, Philip of Delos, the taste of wine does nothing but increase my longing for you. Here…" She handed him a goblet. Lifting hers, she said, "To us…"

Jake held her sloe-eyed gaze, his body hardening almost to the point of pain. Gulping down the wine, he noted she didn't touch hers.

"Why do you not drink?" he demanded, handing her back the empty goblet.

Smiling softly, Tullia leaned over and ran her mouth across his. "Because, my heroic soldier, I want to taste my wine from your lips…."

Hers were pliant and luxurious, and Jake reached up to pull her down on the couch beside him.

Tullia gracefully spun away once more, laughing and swaying her hips as she walked over to the table. She set the goblets down next to the pitcher.

Turning, she watched Philip as he shoved off his boots. Already she could see a dazed look in his eyes. His hands moved with a little less precision as he removed the metal brooch that held his cloak around his body. His dark brows drifted down as the pin dropped to the floor with a clatter.

"What's this?" he growled. The room began to spin. Tullia's beautiful features began to dissolve. Gripping the couch for support, Jake felt as if he was going to pitch forward.

Moving around the back of the couch, Tullia caressed his shoulders and slid the cloak off. "Ah, it is nothing," she whispered, teething the lobe of his ear. He groaned with pleasure. Keeping her hands on him, Tullia guided him down on the couch. Already his ability to coordinate his limbs was rapidly diminishing. The herbs had worked astonishingly fast, she thought. "Lie back, Philip, and allow me to slowly undress you…"

With a groan, Jake stretched out. Every time he opened his eyes, the room whirled wildly around him. Tullia's expert hands slid from his ankles upward. She placed warm, slow kisses on each area in turn, inching higher and higher. Feeling weak, Jake tried to speak, but the words remained stuck in his throat.

Laughing huskily, Tullia watched the Greek's

eyes close. His hands lifted, but then fell helplessly to his sides. His face relaxed, sweat popped out across his brow and his body suddenly sagged into the couch. Within the next minute or so, the herbal drug would take full effect and he would be rendered safe enough to approach. All she had to do was wait.

The sleeve of his tunic reached to his elbow. Tullia moved to his right side, stepping lightly. Philip was snoring now, limp as a sack of wheat, and smiling triumphantly, she tested his reflexes. She did not want to get caught stealing his armband. Being patient was an attribute she knew would keep her safe.

Convinced the warrior was indeed unconscious, Tullia made her move. She slid her fingernails provocatively from Philip's wrist up to his elbow. Not a twitch. Nor did he make a sound except for the heavy, slow breathing indicative of a deep sleep.

Coming around the couch, Tullia slid his right sleeve up.

There, above his bulging biceps, was the silver armband with the clear quartz stone.

Studying the piece, she admired the smooth, silvery metal as she opened it and gently removed it from his arm. Once she had it in her possession, she tucked Philip's arm back across his belly and slipped the bracelet into a fabric pouch at her waist. Turning, Tullia scanned the room to make sure she'd left no evidence. She pinned on her cloak, gathered up the pitcher of wine and goblets, and quietly departed.

Tullia knew the layout of Servilia's *domus* from many banquets she had attended in the past. Hurrying down the empty hall, she went to the kitchen. Slaves were rushing around, preparing food for the next meal, and savory scents of rosemary and thyme filled the air. The slaves looked up but did not speak to her. They knew she was freeborn, and they would never question any of her actions.

Dipping into a side hall, glad to escape the over-heated kitchen, Tullia pushed another door open with the toe of her sandal. Outside, she poured the wine into the bushes, then brought the goblets and pitcher back to the kitchen and handed them to a slave. "Wash these well," she ordered.

"Yes, mistress," the young girl replied, keeping her eyes downcast.

Leaving the kitchen, Tullia made her way to the atrium. Sun was glinting through the wintry clouds. The guards at the entrance knew her on sight and quickly opened the gates to the street. As Tullia stepped onto the cobblestones, a Roman cavalry unit trotted by. She flattened herself against the wall to avoid being hit by them. Shoppers of all kinds, riding donkeys or on foot, were carrying bags of provisions home from the markets.

Breathing deeply, Tullia slid her arms beneath her warm woolen cloak and hurried up the street. She could feel the metal bracelet bumping lightly against her hip as she skipped toward the temple of Diana high atop Aventine Hill.

Kapaneus would be very happy with her.

Torbar waited impatiently. Why wasn't Tullia back? The afternoon sun was hidden behind rain clouds as he stood tensely at the window overlooking the busy street. General Marcus Brutus had a large walled house off the main avenue. Tullia should be coming up the way by now. Where was the bitch?

Turning, Torbar strode back and forth in Kapaneus's small apartment. Outside he could hear the coming and goings of men who were seeking the general's favor at this hour of the day.

With a curse, Torbar sent out a telepathic search for Tullia. She was an empty-headed female at best and it would be easy to find her. Closing his eyes, he concentrated on picturing her face. He had done this before, ruthlessly searching her mind to make sure she was trustworthy enough to take on such an important project. Satisfied that Tullia could carry out the mission, Torbar was more than happy to give her a gold aureus for her services. The money would provide her the best of food and rich fabrics to wear for some time to come.

Torbar snorted. His eyes flew open. Where was Tullia? He couldn't find her! That was odd. Feeling uncomfortable, Torbar made a decision: he'd find the prostitute himself. Striding to the door, he jerked it open. Maybe she was still at Servilia's house, which was less than two streets away from where her son, the general, lived. Perhaps Tullia was still sexually engaged with the Greek?

Impossible! Torbar had carefully orchestrated the wine being laced with a drug. He'd lied and told Tullia it was a powerful herb, but it was really a medication from his own world. He'd assured her it worked fast and she would be able to remove the armband easily, and that was true.

Where was she? The guards at Brutus's gates opened them for Torbar as he threw on his dark cloak to ward off the chill. Outside, he turned left and hurried down the busy cobblestone street. The wind was sharp and cutting, the odors of frying meat and cooking onions filled his nostrils as he strode along.

At the first corner, he turned right. Frowning, he

saw a huge crowd gathered midway along the street. Two chariots with fractious horses were surrounded by a growing multitude.

Torbar heard arguments, loud and heated. Women standing at the edge of the restless throng had horrified expressions on their faces. At least fifty men surrounded the Roman chariots; some of them soldiers. The drivers of each chariot, no doubt slaves, looked distraught as they tried to contain their two-horse teams, which were tossing their heads and snorting nervously. As a Centaurian descended from horse ancestors, Torbar could feel the animals' agitation and terror.

Why terror? He pushed through the gawkers, but as he broke through the throng, shock bolted him to the spot. Tullia was lying dead on the street between the chariots. Blood purled from her lips, and her eyes were open in death, her body limp and broken.

"What happened?" Torbar snarled to a farrier standing next to him.

"The chariots were coming from opposite directions," the heavily muscled man told him. "The woman didn't see them. She must have been blind! The chariots tried to avoid her, but they had nowhere to go. The walls of the houses on either side prevented them from swerving to save her life." The man shook his head. "It was dreadful. I was at my livery over there. When she was struck and run over, a number of urchins dived out of the alley. In seconds, they stripped her of her jewelry. Dreadful…"

Tullia's cloak had been torn and ripped by the impact, Torbar saw. She lay at an odd angle. Moving to her side, he knelt down and searched her clothes. There had been a cloth pouch at her waist. She was supposed to place the armband in it….

It was missing!

Torbar now understood why he couldn't connect mentally with Tullia—she was dead.

Taking charge, he ordered two of the men to carry her body to a funeral shop at the end of the street; he had the air of authority and the money to make it happen. Glaring at the soldiers standing near their chariots, Torbar knew he could not blame them. In Rome, pedestrians quickly moved aside when chariots came thundering down a street. Why hadn't Tullia heard them? Shaking his head, Torbar gestured for the two men to follow him. They wouldn't receive payment until they'd completed the task.

Tullia's slender frame was obviously broken in many places and hung limply between the men. Torbar took the lead to show them where to transport her. When he got to the mortuary, he gave the owner a gold aureus. Tullia's body would be wrapped in linen and given a fine burial. Torbar paid the two men and they quickly left, holding their noses. Then he ordered the owner to leave him alone with Tullia in the stinking back room.

With so many dead bodies—most of them bloated and waiting for burial—the place reeked. He made one last search of Tullia's torn and bloodied tunic and stola. The armband was gone. One of the men, the farrier, had told him some ruffian children had probably stolen it. And if they had, how was he ever going to find it? He didn't want to think of Kentar and what he'd do to him if Torbar didn't retrieve the armband. Sweat popped out on his brow as he left. Unable to linger because he was the chief scribe for the general, Torbar headed back to the *domus.* He would make up some excuse and quickly come back here and search for whoever had the armband.

Jake awoke with a low, painful groan. He sat up slowly, his head feeling like an overinflated balloon. Hearing a door open, he turned and saw Delia standing there.

"You look like hell," she said, shutting the door behind her. "What's wrong?"

He rubbed his face. "I don't know. My brain feels...scrambled."

Walking over, Delia saw that his boots were pushed to one side of the couch. "It's dinnertime. I just woke up. Have you eaten yet?" Jake looked pasty. The stubble of his dark beard made him appear gaunt.

"No...God, I feel like I was hit by a Mack truck." He felt how sensitive the skin across his scalp had become. When Delia sat down on the couch beside him, he added, "Something happened, Del. My mind feels raw. I can't remember anything.... But I keep seeing Kapaneus."

Her brows arched. "Here? At Servilia's home today?"

Groaning, Jake forced himself to his feet. Unsteadily, he headed to the table, which held a pitcher of water and a large bowl. "I...don't know. Damn. What the hell happened to me?" Pouring water into the basin, Jake splashed his face several times. A soft towel lay nearby and he grabbed it and dried his face. Straightening, he blinked. His vision was beginning to clear. Looking around, he smelled perfume. And then he remembered seeing Tullia with Kapaneus in the atrium.

"If I didn't know better," Jake muttered, sitting down on the couch, "I'd swear I've been drugged."

"You don't look very good," Delia murmured sympathetically. Worriedly, she searched Jake's bloodshot eyes. "It's almost as if you were binge drinking. That's not like you."

The word brought another memory. Jack sucked in a breath. "Son of a bitch!"

"What?"

Glaring toward the door, he growled, "Kapaneus was here with Tullia earlier today. I saw the scribe in the atrium and he gave me…a funny look. And then—" Jake rubbed his temple "—something happened to me after that, but I'm damned if I know what."

Watching Jake struggle to remember, Delia said, "I was asleep, Jake. I didn't hear anything. Do you know why he came here with Tullia?"

Shaking his head, Jake desperately searched for answers. He couldn't remember anything. He felt Delia get up. She brought back a wooden cup and held it out to him.

"Maybe if you drink water, it will help," she offered gently.

As his hand curved around the cup, he grazed her fingers. And the contact with her warm flesh brought up more images. Jake slugged down the water, set the cup aside and muttered, "Damn…"

Delia saw his face twist with frustration. "More memories?"

Looking around the apartment, Jake stated, "Tullia was in here. That's why I smelled her perfume just now."

Jealousy suddenly ate at Delia. Her voice dropped into a whisper. "What the hell was she doing here again?"

Hearing the edge in her husky tone, Jake said, "It's not what you think, Del." He'd been about to say that he wanted *her,* but realized that admittance would sound lame as hell right now. As Jake looked up and saw anger flashing in her golden eyes, he realized the extent of her rage. "Delia," he pleaded, "something happened...."

"Yeah," she said sarcastically, "I'm sure it did! Well, I guess I shouldn't be judging who you take to bed, Jake. There's nothing between us, after all. You're free to do what you want."

"Damn it, Delia, stop! I did *not* want Tullia! Kapaneus brought her here for a reason." Jake rubbed his face savagely and tried to fit the pieces together. Faces and scenes he saw just didn't make sense.

Delia moved away from the couch, feeling angry and hurt. But why should she? Jake was single, after all. He could cavort with any woman he wanted. Yet jealousy filled her heart. "He was here to see *you?*"

Jake watched her pace the perimeter of his apartment, anger clearly present in her eyes and the stubborn set of her chin. "I think so. But what do I have that he wants? Did he bring a prostitute here to…engage me? Again? Why?"

Delia halted and turned. "Jake! Is your armband still on?"

Frowning, he lifted his sleeve. "No!" he rasped, leaping to his feet.

"Tullia stole it! And Kapaneus *is* a Centaurian." Delia gulped, her eyes growing huge. "He must have put her up to stealing the band from you."

Delia began to search the apartment. She lifted blankets and threw them on the floor. Getting down on her hands and knees, she checked every shadowy corner.

Jake's head was hammering and it hurt to bend over. He hunted for the armband with Delia despite how awful he felt. They ended their search gazing at one another across the room. "Tullia took it," Jake agreed.

"Kapaneus must have paid her a hefty sum to come in here and lure you to bed, Jake." Delia glared at him. "And like any man, you fell for the ruse, damn it."

Raising his hand, Jake said, "Hold on, Del. My mouth feels like crap. I remember Tullia giving me some wine."

"Wine? Maybe she drugged you and that's why you're feeling like this?" Delia tried to control her breathing. The only way Jake could get back to the present was if he was in physical contact with her when she pressed the button on her own armband. Otherwise he would remain stuck in this period. Losing the band was a critical, unforgiving error.

"I think…she did. I remember…God, my mind is like fog, Del." Jake rubbed his wrinkled brow. "I remember her handing me a goblet of wine." Snapping his fingers, he groaned, "Yes! I drank mine but she didn't drink hers. I remember that now. And I asked her why. She laughed and said she'd rather taste it off my lips."

Scowling, Delia muttered, "Great line. Save it and you can use it on the next bimbo you meet. So, how far did this go, Jake? Did you have sex with her?"

He shook his head, flinching from the pain. "I don't think so. I think I must've passed out right after I got my boots off." Jake decided not to tell her that Tullia had been kissing his lower legs when he started losing consciousness. Noting Delia's furious gaze, Jake didn't want to add insult to injury. It amazed him she was so angry over Tullia coming to his bed. He realized then as never before that Delia cared a lot more for him than she'd ever admitted. Despite her fury and jealousy, it gave him hope for them.

"This is bad, Jake," Delia whispered. "Your missing armband could be in the scribe's possession. If he is an alien, think what he could do with it. Track down Professor Carswell in the twenty-first century? Maybe we should go back now to warn her! Anyone pressing that crystal is going to show up at the lab. What if he does that? Our people in Flagstaff don't know about the alien angle yet. We have no way to warn them except to go back and fill them in."

Jake sat down heavily. Holding his aching head between his hands, he tried to think. "Let's see what we can find out about it first. We need to get to Tullia for some answers."

"She lives in a small house about four blocks from here," Delia said. "And Jake, from now on you have to stay with me at all times. Without your band, you won't be able to leave here.

Raising his head, he met her gaze. "Yeah, I know that, Delia. We're going to have to stick close to one another. The only way you could get me through a time jump is if we're holding on to one another."

Giving him a dark look, Delia snapped, "Right now, I'd like to throw you into the Tiber River and let you live here the rest of your miserable life, Jake. Damn it, that scribe and prostitute tricked you! Sounds like they drugged you in order to steal the armband. And I'll bet you anything that Kapaneus has it. If he does…."

"First things first," Jake muttered. "Let's go over to Tullia's house and see what we can get out of her. We can't afford to overreact, Del. Take this one step at a time?"

Glaring, she jerked his heavy winter cloak off a peg on the apartment wall and threw it at him. "Let's get going. Right now, our lives and maybe the entire Time Raider program are in danger."

Chapter 16

Delia was amazed how well her healed thigh felt. She was in great shape for what she knew was going to be a difficult mission.

Before they left for Tullia's home, she checked with the head slave to find out if Servilia needed them in the next two hours. He said no.

Grabbing her armor and putting on her sword belt, Delia met Jake in the atrium. The sky was once again dark and heavy with clouds. The chill and dampness leaked through her thick wool cloak as they walked to the stable.

In a matter of minutes they were out in the traffic,

picking their way among the hawkers, the vendors, the people buying food and other goods. It was impossible to ride abreast of Jake in the congestion. Wagons drawn by horses, donkeys or oxen, and much swifter chariots claimed right-of-way in the seething, ceaseless flow.

Turning down another street far narrower than the original one, they found the going much easier. Jake rode up beside Delia.

"Tullia's *domus* is down there on the left," he said, pointing toward a group of reddish colored, two-story stucco buildings.

"Red," Delia muttered, frowning. "That's a real symbolic color for her and her kind."

"Don't be too judgmental," Jake counseled.

Delia knew that women in the past had been dealt bad hands time and again. Someone like Tullia, who was beautiful and gifted, with a sense of politics and guile, could use her body to upgrade her situation in life. The same went for Servilia, who had been married, but later in life had become Caesar's mistress.

Dismounting, they saw a slave in the street near the apartments. Jake asked him where Tullia lived. The brown-skinned, black-haired youth was crying as he bowed to them.

"My mistress is dead!" he sobbed. Bowing again,

he sniffed, "I am sorry, master, but we just found out Mistress Tullia was run over by a chariot not more than two streets away from here."

Scowling, Jake growled, "Dead? Tullia is *dead?*"

Delia walked inside the arched brick entrance. She could hear several women wailing from the second floor of the beautiful home. Mouth tightening, she walked back to where the two men stood with the horses.

Jake looked at Delia, then handed her the reins of her gelding. "She was struck by chariots on the main street we took to get here."

"When did it happen?" Delia asked, mounting her horse.

Jake followed suit. "No more than an hour ago."

"Where's her body?"

"Taken to a funeral shop not far from where she was killed, apparently."

"We need to look at her. Maybe she's got the armband on her."

Nodding, Jake touched his heels to his gelding. They began to gallop down the street, the clatter sharp and urgent as they moved through the scattering pedestrians. At the corner, Jake slowed his mount to a trot. Rounding the corner, he headed toward the establishment where people were prepared for burial.

The mortuary was a nondescript building set apart from all the rest. After they dismounted, a red-haired slave with blue eyes, a boy about ten years old, took charge of their horses, bowed and gestured for them to enter. Jake thought the child looked Celtic, but said nothing. Julius Caesar had brought many slaves back from Britain.

Pushing open the door, Jake entered the darkened room. The stench of rotting corpses struck him immediately, and he breathed through his mouth to better handle the sickening odors. The thin light from mica windows at the front revealed the owner sitting at a wooden table. The short man, in his forties, wore a long-sleeved tunic, his legs wrapped in cloth, with thin strips of leather to keep the material in place. His face was round, his well-kept black beard making it look even broader.

"What can I do for you?" he asked, lifting his head from the parchment he was writing on.

"We're looking for Tullia. Is her body here?" Delia demanded, coming up to the table.

"Yes, she is. Are you kin?"

"We are," Delia lied, her voice hoarse as she swallowed convulsively to stop from gagging at the smell.

"She was struck and run over by chariots," the man said in a monotone.

Delia didn't notice any regret in his face or voice.

As an embalmer, he must be used to dealing with death every day. Why should Tullia's demise be any different from the hundreds of others? "And she is where?" Delia managed to rasp.

He lifted his thumb. "On a table in the back room. Go take a look if you must. I warn you, she's broken up. She's next to be wrapped in linen, and then my grave diggers will take her to be buried."

Jake didn't wait for any more talk. He grunted and pushed the dark linen curtain aside. The odor grew worse as they made their way around several tables where bloated bodies were lying stiffly. Some had linen fabric laid across them. Others, the poor ones, lay as they'd died, without being straightened. The whole scene was grotesque and nightmarish to Jake.

Holding his nose, he spotted Tullia's twisted form. "There," he croaked, moving between the tables.

Delia choked, and her eyes watered as she pressed her fingers to her nostrils. Blinking several times, she hurried toward the table closest to the wall.

Tullia's body *was* badly mangled. Delia could see by the way her spine was distorted that she'd probably died swiftly from a broken back. Her once beautiful face was bloody and battered. Delia watched as Jake quickly rummaged through her bloody garments, then checked her limbs for any sign of the armband.

"Nothing," he growled. Holding his breath, he rolled her stiffening body on its side and carefully checked the rest of her garments.

Delia stepped closer. "Don't you think if there was any jewelry on her body the owner would have stolen it?"

Nodding, Jake gently deposited Tullia on her back once more, his hands bloody from the exercise. "Let's get out front," he grunted.

Delia pushed the curtain aside. She spotted a pail of water near the owner's table. Jake saw it, too, and washed his hands. Straightening, he wiped them on the sides of his tunic.

"Did you take anything from Tullia's body?" Jake demanded of the owner, who was eyeing them cautiously.

"No...no, I didn't. Two men, merchants from up the street where she was run over, brought her in here." He glared at Jake. "If something is missing I suggest you talk to them. One is the baker, the other a farrier."

Delia dived out the door of the building. Coughing, she held her throat, afraid she was going to heave. Then she felt Jake's hand on her shoulder.

"Hang in there."

Trying to shake off the odor that now clung to her clothes and her hair, Delia quickly mounted her horse. "God, what an awful place!" Wheeling her mount, she quickly caught up with Jake.

The street was busy and they had to watch where they rode. Most people knew to get out of the way of horses. "Helluva place," Jake muttered, wiping his nose with the back of his hand.

"How can that guy work in there?" Delia wondered, hoping the crisp February air would rid her hair of the smell of death.

Shrugging, Jake said, "He's used to it. He probably stopped smelling dead bodies a long time ago."

"What a job to have!"

"Makes living in the twenty-first century look good in comparison, doesn't it?"

Shaking her head, Delia remained close to Jake as the crowds parted in front of them. "No contest," she agreed grimly.

They turned the corner and went up the busier street. In no time they'd located the bakery by the wonderful fragrance of bread in the oven. Delia held the reins of Jake's horse after he dismounted and went to talk to the owner, who had blood on his tunic, likely from carrying Tullia's body to the undertaker. The stout man frowned as Jake began to question him, and Delia saw distrust in his narrowed hazel eyes. When he pointed to the farrier across the street, she saw Jake nod and turn away.

Walking past her, Jake growled, "Nothing. Bring the horses over to the livery. I'll talk to that big guy with the black curls."

Leading Jake's horse, Delia saw a short, burly man who was massively muscled. He was outside in the courtyard, standing near a fire, while a young slave boy pushed bellows to keep the flames hot. The man hammered relentlessly on an iron shoe for a horse that stood nearby, bridles held by another slave.

Jake approached the blacksmith as he plunged the red-hot iron into a leather bucket filled with water. Steam spat, then billowed upward in a roiling white cloud. Soon the farrier was deep in conversation with Jake. He pointed to an alley next to the bakery and then shook his head, a remorseful expression on his bearded face.

Jake came over to Delia and said, "The smithy witnessed a gang of children swarming Tullia's body seconds after she'd been hit, apparently. He said he saw a tall blond kid, who seemed to be the leader, grab a silver bracelet out of Tullia's pouch." Jake studied the lane next to the bakery. "The guy said the children ran off that way."

"Great," Delia muttered. "Did he know where these kids live?"

Jake mounted. "The farrier referred to them as 'the rats of Rome.'" Swinging his horse around, he paused next to her. "The runaway children of slaves, they steal to survive. Roman soldiers try to capture them, but there are so many and they move around so much, it's impossible to catch all of them."

"So, we're going to try and hunt down this blond kid?" Delia asked, feeling sorry for such children. "Because if he presses that crystal, he's going to get transported back to Flagstaff and the lab. Imagine Professor Carswell's surprise."

Jake grimaced. "I know. I'm not happy about this, either." His head ached from the drug that had been used to knock him out. "But there's nothing we can do until tonight, anyway," he murmured as he urged his horse across the street.

"You mean steal the relic at the temple?"

"Yes."

Their legs brushed from time to time as they walked their horses down the narrow alley. On either side were gray stucco buildings, some two-story.

The lane was paved with cobblestones, smooth and well-worn from much foot traffic over time. A chariot could never squeeze through here and many people utilized it as a walkway. Delia spotted a beggar down on the left peeing against one of the stucco walls. A woman was squatted and defecating farther down on the right. It seemed no one was even mildly embarrassed about such things. Delia realized that for most of the Earth's inhabitants, the great outdoors had always been their toilet. Did humans in the twenty-first century realize how fortunate they were? Time traveling had taught her to be far more appreciative of modern conveniences.

Jake spotted a group of children in ragged-looking clothes. "Hey!" he said, and set his heels to his horse.

Delia saw a tall, thin young man with blond hair at the end of the alley. Seven children of varying ages were attacking a one-armed beggar, who was trying to fend them off with his crutch made from a gnarled olive limb.

Jake jumped out of the saddle as his horse slid to a stop. His focus was the leader, the youth with the blond hair. He was probably in his mid-teens, and on his arm was the bracelet.

Jake lunged forward, hand outstretched. He grabbed the kid's shoulder and ripped at the thin material of his tunic.

With a cry, the blond lurched sideways, off balance, arms pumping like windmills.

Jake felt more than saw the rest of the pack disappear. He heard Delia yelling at them. Gripping the boy, he took him down. The youth's narrow face was drawn in rage, and he swung his balled fists with lethal intent.

"No you don't," Jake grunted. He planted his knee on the youth's thin chest and pinned him there. "Don't move!" he growled, and reached for the band. Taking it, he settled it back on his own arm, hiding it from view beneath his sleeve.

"I got it," Jake said, hearing Delia's horse pull up behind him. He eased off the ruffian, who was glaring at him. The boy's teeth were yellow, the front ones missing. "Get up and get out of here," Jake growled at him.

Scrambling to his feet, the youth took off at a run, disappearing around the corner. Jake looked at the beggar, who was lying against the building, his nose bleeding. Picking up his crutch, Jake took it over to him.

"Thank you, strangers," the man said. Squinting up at them, he whined, "They took my coins." Opening his hand, which had two fingers missing, he pleaded, "Can you give an old soldier a few coins?"

After digging into his pouch, Jake pressed some into the man's hand. "Here, take these and stay out of this alley. Those children will be back."

Getting to his feet, the bearded beggar hobbled away, the coins clenched in his hand. "My thanks to you. May Aries bless you."

Jake remounted and shot Delia a look of triumph. "We're back on track."

"We got lucky," she countered gruffly. They rode down the alley toward the street. It was time to get back to Servilia's.

"The kid obviously didn't know what he had," Jake said as they rode. "Unless that crystal is pressed hard, it won't trigger the jump sequence."

"Professor Carswell designed it like that on purpose." Flexing her mouth, Delia said, "I'm not going to stay upset about this, Jake. I'm just glad we got it back. Without it, we were vulnerable."

Jake nodded, knowing how tricky it would be, getting back to the future without his armband. Remaining behind in ancient Rome was not a pleasant prospect. "I'm not the first to lose an armband," he said defensively. "Others have, too."

"Yeah," she snorted, giving him a dark look, "but no one had it stolen by a prostitute. Only you, Tyler."

"I was drugged."

"So you say."

Nostrils flaring, Jake turned his horse into the busy traffic of the street. "Damn it, I would never have invited that woman into my bed. I was targeted and drugged. She knew exactly what she was doing."

Delia ruffled her gelding's black wiry mane. The horse twitched its ears in response. "What I want to know is who put her up to this? Do you think she knew what the armband was? What it could do?"

"No, I don't." Jake rubbed his chin and muttered, "My instincts tell me Kapaneus was behind this."

"He's the one with the red aura. And my intuition is screaming that he's a Centaurian."

"So the real question is can he read minds? Does he know what this bracelet is? Is he aware that Tullia's dead? If he put her up to it, that means he'll likely try something else to get an armband away from one of us."

"Well," Delia said, swinging her horse under the archway of Servilia's home, "that isn't going to happen. We know enough to watch him." She gave Jake a pointed look. "And you can bet he's going after you again."

Smarting, Jake dismounted and gave his horse to the waiting slave. When Delia joined him, they walked toward the house. "You think he'll send another woman to drug me?"

"Kapaneus is clever," she answered. "He'll think of some way to get to you, not to me."

"Why do you say that?" Jake halted at the entrance to the house, not wanting their conversation to be overheard.

Delia laughed. "Centaurian men see women as

weaklings. Kapaneus envisions you as the leader. He's wrong, but that's how it is."

"Makes sense," Jake admitted. Looking around, he saw a number of slaves hurrying about, arms filled with laundry. "Tonight," he whispered, "we go to the temple, take the fragment and then get the hell out of here."

"Right. We have to make sure Kapaneus isn't around, or that he doesn't suspect what we're going to do." Delia wasn't sure the alien wouldn't guess their next strategy.

Feeling the skin on the back of her neck crawl, she rubbed it. That was a bad sign.

Chapter 17

Torbar was furious that Marcus Brutus had delayed him. The general had demanded that a clay tablet be written and then sent by messenger to Servilia, his mother. Impatient and angry over the disruption to his plan, Torbar had practically run back to the place where Tullia had been struck and killed.

Halting, he stood across the street from the bakery. Mentally scanning the inhabitants of the shop as the delicious smell of baking bread wafted toward him, Torbar managed a hit. The owner had witnessed the accident, and the scene replayed for him. Distracted by a cry of a woman across the way, Tullia had stepped out in front of the chariots, much to her misfortune.

Torbar held the energetic link with the baker. He saw through the man's memory that a gang of children had sprung on her corpse moments after she was struck. The young ruffians reminded him of flies descending upon a carcass. The leader was a yellow-haired youth who was pathetically thin, his face set in a perpetual sneer. Torbar saw him rummage quickly, like the good thief he was, through Tullia's bloodied clothing. And when he pulled the silver armband out of her pouch, Torbar cursed again. They ran off into a nearby alley, vanishing as promptly as they'd appeared.

Standing with his back against the wall of the butcher's shop, Torbar closed his eyes. Ruthlessly, he sent out a huge mental scan about a thousand feet in radius around him. He was hunting for the yellow-haired thief who had the bracelet. Find the boy and he'd find the armband.

Nothing. Torbar opened his eyes and scowled. That pack of feral children lived on whatever they could scrounge in order to stay alive. Feeling disgusted, he was glad Centaurian society no longer had such problems. Thousands of years earlier, any beggar or thief who used to live in his star system was captured and put to death. Now the society hummed along like it should. There was no poverty, no starvation. Everyone was well fed, told what career path they could follow if they were males. Females with prime DNA remained as broodmares to perpetuate Navigator genes, so their race would continue to prosper.

A Navigator could scan and blast anything with his mental powers. Well, just about anything. The problem here on Earth was that humanoid females could be immune to his powerful mental capabilities if their own genes were strong and dominant. If they weren't, the recessive Navigator gene in a woman might give her a strong intuition, perhaps one metaphysical skill, but little else. Torbar had been assigned to many off-world missions, but Earth posed new and unusual challenges for him. However, since the males on Earth did not possess the gene, it should be easy to locate this sniveling yellow-haired thief.

Sending out a larger telepathic scan of the populace, this time two thousand feet in radius, Torbar still did not receive a hit. Not yet…. Again, he enlarged his mental net.

A hit! Instantly, Torbar dug into the thief's mind. The boy was standing near another bakery, waiting to steal a loaf of bread from an old woman who was hobbling toward the door with the help of a cane.

Running down the street, Torbar maintained an energy hook in the thief's mind, so he could track him without a problem. Dodging pedestrians, he ran effortlessly into an alley. All Centaurians were in peak physical condition, and no matter what body they inhabited while on assignment, they could infuse that physical shell with the power of their race—which was consummate.

The wind tore through his hair as he ran with long, even strides for several blocks. Finally, Torbar slowed. He rounded a corner onto a very busy, wide street. Ahead, he could see the colorful red-and-gray-brick wall that surrounded the city of Rome. There was a large wooden gate in the barrier where at least ten Roman soldiers, clad in scarlet tunics and leather armor, stood on duty—Portal Lavernalis, a mental scan told Torbar. A small bakery shop sat nearby.

He didn't want to snare the attention of the soldiers, whose duty it was to check the identification of everyone entering Rome. The last thing he needed was to have those guards interested in what he was doing.

Maintaining his link to the yellow-haired thief, Torbar spotted the boy standing just outside the open door of the bakery. He saw the old woman, her hair gray and frizzled. Her spine bent with age, she hobbled unsteadily away from the shop with a loaf of fresh warm bread tucked beneath her arm.

Switching to another scan, a telepathic one, he dug deeply into the thief's memory. Startled, Torbar grunted. He saw the Greek mercenary capture the ruffian and repossess the armband!

Snorting violently, Torbar waited on the street. Releasing his energy tentacles from the thief's mind, he watched the boy push the old woman down and grab the loaf of bread. The crone fell with a shriek, drawing the attention of the soldiers at the gate.

The thief was fast; Torbar would give him that. Within seconds, he had disappeared into the nearest alley, running as fast as he could.

Ignoring the old female Earthling, Torbar turned and walked rapidly back toward General Brutus's *domus*. The armband was again with its owner. Repeatedly clenching his fists, Torbar tasted rage over the turn of events. He intuitively knew the armband was important. As he strode through the streets, the wind biting and tugging at his cloak, Torbar strategized.

Back in the house, he locked the door to Kapaneus's office. Sitting down in a carved black ebony chair that had been brought from Egypt, he calmed himself. Why not make things easy? He'd been stupid to think it would be simple to finesse the armband from the male Earthling. Why not find out more about it by simply razing the man's mind?

Laughing at himself and his idiocy, which wasn't like him, Torbar gathered the necessary energy. Centaurians' mind beams had their limits, depending upon the genetic capability they were born with. He could usually send his telepathic energy about a mile, and Servilia's home was closer than that. He would try it. If it didn't work, he would have to visit Servilia and find those two Greeks.

Even Centaurians had problems with their telepathic energy beams at times. Torbar had been using his continuously, so his own battery had been depleted. It took one turn of the planet he was from, twenty-eight hours, to recharge the energy in his aura to full power once more. While he couldn't send his telepathic energy into someone else's mind at a distance, he could if he was in close proximity. Knowing that, Torbar wasn't too hopeful his scan would work. But if it did, it meant he could remain unrecognized. The Earthling would have no clue as to what was happening except for an excruciating headache after Torbar got done rummaging around in his mind.

Sending out his mental hook, Torbar could feel how tenuous the thread of energy had become. Grimacing, he searched, but couldn't find Philip even though he had visualized him. Nothing. Well, he knew the Greek wasn't dead, so it meant going to him and then pummeling his mind at close range to find out about the armband.

Opening his eyes, Torbar grinned. At least Tullia had given Philip that medication that would knock out a horse. The Greek's mind would be easy to access, given that he was still recovering from the powerful drug.

Rubbing his hands together, Torbar realized it was near sunset. He would drop by and see Servilia. First, he would find out if the general had any other message for his mother. Perhaps another clay tablet that he could personally deliver to her? Torbar was sure Brutus probably did; the mother and son were close. And that would provide Torbar the perfect reason to visit. Once there, he'd be close enough to access Philip of Greece once and for all.

"What I'd give for a mocha latte triple shot," Jake groused to Delia. They sat at the table in her apartment, eating a dinner of olives, cheese and freshly baked ham.

Delia, who sat across from him, gave him a smile. "Sorry, no Starbucks in ancient Rome, Tyler. Serves you right for taking that wine that Tullia or Kapaneus had spiked with something."

Rubbing his brow, Jake growled unhappily, "I've still got a headache. Whenever I'd get one before, I'd just down a triple-shot latte and it would go away."

Delia's curly hair framed her smooth, glowing face. Drowning in the warmth of her gold-brown eyes, he sensed she really did feel sorry for him.

Jake popped a tasty olive into his mouth, studying her as he did so.

"Why are you giving me that funny look?" she demanded, cutting a piece of the ham with her knife.

"You aren't still angry about Tullia are you?"

She snorted and gave him a narrowed look. "What she did to you?" Laughing heartily, Delia said, "That's rich, Tyler! Men are so predictable! You see a pretty face, swaying hips and nice breasts and you're lost."

"Come on, Delia…."

"Stop giving me that 'poor me' look. You're an adult. You made choices. And you decided to take that woman to bed, pure and simple."

Shrugging, Jake muttered, "I swear I did not. I did not go to bed with Tullia. Or any other woman." He gave her a flat stare. "I only have eyes for you."

Her heart galloped momentarily. The olive she was about to eat halted midway to her mouth. There was brutal honesty in Jake's eyes. Putting the olive down on the wooden plate, she said, "Okay, if that's true, how do you explain why you were so help-lessly drawn to Tullia?"

Shaking his head, Jake said, "I really don't know. All of a sudden, out of nowhere, I felt pushed toward her, Del. Obsessed. What I felt was...well, pure lust. And now that I think about it, it seemed like an outside force *was* pushing me." He paused and looked at her. "You don't believe me, do you?"

Delia snapped her fingers. "Wait! Adonia told me that a Centaurian could make a person do something they didn't want to. She called it a 'mind blast.'" Looking at Jake, her jealousy receded. "That scribe was with Tullia. He could have blasted you and made you want her even if you didn't. And then, she drugged your wine."

Nostrils flaring, Jake stared at her. "That makes sense, Del. I never felt that way about Tullia when I met her the first or second time. I remember this light exploding in my head. I went from not wanting Tullia to desiring her."

Nodding, Delia said in a thoughtful tone, "That scribe made you want her with the intent of getting Tullia close enough to drug you and steal your ESC armband. Damn, he is dangerous."

"I think you're right," he muttered, taking a piece of bread and wiping up the ham drippings on his plate. Chewing stoically, he eyed Delia.

"Centaurians can manipulate our thoughts and emotions."

"We came close to having someone press that crystal and show up back at the Flagstaff lab. Can you imagine the chaos that would cause? Not to mention General Ashton and the professor skinning us alive once we got back. If we got back at all." Delia's brows fell. "Strategically, our flank was wide open to the aliens. Our only protection is that band." She pointed at his arm. "We got lucky."

Grousing under his breath, Jake said, "Yes, we did."

Just then, there was a knock at the door.

Frowning, she glanced over at Jake. "You expecting anyone?"

"It's your apartment. Who are you expecting?"

"Yeah, right. I saw a good-looking stud of a Roman soldier, so I asked him to drop by and visit me after his watch was over."

Grinning sourly, Jake knew Delia had never been the type of woman to bed hop. She was a committed person. He turned toward the door to see who was knocking as Delia called out, "Come in."

Jake saw Kapaneus step through the opening. The scribe carried a scroll in his hand. This was the man with the red aura.

Sensing his powerful vibrations, Jake quickly shielded himself.

"Kapaneus?" Delia said, her voice wary. "What do you want?"

Torbar saw the instant distrust on the Greeks' faces. He made an effort to be obsequious, and held up the scroll. "Greetings. I am looking for the lady Servilia. I have a message from her son, the great general, Marcus Brutus. Do you know where she might be?" As he spoke he sent a huge mind blast at them both.

On the way over he'd decided to just knock them out and steal both their armbands. The mind blast was the most powerful of all the skills a Navigator had at his disposal. It was akin to an explosion that would render the recipients unconscious without laying a hand on them.

Torbar saw the energy leap from his mind. And he saw it sail straight and true toward the Greeks. In the next second, he saw a huge flash of red light erupting.

It was the last thing he remembered.

Chapter 18

"What the hell just happened?" Jake demanded. He stood in shock as something invisible seemed to strike the scribe. The man collapsed in the doorway, unconscious.

"He attacked us," Delia said, leaping forward. "And it backfired on him because our walls were up and deflected it—right back to him." She dragged the scribe inside the apartment and shut the door so no prying eyes could discover what had just happened. "I saw him send a red ball of energy toward us."

"We deflected it with our auras?" Jake asked,

leaning over and rolling the scribe onto his back. Putting his fingers to the man's scrawny neck, he felt a slow, strong pulse.

Delia removed the headband the scribe always wore, and studied it. "That's right. He wanted to knock us out, Jake. I don't know why. That's your department." She glanced over at him.

Jake stood scowling down at the scribe. "I can't read the mind of someone who is unconscious," he reminded her. "What's that?"

"This thing he's wearing sure looks like Professor Carswell's headband, don't you think? It's a lot thinner, but there are two oval crystals on each side, just like the one she has."

Delia handed it to him to inspect.

"You're right," Jake muttered, closely examining the object. The circlet was made of a fine, thin silver metal and was designed so that the crystals would lie flat against the wearer's skull. The device Professor Carswell wore was much larger and thicker, and yet just as lightweight. "We know that headband she has came from the UFO crash at Roswell." He handed it back to Delia. "This man has to be an alien. The headband is too similar to ours not to come to that logical conclusion."

"No disagreement," Delia muttered. She tucked the headband into the soft leather pouch she wore on her belt. "He's not getting it back. I intend to take this to the lab and let the professor examine it." Glancing around, Delia added, "Jake, we need to get out of here. Kapaneus may have buddies. If he is alien, we'll never be able to pick his friends out of the crowd unless I constantly maintain surveillance for red auras."

"I know you can't be 'on' all the time," Jake said. Delia had only so much energy for use of her psychic skills. As with his, there were limits. "Plus, we have to be quiet and centered in order to see such things, and right now, that isn't happening."

Delia grabbed her cloak and swung it over her shoulders. "The scribe will wake up sooner or later." She grinned briefly. "Serves him right. He got a dose of his own medicine. Sometimes revenge is sweet."

Jake nodded and put on his own cloak. "I wonder if he has any powers without that headband in place?"

Delia patted the pouch where she'd placed the device. "I know one thing for sure—he's going to have one hell of a headache when he regains consciousness."

Jake dragged the scribe across the room and laid him on the couch. After covering him with a blanket, he turned to Delia. "Anyone who comes in will think he's asleep and leave him alone. That will buy us time to get to the temple and find the fragment."

"Good plan," she agreed. Touching the hilt of her sword, which hung in its scabbard at her right side, she met Jake's narrowed blue eyes. He was efficient and in soldiering mode. "I don't like having to get that relic in broad daylight. I wish we could wait until dark."

"We don't have a choice," he said. "We know this alien is on to us. Considering his headband looks so similar to the professor's he may be alerted to what we're doing here."

Giving Kapaneus an angry look, Delia said, "We don't have time to sit here and wait until he wakes up. Besides, if he knows who we are, he's going to spread the alarm. As a scribe to the general, he'll send Roman soldiers after us as soon as he wakes up." Rubbing her brow, she growled, "No, we have to get out of here now."

There would be much danger attempting a daytime theft of the fragment. Delia walked with Jake out of the house to the stables, where slaves hurriedly saddled their mounts. The two of them said nothing about where they were going. Stomach tied in knots, Delia hoped Servilia didn't see them leaving.

Pushing their horses into a trot, they swung around one end of the *domus* and headed for the closed gates. The guards on duty saw them coming and quickly opened the barriers.

A feeling of relief trickled through Delia as she lifted her hand in thanks as they rode out into the street. It was much less busy now, as the February sun neared the horizon. The air was growing chillier as evening approached. Rome took on a pinkish hue, making the white columns of the temples on Aventine Hill above them look almost magical.

As they trotted up the cobblestone street toward them, Delia worried about Kapaneus regaining consciousness. In her gut, she knew the scribe was an alien in disguise. Was he harmless without his headband, or not? How many more of his kind were in Rome? It was impossible for her to be psychically searching for red auras all the time. She would have to rely on her powerful intuition to warn her.

As Delia dug her heels into the flanks of her horse to climb the hill toward the temple, she wondered if Kapaneus might die. Maybe the charge he'd hurled at them had been a lethal one, meant to kill. Jake had said he got a pulse, but who knew?

Torbar groaned loudly as he awoke. He was covered with a wool blanket and lying on a couch—

but where? Head aching as if a horse had nailed him with a kick, he slowly sat up.

When he raised his hands to touch his head, his grogginess turned to alarm. Where was his headband? Opening his eyes fully, he quickly searched the area around him. *Nothing.* Getting up dizzily, he clung to the couch and scanned the dimly lit room. His headband was nowhere in sight!

Panic ate at him. Without his headband, he was literally marooned in this time and place. A Navigator could not make time leaps or move from one part of the galaxy to another without it. Pushing himself to begin a search, he stumbled, and would have fallen except for his grip on the couch. Mind churning with questions, Torbar anxiously combed the apartment, but couldn't find the missing headband.

Sitting back down, he leaned forward and buried his head in his hands. He could hear voices outside the door. It was almost dark in the room except for two braziers in the corners, which provided feeble light. The smell of burning oil made him wrinkle his nose.

Closing his eyes, Torbar reviewed what had happened. He had sent a mind blast at the Greek mercenaries, whom he suspected were time travelers. And instead of knocking them unconscious, the energy had been deflected back, striking him instead. Raising his head, Torbar stared at the door.

Could primitive humanoids have the strength to repel a Centaurian's mind blast? No one in the galaxy was immune. In this case, Torbar had wanted to knock the pair out, to steal their armbands....

It hurt to think. But he had to, because his life depended upon it.

Was it possible the woman, who clearly possessed the Navigator gene, had reflected his mind blast back to him? What about the male? Did he have the same genetic trait? Torbar must have received a double blast back upon himself. By Chiron, nothing like that had ever happened to him before.

In class as a young trainee, he recalled, the possibility had been discussed. If two Navigators squared off to fight one another, and sent lethal mind blasts at the exact same moment, they could deflect them. That was theory. Torbar had never sent a mind blast at another Navigator; it was against the law. Centaurians never fought among themselves.

They controlled humanoids with mind blasts when necessary. They could use them to manage an angry crowd, for example, rendering everyone passive in seconds. Humanoids were always helpless to fight off a mind blast from a Navigator; that had been shown time and time again, in all the star systems of the galaxy. It was the greatest skill his species possessed, and a natural defense.

Without his headband, however, Torbar was almost relegated to the level of Earthling. His Navigator skills were harmonized and focused by the crystals in his headband, their potency increased a hundredfold.

Torbar had spent twenty years of his life, from babyhood on, learning to become a Navigator. Rubbing his watering eyes now, because the pain in his head was so great, he wondered how this Greek woman soldier had gotten her training.

Was it possible she was a rogue Navigator? Torbar had heard whispered stories about a few Centaurian women being trained in secret. No one dared talk about this in public, for fear of being branded a traitor and killed outright for spreading such gossip.

If she was such a rogue, then she had escaped the star system and was making her life in a place where she was not likely to be discovered by the Centaurian network, which spanned the galaxy. Torbar knew it was possible that if a Navigator wanted to defect from their home world and responsibilities, it could be done. But he knew of no one who had attempted it. Only whispered tales told by retired Navigators mentioned such a possibility.

Was he up against another Centaurian? A rogue female Navigator, of all things? He must be, for it was inconceivable to Torbar that a mere primitive Earthling could deflect his mind blast. Worse, he had no way to warn Kentar or his star system of this anomaly. Right now, he was marooned on this planet. And if Kentar did not send another Navigator to check up on him when he failed to appear at the appropriate time, Torbar was destined to live and die in the body of this scribe.

Groaning, he cursed, "By Chiron, this cannot be happening!" Fortunately, because he was Centaurian, he had a magnificent aura and powerful energy. And even though the scribe's body had been battered, Torbar could feel his strength returning. If he had to remain captive within Kapaneus's possessed form, at least he could dispense with the spirit of the man.

As a Navigator, he'd been taught how to temporarily inhabit and share another's body. But if a Navigator, for whatever reason, had to live out his life in a foreign humanoid body, he knew how to cut the cord and release the original owner's spirit. That way, he had full ownership of the physical form. Right now, Torbar did not want to do that. He needed the scribe's memories and knowledge to live undercover here in Rome.

Where were the two Greeks? The time travelers? Torbar was sure they had used the armbands they wore to get to this age and place. But why? Rubbing his head, he was glad to find the pain was beginning to recede. Standing again, he felt solid and grounded, no longer dizzy or weak. The mind blast was finally wearing off.

Getting up, he jerked the door open. Finding a slave, he asked her where the Greeks had gone.

"Master, they left on their horses."

"Where to?" he demanded.

The young slave blushed and said, "I do not know."

"Who would know?"

"The stable manager."

Hurrying out the back door of the house to the stable area, Torbar found a Nubian man in his early thirties. "You there," he snapped, "where did the Greeks go?"

The slave bowed deeply. "Master, they did not say."

"What direction did they go when they left?" he growled impatiently.

"Toward Aventine Hill and the temple of Diana. The guards at the gate saw them taking that route."

Frowning, Torbar turned and walked quickly back into the house. What was at the temple of Diana? Why would they go there? He relentlessly reviewed a list of people who might have the answer.

Torbar decided that Servilia would know. Rubbing his brow again, he found the ache had disappeared. How good was his mind reading without his precious headband to amplify his natural psychic abilities? Torbar wasn't sure. He needed to prowl into the Roman woman's mind to find out.

Servilia was in a large, open room reading a parchment lying on a lavishly carved wooden table. Not wanting to let her know he was there, Torbar pressed himself to the outer wall. Luckily, there was only one way in and out of the room, through a narrow, dimly lit hall. He could see who was coming, and leave before the mistress of the house detected him.

Closing his eyes, he marshaled all his energy and focused on Servilia. Picturing her face, he sent out a subtle energy that would not be detected by her. To his surprise and pleasure, he was easily able to access her mind. She would never know he was there. His energies were diminished but not gone. Good!

His head began to ache again. The ability to mind read hinged on a laserlike focus. To sift through all the ideas in her mind in hopes of stumbling upon what he was searching for took time. He hated the process. Humanoids had such an avalanche of thoughts it hurt his head to plow through it all.

Suddenly, Torbar froze. *A tidbit. A tease.* He

heard "magical" and "Temple of Diana," and stopped to investigate in that area of her mind. Squeezing his eyes shut, he concentrated harder. He had to get a visual of what she was thinking about. Automatically, his fingers curved into fists at his sides. Without the headband, this was hard work!

A picture slowly congealed and Torbar finally saw an object Servilia called an "arrowhead." Only it wasn't. His heart pounded hard as he realized what he was looking at. It was part of the stamp that the council had been allowed to plant on Earth!

Breathing shallowly, Torbar clung excitedly to the picture. What was of most interest to him was the circle of seven stars, like a crown. That was the Pleiades constellation. Relaxing his fists, he felt a flush of excitement suffuse him. For over four thousand years, Centaurians had tried to find out where these twelve pieces of the stamp had been hidden on Earth. They'd had no leads. No matter what they did, the information had escaped them. *Until now...*

Torbar saw the high priestess at the temple of Diana. He saw where the fragment was hidden. And he saw how it worked. He even recognized Delia of Delos holding it. Snapping his eyes open, he felt panic. If only he had his headband! He could contact Kentar immediately and let him know what he'd discovered.

Shame flowed through Torbar as he stood there thinking of what to do next. He heard Servilia moving around, and quickly exited the passageway. Once outside, Torbar glanced toward the stables. He'd arrived on foot, but was going to ride out of here. Waving at the Nubian, he quickly ordered the man to saddle a gelding for him. The slave started to ask if Torbar had permission from his mistress, but then decided not to. Instead, he barked orders to a young boy in the barn to find the scribe a suitable mount.

Standing on one foot and then the other, Torbar glared alternately at the manager and then at the path leading around the beautiful home. He knew the Greeks were on their way to the temple and why. They were going to steal the fragment. He would bet his life on it. Opening and closing his fists, Torbar was ready to scream at the scurrying lad, who was leading a gray, rangy-looking gelding out of the barn for him.

In swift strides, Torbar stepped forward and ripped the reins from the boy's hand, then leaped into the saddle. As a Centaurian, he was a natural rider. Over millennia, his ancestors had evolved from having the body of a horse to being half horse and half man. One of the most famous centaurs had come here, to Earth. Chiron was still worshipped as

a god, back in Torbar's home world. Chiron had
been a great healer before leaving in search of other
humanoids across the galaxy. And where he found
such groups, he imparted knowledge of healing to
them. He had been one of the few Navigators ever
given permission to promote humanitarian development among primitive worlds.

Gripping the gelding with his thighs, Torbar
leaned forward and spoke in a growl to the animal,
whose ears flicked nervously back and forth. Then,
with a lunge, the horse broke into a fast trot and
rounded the corner of the house, tail held high like
a flag.

Torbar waved perfunctorily to the two Roman
guards at the gate. They recognized him, saluted
him and stood aside as he trotted out into the stream
of traffic. The few people on the avenue this time of
day leaped aside as Torbar pushed the gray into a
gallop down the cobblestone street. Some cursed
him. Others shook their fist as they scattered like a
flock of chickens.

Not caring about the primitive humanoids,
Torbar set his sights on the gleaming temple that
stood atop Aventine Hill. In the last rays of the
setting sun, the structure turned golden. Even Torbar
had to admit that Earthlings had superior architec-
tural skill. His cloak flapping like wings around

him, he pushed his horse relentlessly up the steep street. Vendors dived out of the way and so did the customers they served.

Gritting his teeth, Torbar wished for the hundredth time that he had his headband. He could forge a link with the Greeks and know exactly where they were located. Now, he didn't know. And the temple on top of the hill was huge.

Searching frantically among the patrons of Diana, Torbar did not see the Greeks. There might be much less foot traffic at this time of day, but there was a fair amount of vehicular traffic to avoid. Torbar couldn't just gallop madly into the crowds at the base of the steps of the temple.

Which way did the Greeks go?

He had to stop panicking. He had to *think!*

Torbar pulled his horse to a stop at the bottom of the wide steps. There were at least twenty people currently mounting the stairs to the main part of the temple.

Breathing hard, Torbar sat on his mount, glaring around at the populace, who took little notice of him. Where could the Greeks be? Closing his eyes, he tried to scan. In doing so, he could usually picture a person's face and feel where he or she was located.

There was no response. Opening his eyes, Torbar

cursed softly. This particular skill didn't work at all without his headband in place.

And to try to read twenty humanoid minds was impossible. If he couldn't even send out a scanning beam to search for the Greeks, then Torbar had no idea where they might be in the huge temple complex. He'd seen only one portion of it in Servilia's mind and that section was not visible to him. Even his intuition seemed faulty right now, and he blamed it on the mind blast, which had brutally shaken him up. He hated feeling helpless. Navigators were powerful, indispensable, and they ruled the galaxy. As Torbar sat there on his horse, he realized he was no better than the primitive humanoids who surrounded him right now. That made him bitter and angry. To be marooned here, of all places, among these pitiful humanoids made his stomach roll.

It was the fault of the Greeks, he decided. They had caught on to who he was before he'd realized they were time travelers. Torbar knew that when Kentar found out about his failings, he would be permanently demoted and his Navigator status stripped from him. That is, if he was able survive this mission. Glaring around at the scene before him, Torbar felt rage funnel through him.

No! He would not allow these two Greeks, or

whoever they really were, to win! His family went back four hundred generations. Torbar could not allow himself to dishonor their illustrious name.

One way or another, he would find the Greeks and stop them.

Chapter 19

The braziers were lit and light flickered off the temple columns as Delia quickly walked behind Jake. Dusk was deepening, and soon it would be dark. That suited her just fine.

Jake led her into a room at the rear of the temple where the high priestess kept the sacred objects. Heart bounding in her chest, she felt him grip her hand and give it a squeeze. Surprised, she saw him look down at her, his eyes narrowed, before he released her hand.

She grinned. "Feeling frisky?"

"Yeah, it's the danger," Jake teased back. "Like an orgasm."

"Hmm, that sounds good to me."

"What? The orgasm or the danger?"

"I'll plead the Fifth on that one, Tyler." Delia heard him chuckle as they opened a door and went inside. Standing side by side for a moment, they allowed their eyes to adjust to the gloom.

Jake pulled out a small flashlight and flipped it on. "Don't you love modern technology?" he drawled, as they walked toward another door.

"Makes you really appreciate it at times like this," Delia agreed. She opened the second door, which was heavy and creaked in protest. The oily smell of the braziers made her wrinkle her nose. "You stay here, on guard," she told Jake. "I'll get the piece."

He handed her the flashlight, since the inner room was totally dark. "Go for it."

Hurrying inside the tiny, airless room, she saw a wooden table with a beautiful white linen cloth across it. In the center was the box that contained the fragment. Hands shaking, she quickly opened it and dug out the relic. At once, her fingers started tingling.

Delia held her breath. She opened a small pouch she had inside the larger one at her waist, where she'd tucked Kapaneus's headband. Delia placed the precious relic into the smaller pouch, then hung it around her neck on its thick leather thong, pushing the pouch beneath her tunic, where it couldn't be seen. Relief rushed through her. It seemed the relic was not going to whisk her out of her body, to travel the galaxy again. *Good!*

As she closed the box and smoothed the linen back into place, she wondered why the high priestess did not guard this relic. But then, Delia thought as she turned to leave, Romans would never think of coming in to steal such a sacred object, for fear of reprisal from the god or goddess involved. She opened the door and stepped out. Jake was standing where she'd left him, his brows drawn and his eyes alert.

He held up his hand and pointed toward the door.

Delia scowled and tiptoed across the stone floor to where he stood, noting tension in his shadowed face.

"I'm picking up a lot of sudden mind activity here in the temple," he warned her in a whisper. "Let's press our armband crystals and get out of here right now."

Delia nodded. They could time-jump from anywhere. She didn't want to risk being found out. "I've got the relic on me," she whispered back, patting the area between her breasts.

"That's all we need…."

Delia stood next to him. Both of them lifted their sleeves, reaching for their armbands.

"Ready?" Delia asked in a whisper. Outside, she could hear running footsteps—and hobnailed boots. Roman soldiers were coming this way.

"Ready," Jake growled.

"Count of three. One, two, three…"

Delia pressed the oval, flat crystal hard with her index finger. She waited. Nothing happened.

"What the hell?" Jake growled.

Confused, she looked at him and then pulled off her armband. "Take it off. Maybe we need a more direct pressure on the crystals."

Hurriedly, Jake did as she suggested. He heard the Roman soldiers just outside the door. And they were coming in.

"Now!" Delia whispered, and pressed her crystal as hard as she could. It had never *not* worked before. Why wasn't it transporting them back to the lab?

The door was shoved open by two grunting Roman soldiers. Jake was shoved violently, and landed on his hands and knees. The armband clattered on the floor and bounced away from him.

Delia cursed and started to pull her sword out of the scabbard as the room filled with Roman soldiers, their own swords drawn, their faces dark with threat.

"Hold!" the centurion barked. "Don't move!"

Jake scrambled to his feet. He leaned down

and grabbed the armband, shoving it into the pocket of his tunic. By now five soldiers had their swords aimed at him. Breathing hard, he saw Delia slip her armband into her pocket also. She raised her hands.

"What's this about?" she demanded angrily.

"General Brutus's scribe accuses you of theft," the centurion barked. "Now, move forward!" He gestured for Delia to step his way.

Jake could see Kapaneus, tense and angry, standing just outside the door. His eyes were glittering with rage, arms crossed on his chest. The scribe smiled lethally as Delia was pushed out ahead of the Roman soldiers. Jake felt a sword nudging his back and he stepped out in turn.

There was a crowd gathering, of temple priestesses as well as the populace. The braziers flared, sending light dancing across the faces of the fifty or so people who stood around the outer door.

Jake's gaze never left the scribe. The smirk on Kapaneus's face made anger burn deep within him. How badly Jake wanted to plant his fist into the bastard's bearded jaw. Turning, he saw Delia being shoved toward where he stood. And then, it hit him. Even without his headband, Kapaneus was able to stop them from time jumping! That was why the ESC didn't work! Jake's mind spun. How far away did they have to be from this alien before his mind no longer had control over their ESC devices?

"Now!" Kapaneus yelled. "Search them, Centurion! They have my headband on them somewhere. And they came here to steal the arrowhead of the goddess Diana! They deserve to die!"

The centurion, a man of near forty and a grizzled veteran of many campaigns, glared over at him. "Hold your tongue, scribe. You may work for General Brutus, but I am in charge here."

Breathing shallowly, Delia stole a glance at Jake, less than two feet away. The armbands did not work! Her mind spun with questions that couldn't be answered.

Kapaneus stood to one side, his narrowed gaze on her. Even now, Delia could see the glowing red of his aura.

"Now then," the centurion growled at Jake, "hand over what you've stolen."

He opened his hands. "Search me. I have nothing that belongs to the scribe or to this temple. He's framing us," Jake accused, pointing at the scribe. "We are personal guards of the mistress Servilia, General Brutus's mother. Surely, this is wrong! We've done nothing! We came here to worship the goddess Diana."

The centurion halted and frowned. "You are

Greek mercenaries working for the lady
Servilia?"

"Yes," Delia said hotly, "we are! This scribe is
jealous of us! He has set us up, Centurion. How is
it that we cannot come here as freeborn citizens of
the Roman Empire and worship whom we please?"

Delia saw the dark eyes of the old soldier
abruptly narrow. He turned and glared at the scribe,
whose mouth had fallen open. And then he studied
the two of them. Knowing that his commander,
Marcus Brutus, would be furious with him for
stopping the Greek mercenaries who had saved his
mother's life, he hesitated.

"They lie!" Kapaneus shouted. He strode
forward and pushed his way between the soldiers.
"Search them! They have stolen my headband! I
know they have it on them!"

The centurian glared at him. "Step back,
Kapaneus. You may be educated, and write on
papyrus, wax and clay tablets for General Brutus,
but we do not arrest people without proof."

Snorting violently, Torbar lunged at Jake. The
Roman soldiers stopped him and threw him back.
He nearly fell, but caught himself as the crowd
around them murmured.

Regaining his balance, Torbar wished mightily
for his headband. If he had it, he could mind blast

these simpletons and get hold of that intriguing relic. But as things stood, he was vulnerable. It was a pulverizing realization. Still, he had enough energy to freeze the capacity of their armbands. At close range, Torbar could stop these time raiders from going anyplace. But if they were too far from his physical presence, he could not control the armband. The leader of the soldiers was hesitating, he saw. The man probably did not want to get in trouble with the general by arresting his mother's bodyguards. Of all things! Gritting his teeth, Torbar snarled, "I tell you, they have my headband! You must search them!"

Delia laughed harshly and lifted her chin. "We must return to the mistress Servilia. Do not hold us up any longer. We have nothing that belongs to the scribe." She raised her hands, her palms toward the leader.

"Get out of here," the centurion growled to them. He jerked his thumb toward the front of the temple. "Leave now!"

"Wait!" a woman's voice from within the sacred room cried out.

Delia didn't hesitate; she lunged through the opening provided by the Roman soldiers, with Jake on her heels, then pushed her way through the crowd.

In seconds, they were clear and free. Delia dug

her boots into the smooth marble floor as she ran. "The horses!" she cried.

"Yes!"

Delia heard a roar go up behind them. She'd already guessed that the priestess had gone into the sacred room and found the relic missing. She hated being a traitor to these women who had trusted her. The ring of hobnailed boots echoed loudly through the temple.

They hurtled down the white steps, which appeared gray in the dusk. Delia saw their mounts tied to an olive tree to the left. Jake leaped ahead of her and raced for them. Behind her, she heard the soldiers yelling. They were gaining on them....

Jake got to the startled horses first. They danced around in panic as he stripped the reins from the tree. Delia leaped onto the back of her gelding. Jake threw her the reins.

"The Tiber!" she yelled, whirling her mount around. The Roman soldiers, led by Kapaneus, were charging down the steps. While Jake jumped upon his horse, Delia leaned forward and dug her heels into her gelding's flanks. The animal grunted and leaped forward just as the closest soldiers rushed at them.

The hooves of the horses clattered loudly on the cobblestone street. Several spears were thrown, clanging as the iron tips hit the pavement. Wind rushed by Delia as she raced down the now nearly deserted avenue. It was nearly dark—dinnertime for Romans. The streets were clear except for beggars here and there.

Jake galloped up beside her. "Why the Tiber?" The river flowed outside the walled city of Rome.

"It's our only escape!" she panted. "They'll shut the gates on us. We'll be trapped inside the walls! Once that centurion sends a messenger by horse-back to the nearest gate, we're doomed! If we reach the river, we can dive in and swim. They won't catch us that way and we'll be outside the walls. It will give us time to figure out why our armbands aren't working."

Jake nodded. "Hey! I figured out why our ESCs didn't work. Kapaneus used his mind to freeze them. I don't know how far away we have to be from him before they will work." The street was dark now except for braziers lit in front of wine shops. The cobblestone was slippery and their horses were in jeopardy of falling.

"Look out!" Delia cried. She hauled back on the reins. Her mount skidded to a stop, its iron shoes making sparks fly.

Ahead of them was a small contingent of cavalry. Delia was stunned by how swiftly the soldiers could communicate. There was no radio to call ahead and alert one another about a crisis. Whirling her horse around, she yelled to Jake, "I know another way to the river! Follow me!"

Behind them, the clatter of the cavalry unit swelled. Ten Romans mounted on horses sent a loud echo up and down the avenue. Beggars scurried to either side, pressing themselves up against walls to escape being run over.

To Delia's chagrin, she saw Kapaneus mounted on a white horse riding hell-bent for leather toward them. Somehow, he knew they would take this route to the river. Realizing the scribe, or whoever the bastard was, wanted the headband, Delia started to dig it out of the pouch tied to her belt. It was hard to get hold of as they flew along the narrow, twisting street.

Up ahead, Delia could see the smooth black waters of the Tiber. It was a wide, deep river, with strong currents.

Kapaneus was gaining on them. Their own mounts were lagging, because they'd been running for miles now and were tiring out. She saw the scribe whip his horse repeatedly. The white gelding surged ahead, only ten feet behind Delia's horse now. If she could force Kapaneus off their track, his mind energy would wane and their ESCs could work.

Breathing hard, she dug for the headband, finally

curling her hands around the damn thing. Holding it up so that the scribe could see it, she swerved her horse to the right, cutting off his own mount. They nearly collided. The white gelding grunted and slid, almost unseating the scribe. At the last second, he grabbed its mane and hung on.

Delia made it to the banks of the Tiber and halted her horse. The scribe was riding hard to catch up.

"Here, Kapaneus!" she shouted, waving the headband in the air.

"Give it to me!" he screamed as he galloped down the bank, straight toward her.

Laughing, Delia threw the headband out into the Tiber. "Go get it!" Then she whirled her mount away from the scribe and headed toward Jake.

Torbar screamed in rage and launched himself off his galloping gelding. Landing hard, he rolled several times. And then, scrambling to his feet, he dived into the black waters, searching frantically for his headband.

The Tiber was not shallow. As Torbar leaped into the water, he discovered it was cold and deep. Making several dives, his hands outstretched and searching, he met only mud. Where was his headband?

Again and again, he dived, groping blindly. Out of breath, he surged to the surface, gasping loudly.

It was nearly dark. To his left, he saw the two Greeks abandon their horses on the bank about half a mile downriver. He felt his mind energy dissolving as they rode farther away. He knew that shortly their armbands would work once more and they'd be able to time jump. He didn't care. Getting his headband back was far more important! In seconds, they leaped into the Tiber, swimming strongly away from the shore, to avoid being shot at with arrows or spears hurled by the Romans.

Cursing, he saw the cavalry arrive—too late. They hurled their spears toward the fleeing swimmers, but all fell short because the Greeks had already reached the center of the wide river. And then a group of Roman archers raced to the bank to try and shoot them. Standing in waist-deep water, Torbar watched.

There was no choice—holding his breath, he sank beneath the surface, hands moving relentlessly across the muddy bottom, trying to find the only thing that would get him off this accursed planet.

Gulping and spitting out cold river water, Delia heard Jake cry out behind her. The current was strong in the center of the Tiber and was quickly carrying them out of range of the archers. Her boots were filled with water and dragging her down. She'd already jettisoned her sword belt and weapons in order to remain afloat.

Floundering in the icy river, Delia twisted toward Jake, who was about five feet behind her. To her horror, she saw an arrow sticking out of his left shoulder. Giving a cry of alarm, she swung her arms outward and battled against the current to reach him. Delia could see his teeth were clenched and pain clearly written across his wet face.

"Jake!" she shrieked, noting the current had moved them out of the archer's range. She gasped and splashed toward him. Grabbing his upraised right arm, she used all her strength to keep his head above the water, which was turning even darker with his blood. "Hang on!"

Jake groaned. He felt Delia's arm snake across his chest. She was drawing him onto his back so that she could help keep him afloat.

"I—I can't use my left arm!" he said through gritted teeth, his head tipping back against her shoulder. They swam together, the night swallowing them up. "We have to make it to the other side of the river!" Water rushed into his mouth. Jake spat it out. Delia was gasping as she jerked him along with slow, strong strokes of her arm and legs. She had one free arm to swim with now.

Jake knew they'd never make it to the other shore. It was too far away, and the icy water was already causing hypothermic symptoms. In a matter of minutes, Delia would be growing numb, the river stealing the life heat from this courageous woman's body. She would begin to flounder, and eventually they'd both sink and drown in the Tiber.

Something told Jake to reach for the armband he'd stuffed into his left pocket. Could he move his hand? The arrow in his back made it difficult. Each attempt sent white-hot pain through him. Gritting his teeth even harder, he forced his left hand beneath the water. Fingers searching, he finally located the armband. Turning the smooth metal, he fumbled for the crystal, but his fingers were cold and refused to bend.

Jake tried one last time. He'd never known an armband not to work when the crystal was pressed but Kapaneus had interfered with it. Still, his gut screamed at him to try pressing it one more time. Maybe they were out of range of the alien's controlling energy over the ESC. With a final effort, he got his fingers around the metal.

With water sloshing continuously into his face, blinding him, he finally felt the crystal with his nearly numb fingers. "I'm going to try pressing the band," he called out. His voice was ragged. He was losing a lot of blood and growing weaker with each minute that passed.

"Do it!" Delia gasped, lunging time and again as

she angled them toward the far shore in the darkness. Coughing, she spat out water. Only the strength of her legs kicking violently kept them afloat.

His thumb found the smooth, glassy surface of the crystal. Jake prayed it would work this time as he pressed the stone. Instantly, pain shot up his arm to where the arrow was stuck in his back.

Seconds later, he felt the familiar spinning sensation that always signaled a jump had been initiated. Letting out a groan of relief, he felt himself and Delia begin a slow, circular spin. That meant the time jump was under way.

Since Delia was physically touching him, she, too, would be part of the jump.

His body was filled with pain, his mind roiling with questions as to why the armband hadn't worked before. It didn't matter. Closing his eyes, Jake felt his awareness of his surroundings fade. He knew from Professor Carswell's experiments in the lab on inanimate objects that their molecules would begin to draw apart. As they did so, their bodies would literally disappear. When called back with the crystal resonation, the molecules would reassemble at the other end, into physical form once more.

That was the last thing Jake thought before everything began to dissolve.

Delia's warm, strong arm around his chest made him feel hopeful that they would wake up at the other end of their journey and find themselves once more in the glass cylinder. There, he could get medical help. There, they would be safe....

Chapter 20

Athena concentrated until she heard General Beverly Ashton call out, "They're back!"

Instantly, Athena opened her eyes and broke the connection she had maintained via the headband to the armbands the Time Raider team wore.

"Get a corpsman!" Ashton ordered a lab tech.

Jumping out of the comfortable chair where she orchestrated the time jumps, Athena rushed into the other room. There, in the glass cylinder, were Jake and Delia. She lay beneath him, her arm across his chest. Water pooled around them on the floor of the cylinder; they had obviously been swimming when she'd connected with them.

Gasping, Athena saw an arrow sticking out of Jake's back, and blood covering his left arm and shoulder. Her stomach knotted. She was no good at emergencies like this and relied heavily on Beverly, who could remain calm and cool during such a crisis.

Athena stood aside as two paramedics carried Jake, who was unconscious, out of the glass cylinder. Both he and Delia were sopping wet, the civilian clothes they'd worn for the time jump clinging to their bodies. Athena saw the anguish in Delia's face as he was hurriedly wheeled out of the room on a gurney, to be taken to the nearby Flagstaff hospital.

Only when the door to the lab closed did Athena move to Delia, who had staggered out of the time capsule cylinder under her own power. Her curly black hair was draped wetly around her glistening face. She was tugging on a leather thong and pulling up a leather pouch that had been hidden inside her tee. If an object was retrieved in a time jump, it automatically returned with the person.

"Athena?" Delia said, her voice hoarse. "This is the piece. The fragment!" She handed the pouch to the professor. Right now, all Delia wanted to do was be with Jake. She knew he had lost a lot of blood. Would he die? Would he live?

"Thank you!" Athena exclaimed, giving her a warm and deeply grateful look. "Are you okay?"

"Yes, but I'm tired. We had to jump into the Tiber in order to escape," she explained, pushing the wet curls off her brow. Ashton took a dry towel from a lab assistant and handed it to her.

Athena's hand was tingling wildly. She gazed down at the soaked pouch. Excitement was tempered by Jake being wounded. "That was a close call. I'll take this to the conference room and open it up."

A surge of joy made Athena feel giddy. They had found the first piece. But at what cost?

"Jake will need surgery," the general told them grimly. She looked at Delia. "Change your clothes and grab a shower in the locker room. Then give us a quick report. Afterward, I'll have one of our lab techs drive you over to the hospital so you can stay with him."

Delia nodded with relief. Athena had opened the pouch and produced the fragment. They all looked at it and marveled. "This is a powerful piece," the professor said reverently.

"Yes," Delia said, "it is." And she gave a short version of what had happened when she'd held it during the ceremony at the temple of Diana.

Ashton put her hand on Delia's sagging shoulder. "Go get cleaned up. You need to be with Jake. I'll call over to the hospital right now and get a status report on his condition." Beverly was fully aware of their relationship from the past. Judging from Delia's worried expression, she knew it was important for her to be with Jake as soon as humanly possible.

Delia hurried out of the main lab to a small locker room. Standing under a hot shower was wonderful. She washed the river smell of the Tiber out of her hair and then scrubbed her body with a fragrant raspberry gel. Though she felt exhausted, her thoughts stayed with Jake. *How was he?*

Choking, the warm water streaming down her face and across her closed eyes, Delia fought back the tears. Somewhere along the line, she'd fallen in love with Jake all over again. When had it happened?

As she rinsed herself and shut off the tap, Delia had no answers. Jake had been trying to change, that was for sure. She had never expected him to be able to do it, but he *had* changed. All for her. He had been more vulnerable. She had seen him struggle to be open and intimate with her.

After drying off with a thick, light blue towel, Delia went to her locker and opened it. Inside were clean black velvet pants, a white angora cowl-necked sweater, her lingerie and a pair of no-nonsense black leather shoes.

The door to the locker room opened. A lab tech, a young woman by the name of Arlene, stepped in.

"General Ashton called over to the hospital, Delia. Jake is in surgery right now. The doctor who examined him says that if all goes well, he'll live."

Relief shot through her. "Thanks, Arlene."

"I'll drive you over to the hospital as soon as you give your report to the general and professor."

"Thank you." Delia sat down and shoved on her shoes. Grabbing her deerskin jacket, which was fringed across the back, and sported a beaded Navajo design of the rising sun, she shrugged it on.

Moving to the conference room, she saw the group anxiously waiting for her. Typically, on a completed mission, the time jumper would immediately give a verbal report, while all the facts were still fresh. The words were fed into a computer and turned into a version to be studied by the whole strategy and tactics branch of this clandestine operation.

Sitting down, Delia nodded to Professor Carswell, who sat opposite her at the oval maple table. General Ashton and her aide, Captain Sarah Stanton, sat at one end with the computer and other devices, ready to log Delia's every word.

Hurriedly, she gave them the bare bones of what had happened.

The general's face drew dark when Delia mentioned Kapaneus, the red aura around him, and that they suspected him of being an alien. And when she brought up the headband they'd stolen from the scribe, Professor Carswell gasped.

"Can you draw us a picture of what it looked like?"

Delia nodded. "It's much thinner and finer-looking than the one we have, Athena." Delia used her hands to show how Kapaneus wore it around his head. "He came after us to retrieve his headband," she told them. "He seemed desperate to get it back."

Athena gave the general a quick look. "This is something new, Bev. None of our Time Raiders have ever encountered anything like this."

Ashton frowned. "This is the first team we've sent looking for pieces of that stamp. Maybe it has triggered an alarm back to the alien culture? Is that why they sent this scribe, Kapaneus—in disguise? Maybe his job was to intercept you?"

Delia shrugged. "I don't know."

Tucking her lower lip between her teeth, Athena searched Delia's exhausted-looking features. It was obvious to her that Delia and Jake had made amends in their relationship. "You need to be with Jake. We've got plenty of info from you with this cursory report. We'll sit down with you and Jake later for an in-depth debriefing."

"Thanks," Delia told them. Even though she knew Jake was going to live, she still wanted to be at his side.

"Yes, get going," Ashton ordered. "We'll meet here at 0900 tomorrow to start the complete report. That will give you time to be with Jake and then catch a good night's sleep."

"Yes, ma'am," Delia said. She rose, pulled the strap of her leather purse over her shoulder and turned toward the door. "I'll see you tomorrow."

Arlene was waiting outside the door of the conference room. A young woman in her early twenties, she had short, shiny red hair and wore clothes typical of a college student. One of the many things Athena and the general insisted upon was fitting in with the students on campus. No one knew what the lab was about except for the people hired to work here. And the only way an individual could enter was through retinal identification.

"I'm ready...let's go!" The redheaded woman gave a quick smile and ushered Delia down the hall toward the reception area.

Jake was conscious when Delia walked into his private room at Flagstaff Memorial Hospital. His left arm was in a sling and a thick dressing wrapped around his shoulder.

"You look like hell warmed over," Delia said in greeting, closing the door and hanging her purse over a nearby chair.

He smiled wanly. "And you look like an angel to me." Holding out his right hand as she approached, he rasped, "Thanks for saving my life, sweetheart."

Warming to the endearment he'd always used for her when they were together in Afghanistan, Delia reached out and gripped his fingers. His skin was cool to the touch. She stood by the bed, his hand wrapped between her own. Gazing at him, she saw that his eyes were still fuzzy-looking from the anesthesia and surgery.

"You saved our lives, if I recall. You're the one who pressed the ESC to get us home. In my eyes, you're the hero." She leaned down and settled her lips across his. When his hand tightened around her fingers, she pressed it to her breasts as she continued to gently explore his very male mouth. His lips moved hungrily with hers, and she smiled.

"You might be half-dead, Tyler, but you still can kiss…." she whispered.

Jake relaxed against the pillow and enjoyed the continued exploration of Delia's lips against his. When she broke contact, he felt a sharp pain in his heart. Opening his eyes, he saw her face hovering close to his. Her eyes were warm and golden, with love radiating in them—for him.

Was there still a chance for them as a couple? Had their time together in Rome served to reunite them? Or was Delia being kind because he'd been shot by an arrow and nearly bled to death? Jake didn't want to believe that as he searched her sunlit eyes and parted lips.

"I love you, Delia," he told her huskily. The tube they'd put down his throat during surgery made it sore, and his voice wasn't his own yet. He squeezed her hand as she straightened.

"What *are* we going to do, Jake?" Delia gazed into his hooded eyes. His mouth was strong and so beautifully shaped. It drew her again, and Delia had to stop herself from swooping down again and kissing him hotly.

"I want to start all over with you, sweetheart. When I woke up, about twenty minutes ago, the first thing I did was look around for you."

Heart squeezing at the note of anguish in Jake's rumbling tone, she released his hand. "I had to give a report first. You know how that goes."

He lifted an eyebrow. "While giving the report did you really want to be here instead? With me?"

"Yes, Jake, I did." She leaned over and brushed

several strands of hair off his forehead. His color was slowly returning and that lifted her spirits as nothing else could. Jake was going to live. He'd survived.

When he gave her his best smile, her heart skipped a beat. "In the past all we did was fight, Jake," she murmured, running her fingers up and down his uninjured arm.

"That's true, Del, for the past. We made love, too. Doesn't that count?"

"It does. I want what we started back in Rome with you, Jake."

"You can see I'm trying," he said, feeling relief. "It was true we couldn't do much kissing or other things...but we were on a mission." He reached for her hand again. "We're home now, Del. And I want another chance."

"I can see you're opening up to me, Jake." Her voice cracked with emotion.

She saw Jake's black brows dip. "I'm sorry I've hurt you so much in the past, Del. Men are hardwired differently than women. We don't talk much. At least, not about lots of important things. I realize now that it's important to share. And I'm going to change my ways. Don't you see that?" He searched her face.

Desperation crept through his chest as he

watched Delia lift her head and meet his gaze. Her fingers curved gently around his and she squeezed.

"Yes, and that means the world to me, Jake."

"No matter what world or time we're in, Del, I want you back. Do you hear me?"

Nodding, she grimaced. "I'm afraid, Jake. I'm afraid that if I open up my heart and take you back, you're going to hurt me all over again. It's a stupid reaction, but I need to tell you how I'm feeling about us."

Sighing, Jake turned his head, eyeing the white venetian blinds on the other side of the room. "I deserved that," he told her quietly. Turning back, he added, "Look at me, Del...."

Anguish seared through Delia as she met and held his warm blue eyes. Clearly, she saw Jake's love for her—as she'd seen it in Afghanistan. "What?"

"I promise to try. I won't curl up and go away and stonewall you like I did before."

"I believe you. I also know it won't be perfect. Nothing ever is." How she loved the feel of his strong, callused fingers gripping hers. Delia remembered all too well his hands searching and memorizing her naked body, sending her to the edge of a blissful oblivion. There was no question Jake knew how to make her body sing like a finely tuned instrument. But a relationship didn't hinge on sex alone. There were so many other variables that had to be added to the recipe to make it work for them.

"I will screw up," Jake told her, clearing his throat. "But with your patience and understanding, I'll get back up and keep trying."

"You are beginning to trust someone outside yourself," she said quietly. She saw Jake's eyes go dark and his mouth quirk. This was always the area of contention between them—his lack of intimacy in anyone outside himself. Delia understood this was ground zero for them. Could Jake really overcome a lifetime of stonewalling, and truly let her be a partner to him?

Jake felt the tension build between them and saw the worry in Delia's eyes. It was time to come clean. Time to be honest as he'd never been with her before. Releasing her hand, he gestured to the chair. "Pull it over and sit down, Del. I need you near…"

Searching his eyes, which were dark with pain, Delia ran her palm across his stubbled cheek.

"Jake, thanks for sharing your real feelings with me. It helps me to understand you. By now, you must realize you can make different choices, don't you? You don't have to stay closed up with me any more. I'm here. I'll listen. I'll hold you when you want to be held. I can protect you against the winds of life, just like you can protect me. We can hold one another. What you're realizing, I think, is that the possibility is there. Now. You no longer have to go through life protecting every vulnerable emotion. You can share them with me."

Nodding, Jake closed his eyes and relished the feel of Delia's soft, firm hand stroking his cheek and jaw. Tiny tingles of pleasure radiated outward and he hungrily absorbed the magical connection. "My parents weren't touchers like you, Delia," he admitted, gazing up at her.

"Some people aren't demonstrative, Jake. Sometimes highly intelligent people have a tough time showing their love and emotions to others."

"You're smart but you're a toucher," he murmured, amazed by how her golden-brown eyes clearly shone with love for him. "I like being held by you, Del. In Afghanistan you have no idea how much I looked forward to being held in your arms after we made love. I can't begin to make you understand how much it meant to me."

"Maybe because your parents didn't hold you as much as you needed?"

Nodding, Jake felt another pang tightening his chest. "Probably. It's hard to compare." It hurt to realize how much nurturing he might have missed out on as a child.

"Jake, you never got the emotional support you needed." She pressed a kiss to his hand. "And you know what's good about you sharing all this with me? We can go forward now with better understanding. The next time you retreat, I'll know why. And then we'll talk and we'll hold one another, and you can break that old pattern of reaction. Jake, you can have a completely different life with me, if you want. It's going to take a lot of work. I'm not going to try and fool you about that—or fool myself."

"I want that chance with you, Del."

Those words shattered the last fears she had about having a relationship with Jake. "Music to my ears, darling."

It was so easy for Delia to lean over and gently place her mouth across his. As she did, his lips softened and he groaned. He slid his good arm across her shoulders and guided her down to the bed. She lay against him, her hand framing his jaw and deepening their exploratory kiss.

Oh, she'd almost lost him! As his mouth took hers with a tenderness that brought tears to her closed eyes, Delia moaned. Jake could have died in the Tiber River! There were so many things that could have gone wrong. Somehow his strength, despite his wound, had saved the day—and saved them. In her eyes and heart, he was a true hero.

An ache built rapidly in her lower body. Her breasts tightened as his tongue moved sensuously along her lower lip. Oh, how she wanted Jake! All of him. In every way. His breath was ragged and warm against her cheek. Glorying in the stubble of his beard brushing her flesh, Delia drew in every scent, every contact and sound of Jake as he held her.

Jake had to release Del, and he didn't want to. The pain was becoming too much in his shoulder. He released her, and she sat up and gave him a soft smile that said so much. "Sorry," he murmured, pointing to his shoulder.

"Don't worry about it," she soothed, sliding her hand against his cheek. "I like kissing you, Jake. It's nice to have you back. All of you—your heart, your thoughts…you…"

The wobble in her voice moved Jake. Gripping her hand, he whispered, "More good days than bad ahead of us, Del. I promise you that."

Ruffling his hair, she gave him a tremulous smile. "I know that now. It's a good feeling. We'll make our relationship work."

Feeling suddenly exhausted, he closed his eyes. "Listen, I'm pretty whipped, Del. Can you come back for a visit tonight? I need a little sleep right now."

Smiling, she rose to her feet and placed a soft, searching kiss on his parted lips, noting the dark shadows beneath his eyes. "I'll be back this evening, I promise…."

As Delia left Jake's room and walked down the busy hospital hallway, she shook herself mentally. Right now, she needed to get to her condo, which was near the university, and grab some sleep herself. Time jumps always took a toll on her energy. Once she was back at her condo, she'd be able to relax.

As she stepped outside and looked up at Mount Humphrey's mantle of snow, she wrapped her fuzzy, colorful muffler around her neck. It was a beautiful afternoon. The sidewalks gleamed with crystals of salt for melting the ice that had covered them earlier. The wind was blustery and the sky studded with puffy clouds.

Arlene was sitting in the van and smiled a welcome when Delia climbed in.

As they drove along the recently plowed streets, Delia's mind whirled. As tired as she was, anticipation and happiness threaded through her as she thought of the coming week. The report on the time jump would take several days of thorough and detailed sifting by the team. There would be a lot of hours put in at the lab, meeting in the conference room with Athena, General Ashton and her staff.

Delia wanted to be with Jake all the time, but that was not meant to be. Their time would come later. And how she looked forward to it...

Chapter 21

Jake got the surprise of his life the next morning: Delia visiting him with Professor Carswell. The scientist looked flushed as she carried her beat-up black calfskin briefcase into his room. Athena had left off her ever-present white lab coat and was dressed in a simple black wool pantsuit. She looked like a young professor at the university instead of the genius physicist she really was.

"Jake, good morning! You look great compared to yesterday," she said with a smile. After Delia closed the door, Athena could barely keep the excitement out of her voice as she added, "We're going to try an experiment." Digging into her brief-case, she produced the metal fragment of the seal they'd carried back from ancient Rome, and held it up for him to see.

"I was working with this last night and I got a lot of information from it," Athena said. Moving to the bed, she gestured for Delia to go to the opposite side. "Delia, you mentioned in your report that this relic healed your thigh after you'd gotten that sword wound in the fight at Servilia's home, right?"

"Yes…" And then Delia gasped, making the connection. "Maybe it can heal *Jake's* wound? Why didn't I think of that before?"

Athena laughed giddily. "Don't worry, you love this guy, and you wouldn't be thinking clearly in such a situation. Besides, the first twenty-four hours after a time jump, your brain is muddled at best. Don't be hard on yourself."

Delia felt her face burning. She could feel the heat in her cheeks as Jake's mouth stretched into a grin. *Love?* Yes, it was love. Riding over with Athena this morning, she'd told her about Jake and herself getting back together again. In that moment, Delia realized she'd never stopped loving Jake. She'd just suppressed it and pretended it was over. "I held it against my wound and it healed within seconds."

"Precisely," Athena said. She gave Jake a look of anticipation. "Jake, hold this fragment in your left hand. That's the hand we receive energy with. I want you to close your eyes, hold it and allow the energy that will come through it to heal your arrow wound."

Jake took the object and closed his eyes. Within seconds, the palm of his hand felt as if it were burning. And then energy shot up his arm and he felt intense, swirling heat move into his left shoulder-blade area where he'd been struck.

Delia traded a glance with Athena. They stood with their hands on the bed, anxiously watching his face. He had been pasty looking at best, with a day's growth of beard on his face. Now, as he held the fragment in his palm, his skin tone regained a healthy pink color. Delia bit back a gasp.

Within minutes, Jake felt the heat recede. It flowed out of his shoulder, down his left arm and centered once more in his palm, where he held the fragment. Opening his eyes, he said to Athena, "I think it's done." Handing it back to her, he sat up. To Delia he said, "Undress this wound and let's see what's happened."

"Do you feel healed?" Athena asked, carefully tucking the fragment into the briefcase.

"Yeah, there's no pain when I move my shoulder."

Delia untied his sling and he carefully moved his arm, stretching it in several directions to test it. "No pain," he told them triumphantly.

"I'll be," Delia whispered excitedly. She uncovered the wound. "It's gone, Jake! All that's left is a pink scar." She removed the dressing completely.

Jake sat there, naked from the waist up. To Delia, he looked delicious. A feast for her eyes, heart and needy body, which wanted him so badly.

"Wonderful!" Athena crowed as she moved around the bed and carefully examined Jake's back. "It healed you! Completely! In Argenta's journal she never made mention of the fragment's ability to heal." Giving the pair a triumphant look, she said, "Jake, I'll go sign you out of the hospital. I think it's time you and Delia went home—together. We'll see you at the lab in a couple of days to start the debriefing. Sound like a plan?"

"Nice. Very nice," Jake commented as he sauntered into Delia's condo. The winter sun slanted in through a rectangular window, giving the place a cheery look. Jake had never been in Delia's condo since they'd split up two years earlier, before she'd moved here. Hands in his pockets, he stepped across the bamboo floor into the small living room. Green plants were in two corners, near the couch, with its willow-green and fuchsia flower upholstery. A black lacquered coffee table sat in front of it, with two small upholstered chairs opposite.

"Thanks," Delia said, closing the door. Jake looked completely well, as if nothing had ever happened to him. She was still in shock, but it was a good kind. Placing the keys on the black granite counter in the kitchen, she hung her purse on a hook in the hallway near the door. The hall led to the bedroom, her office and the bathroom.

"Green as ever—your decor," Jake said, turning and giving her a heated look that couldn't be interpreted any other way than that he wanted her—body and soul. He knew she would get the message. He saw her eyes go smoky gold.

Holding out her hand, Delia said, "Green has always been my favorite color. And I love the spare Japanese design of my place. Come on, let me show you where you're going to sleep tonight."

Jake gripped her hand momentarily, then slid his arm around her shoulders as they sauntered down the hall together—like old times. The bamboo flooring shone as sunlight glanced off it here and there, thanks to skylights above. "I don't know about you, sweetheart, but all I want right now is you, in our bed."

Her body tingled wildly in anticipation. Delia

wrapped her arm around his narrow waist as they approached her bedroom on the left side of the hall. "What? Are you sure your wound is healed enough? You aren't starving? Want to eat first?"

"None of the above," he said in a growling tone. "And all I feel in the shoulder area is a little tenderness." He gave her a pointed look. "That's not going to stop me from loving you."

Jake paused at the entrance to her bedroom. There was a king-size bed with a dark green and lavender raw silk spread. Here, too, the decor was cleanly Japanese, with plants and a nubby light green carpet. "Nice," he murmured, looking down at her. He saw the hunger in her eyes—for him. It filled him with warmth as he led her to the bed.

"I'm going to enjoy every second of this," he murmured, brushing her hair with a kiss as he unbuttoned her white cotton blouse. Slipping his fingers beneath the soft fabric, he grazed the silk of her camisole and lightly caressed her firm breasts.

"Still not wearing a bra, I see." He laughed against her curly hair. It felt so right to move his fingertips across her fine collarbones.

"A bra? Not on your life. Not ever…" Delia helped Jake pull the silk camisole over her head. She watched as he dropped it on the end of the bed. Her flesh tingled hotly in the wake of his caresses.

Naked from the waist up, she whispered in a teasing tone, "Now it's my turn...."

Jake grinned and allowed himself to relish each fleeting touch of her fingers as she unbuttoned his denim shirt. "I'm not wearing anything under my shirt, either," he said.

Delia chuckled with him as she dropped his shirt to the floor. "I hope not! You never lose your sense of humor, Tyler."

"Something else to love about me," he whispered into her ear as he moved his hands to the waist of her Levi's.

"Not so fast," she murmured, provocatively sliding her fingers to the waistband of the navy-blue Dockers he wore.

Groaning, Jake felt lightning heat rip raggedly through him as her warm, exploring fingers unsnapped them and then pushed the fabric down his hips.

"Ah, you're not wearing any shorts, Tyler.... Why, shame on you!"

"Well, if you aren't wearing a bra, why should I wear boxers?" he teased, catching her smiling mouth with his. Her lips, soft and wet, nipped eagerly at his. In one swift motion, he lifted her in his arms and gently deposited her on the warm silk coverlet.

Her eyes flew open in surprise, and he gave her a predatory grin. "See? I'm all better. So get that worry that I'm still ailing from that arrow wound out of your eyes, okay?" He moved up on the bed as he unsnapped her jeans and pulled them off her legs.

"Uh-oh, no panties, either... What am I going to do with you, Ms. Del?"

She laughed. "Remember? I hate bras and panties. In two years you forgot that about me?"

Moving his hand slowly up her thighs, he murmured, "Oh, I remember all right. I never forgot that about you, sweetheart...." And he saw her eyes go liquid with desire.

Delia pushed his arm aside as she forced him onto his back. "Not so fast," she whispered wickedly. Jake's Dockers dropped into a heap on the floor. She raised herself up on one elbow and clicked her tongue. "You're armed and ready...."

"Only for you, darling." Jake drew her across his naked body. He felt her warm, firm thighs straddling his own and he groaned as she deliberately rubbed herself against him. Bolts of heat shot through him and he clenched his teeth.

Delia moved her hips sensuously and slid down upon Jake. Her inner muscles rippled as they met and melded. Splaying her hands against his dark-haired chest, she opened her eyes and lost herself in his stormy gaze. When he settled his large, callused hands around her hips and began to move her against him, she uttered a sigh of utter surrender and pleasure.

Two years apart from Jake dissolved into nothingness as he leaned up and brought her against him. The moment his lips captured her hard nipple, Delia gasped in delight. Sliding her arms around his shoulders, she held him, and the pain of the past fled as they moved together. Her heart flew open as it always did when they made hot, sweet love. It was as if those two years hadn't existed at all. Maybe, Delia thought, being Time Raiders, the jumps had indeed dissolved their painful years apart. She hoped so.

Fervently, she leaned forward and found Jake's mouth. With all her strength, with all her love, she kissed him, until they were both breathing raggedly. As his hands moved across her body, Delia gloried in his strength and also the gentleness that had always been a part of him. That was what she'd missed the most: his sensitivity to her needs, reading her correctly and somehow making their love sessions so special. Filled with awe as his rough hands moved to cup her breasts, Delia moaned. Arching into his palms, she felt the white-hot release of her body, as if a volcano had exploded

within her and was sending out tidal waves of incredible pleasure.

Delia felt as if she had become nothing but white-
and-gold stardust in the universe. Then Jake stiffened
against her and she clung to him, moving in sync with
him to enhance his orgasm as he spilled his life, his
love, deep within her glowing, throbbing body.

All too soon, the raw pleasure began to subside
and Delia felt sated. She rested weakly against Jake
as they lay on the bed in one another's arms.
Enjoying straddling him in the aftermath, she
moved her hips teasingly. He groaned, smiled and
opened his eyes, gazing deep into hers.

"I'm glad some things don't change," he
growled, framing her face with his palms.

Sinking into his arms, Delia moaned and let him
know just how much she'd enjoyed their reunion.
Their lips slid together and she relished the power
of his mouth, how it cajoled hers and commandingly took over, making her feel incredibly loved
and cared for.

Later, as they lay in one another's arms, the silk
coverlet drawn up across their waists, Delia stirred.
She rose up on one elbow and placed her hand on
Jake's massive chest. "What do you think?"

"About what? Making love?" Jake grinned and
waggled his eyebrows.

Slapping his chest playfully, she said, "No. And you know I didn't mean it that way. I'm talking about us, Jake."

Sliding his hand up her arm, he rasped, "I know what you meant, sweet woman. And yes, we're going to try again. Those were two damn lonely years without you."

"I wasn't happy about breaking up with you, either, Jake. But your lack of intimacy was just too much to take."

"Well," he murmured, enjoying the feel of her sleek skin, "I'm working on that. I'm going to make the changes, Del, because I don't like being without you in my life."

Nodding, she absorbed the sight of his rugged face into her heart. "I missed you, too, Jake."

"I know…I saw it the first time you laid eyes on me in that lab, before the time jump. I saw your anger, but I also saw something else…. Longing… maybe a little love that hadn't yet been destroyed by our being apart."

Nodding, Delia lay down at his side and nuzzled the hollow beneath his jaw. She slid her arm across his chest and reveled in his embrace as he held her close. "As long as you can change, Jake, I can hang in there with you."

"I'm coming to the realization that we're all

wounded in one way or another," he told her, pressing his lips against her soft, silky curls. "We're all operating in a pattern, but that doesn't mean we can't break out of old patterns and make new ones." He kissed her brow. "I want to make a new pattern with you, starting now."

Fighting back tears, Del lifted her head and met his clear blue eyes, which held such fierce love for her. "Yes...I'd like that, Jake."

He caressed her hair. "Let's sleep for a while. We've earned this time together. For the next little while our lives won't be our own. We're going to be working twelve hours a day over at the lab, putting all our adventures into their computerized system."

Sighing, Delia closed her eyes and gave him a fierce hug. "I love you, Tyler. And yeah, today is ours. Tomorrow, they own us body and soul, but after that, a vacation together should be our reward."

Laughter rumbled through his chest. Delia warmed to Jake's laugh, absorbing the feel of his strong male body. She couldn't see herself ever parting from him again. He'd grown, he'd matured over the last two years, and she knew intuitively that he would make the changes so that they could live together.

With that sweet thought, she spiraled her into
sleep. Tomorrow would begin the grueling report-
ing on their mission, but they'd be ready for it.
Together.

Chapter 22

"After three days of debriefing," General Ashton said, "we've got more questions than answers." She looked around the conference table at Athena, Delia and Jake. A computer technician at the far end made sure the report was fed into a computer and a hard copy produced. Another copy would be encrypted and placed into a vault for safekeeping.

Athena grimaced. "I'm very interested in the Centaurians Adonia spoke about, Delia. I feel Kapaneus was really a Centaurian. More than likely he possessed the scribe's body, but we can't know that for a fact."

"His aura was red," Delia said. "He was the one who owned that headband, which looked like a much improved copy of the one we have. Plus he attacked us energetically at Servilia's home, though somehow we repulsed his assault. It ended up knocking him out, instead, a boomerang effect. He has all the earmarks of someone who has total control over his psychic abilities. That makes him dangerous, and I feel you're right—he's a Centaurian Navigator."

"I believe he is, based upon your conversation with Adonia." Athena studied the notes she'd made on her Blackberry over the course of the debriefing. Pointing to it, she added, "And it's good to get the history on the seal." She smiled briefly. "At least we know who put it here on Earth and why."

"Those are assets," the general said, nodding. "Knowing who our enemy is gives us an advantage. We know the Centaurians have Navigators who utilize the same headband, albeit a more advanced model than the one you use, Athena."

Nodding, the professor studied the drawing Delia had made of Kapaneus's headband. "It's more streamlined, less bulky and certainly easier to wear than the Roswell model. And it appears to be less heavy than ours."

"But it probably performs the same functions," Delia said.

"I'm going to assume it does," Athena told her.

"The question," Ashton said, "is are the Centaurians aware of the stamp?"

"Adonia said everyone in the galactic federation was aware of the stamp," Athena reminded her. "The fragments were put into play because the Centaurians had kidnapped a hundred Earth women to try and figure out our genetics. They just didn't know where any of the pieces were placed. This was the Galactic Council's way of slapping their hand for breaking the law."

"That Centaurian, Kapaneus, knew the seal existed," Delia murmured.

"And we have to assume he got the information back to his home world," General Ashton added.

"But I threw his headband into the Tiber," Delia stated. "If he can't find it, does that mean he's marooned in that time without any means of contacting home base?"

The general shrugged. "We don't know if he found it or not. We don't know if a Navigator without a headband can still be in psychic contact with his world."

"Adonia made a strong point of saying that the headband controlled everything. I threw it into the river because Kapaneus was closing in on us. I knew he'd go after his headband instead of us," Delia said. "And we were swept into the current of the Tiber just as it was getting dark, so there was no way to know if Kapaneus retrieved it or not."

Ashton grimaced and moved uncomfortably in her chair, then folded her hands on the table. "We have to assume Kapaneus found the headband. That means they may try to track us down," she warned grimly. "If they possess time-travel technology as well as the ability to cross space from one star system to another in a matter of moments, we're at risk."

"Also," Jake said, "was Kapaneus sent in after we arrived in that time? Or was he already in place, waiting for us?"

Athena shrugged, then looked at the retired general. "What do you feel about this, Bev?"

Rubbing her chin, the woman repeated, "We simply don't know. What we need to do is assume they followed us into Rome. Time movement creates a rippling effect, energetically, doesn't it, Athena?"

"Yes, any movement disturbs the normal energy patterns within the universe when a time jump is initiated. It would be akin to us throwing a large rock into a quiet pond. The ripples created could be picked up with sensitive instruments. And Adonia said the Centaurians have very advanced technology, superior to anything else in the galaxy, to pick up such perturbations. I believe we must assume they felt me send Jake and Delia back to Rome, and that they responded by sending Kapaneus there to hunt them down."

Grimly, Jake looked at Delia, who sat next to him. Her face still glowed from the lovemaking they'd shared hours earlier, before today's debriefing began. He then gazed at the general, who sat at the head of the conference table. "If that is so, then whoever is sent to locate the second piece of this stamp will alert the Centaurians again. They'll send another agent to track down our mission specialist."

Nodding, Beverly said, "I agree. We must assume they will do that. All we can do is put all Time Raiders on alert."

"The only way we can tell Centaurians are different," Delia said, "is to see their red aura. Not all time jumpers have that particular psychic ability. And did the Centaurian take over the body of the scribe? Or was he really a Centaurian? We don't know. The other red flag is if someone is wearing a headband like Kapaneus's. There's a lot we don't know about these Navigators and their skills. It's going to be tough to figure out who our enemy is."

"That's right," Jake said. "And can a Centaurian Navigator take over a woman's body?"

Athena shook her head. "From now on, we're

going to have to brief our Time Raiders about all this at the beginning of each mission. It's the best we can do."

"One thing for sure," the general muttered, "if the Centaurians get hold of any piece of that stamp, we're screwed. We need all the pieces in order to make this work."

Delia looked around the table at the grim faces. "I wonder if the Centaurians can track us here?"

"No. I've set up a special protection energy grid with the headband." Athena smiled grimly. "As you know, the headband crystals work with the electrical energy of my brain. When we first built this lab, after the Pentagon booted us out of their military program because of so many time-jump failures, I set up the grid protection. If they try to find us *or* the fragment, their energy will rebound back to them. They won't be able to pinpoint us unless they follow us physically to this lab here at the university. Energetically, we're safe. We just have to watch out for spies among us. We can't assume Centaurians aren't in our time right now."

With a shiver, Delia said, "That's a scary thought. That alien was mean."

"Well," Ashton said, opening her hands, "put yourself in their position. The Centaurians know if we collect all twelve pieces of the seal, we're automatically accepted into the Galactic Council. That means they lose their power and control over the galaxy, and their trade will suffer badly as a result. They don't want that and will make every effort to protect what they have."

"Just like down here on Earth," Delia muttered. "They remind me of a megacorporation that will stop at nothing, including murder, to hold on to power."

"I think that about sums it up," Athena said. "By the way, our next Time Raider to be sent back is Tess Marconi." She gave them a slight smile. "I was working with the fragment and discovered that the Pleiadians put in the coordinates and time period for where the next piece is located."

Gasping, Delia said, "That's great! Where will the next specialist be sent?"

"Greece, in 480 B.C., at Thermopylae, where the Spartans stopped the Persian army from advancing."

"The Battle of Thermopylae?" Jake asked.

"Yes, the fragment pinpointed Greece, that time and date," Athena said. "We've decided to send Tess alone, because if the Centaurian is in touch with his home world, they may think we're sending two people again. We're going to send one and hope she evades them."

"Good plan," Jake murmured. "I'd give my right arm to know if Kapaneus found his headband."

* * *

Torbar felt rage rolling through him, painfully tightening his gut as he stood beside the Tiber River. It was the Ides of March, and Julius Caesar had just been assassinated that morning. With the city in turmoil over his death, Torbar had come in search of his headband once more.

Over and over, he replayed that night when that Greek mercenary had thrown his headband into the muddy river. Looking at the lazily swirling water, he felt panic eating at him. Without the headband, he was marooned. Unable to leave this time or place.

He also knew that within a certain amount of time, if he didn't check in with the officials who kept track of his mission, they would send someone to find out why he wasn't in contact. Humiliation plunged through him and he wrapped the thick wool cloak more tightly around his body. When that Centaurian Navigator came to locate him and find out what had happened, Torbar would have to tell the truth.

Cursing softly in his own language, Torbar walked restlessly along the bank of the Tiber. The March day was cold and rain threatened. Rome rose up the hills behind the mighty walls that surrounded the ancient city. How badly Torbar wanted to get out of this body and go home to his own, which remained in repose at the military installation where all time jumps were conducted. So long as he was alive in this miserable scribe's body, his own would remain healthy in his home world.

Hating this time frame and Rome's backward people, Torbar looked up at the churning gray-and-white clouds that moved slowly across the seven hills of the city. The odors of garbage, fecal matter and blood released from the recent slaughter of a sheep or goat filled his nostrils. Turning away, he longed for the refined civilization of his own people.

Along with that thought came terror. *He had failed.* The headband was gone. Torbar had lost count of how many times he'd waded into the muddy water and thrust his hands through the slimy mud to try to find it. Headbands were not foolproof. If a Navigator lost one, there was no way to energetically pick up on its location. Once it was off the person who owned it, the piece shut down.

It was a safety measure that had shortcomings, as far as Torbar was concerned. The Centaurian scientists had built automatic concealment into each devise so it couldn't fall into enemy hands.

Scowling, Torbar glared at the smooth surface of the Tiber. The headband could have been swept away by the strong currents. Or could have been swallowed up by the soft mud at the bottom.

Turning, he continued along the bank, through grasses yellowed and dry from winter.

One thing for sure, Torbar knew he would be stripped of his Navigator status. One never lost his headband. If he did, it meant automatic expulsion from the powerful Navigator society. Torbar's family would be humiliated, tarred forever with a black mark against the Alhawa name. Sickened, Torbar again felt helpless rage. Who would have thought that an Earthling could repulse a mind blast, which would then knock *him* unconscious? Torbar had never heard of that happening. Maybe he could use that as a defense to keep his Navigator status.

When they did come to find him, he knew he'd be taken back to his home world, where he'd have to recount everything in front of a board headed by Kentar himself. The leader did not suffer fools. And Torbar knew he'd be seen as just that: a fool. Fooled by a woman, no less. He would never live that down.

Rubbing his bearded face, he kept pacing along the bank. Up ahead, poor women were washing their clothes by slapping them on stones. How primitive these people were. Torbar longed for the fine comforts of his home world, the good wine, uplifting and informative talks with men, and a bed where he could truly relax and rest. Rome had none of those things, and he hated the place.

Torbar realized that at least discovering that "arrowhead" fragment would be in his favor. Centaurians had long been searching for the trail of pieces the Pleiadians had been allowed to place on Earth. This one discovery could save his career and family name. Curving his hand into a fist as he held the cloak close to his chest, he felt a trickle of hope. Kentar would be overjoyed to hear that one of the twelve fragments had been found. It gave them a path to follow.

Torbar's mind spun with questions—the same questions Kentar would be demanding of the time-travel scientists in their home world. *How had someone on Earth reached Navigator-quality status without any training?* He knew a headband had been lost on that planet. Had someone found that headband? Had it not been destroyed in the crash? Headbands were not indestructible. And normally, in a crash landing on another world, they burned up in the explosion, just as everything else would. They were made to destruct, because Centaurians never wanted a headband to fall into the hands of another race. Ever.

Torbar knew that he'd have no real answers for Kentar. But he knew the leader well enough to be sure he'd send scientists scrambling to find answers now. Smiling briefly, Torbar felt his heart lift with hope. Yes, he had lost the headband, but he had discovered the first fragment of the stamp. That alone might save his name, career and family reputation. He hoped. Most of all, he badly wanted vengeance against that Earth woman who'd posed as a Greek mercenary. She was powerful. More powerful than he, if he was honest.

How could she have protected herself and her male partner against his mind blast? How had she deflected it and then sent the energy back to him? Staring at the Tiber, Torbar snorted. The shame of being knocked out with his own mind blast was almost too much to bear. Kentar would not believe that any woman had such power over a male Centaurian Navigator. And yet it had happened.

Turning on his heel, Torbar walked to where his horse was tied to a nearby bush. He knew that soon another Navigator would be sent to locate him. It was a good thing Kentar knew he was inhabiting the body of the scribe of General Marcus Brutus; Torbar would be easy to find and contact. Rubbing his damp hands together, he mounted the small chestnut gelding. The horses of this world were pitiful in comparison to the breeds of horses kept in the worlds of Centaurians.

As he settled into the saddle and turned toward the gate into the walled city, Torbar smiled. The

Centaurians had, long ago, peppered this world with different breeds of horses from their home world. It was one of the things that Centaurians did even though it was against the laws of the Galactic Council. They would not only steal a certain species from another world and bring it back to their own system, but also release their own animals, insects and reptiles on other worlds. It was a way of claiming them sometime in the future, when the time was right. The council did not have the technical expertise to catch them doing this—yet. That day would come, but until then, Centaurians continued to scatter DNA seeds of their home world into as many others as they could.

The laws of the Galactic Council mandated that if living organisms of one world were similar to a home world, that a claim could be placed upon it. And of course, the Centaurians, knowing that Earth women had Navigator genes, had set out to proliferate many different breeds of horses who took well to this world, to make it as similar to their home as they could. In the future, if there ever was a legal battle to claim Earth, Centaurians could claim that their horses were very similar, genetically, to their own. That would give them first claim to the planet.

Chuckling, Torbar knew that the craftiness of the Centaurians would eventually make this pitiful world their own. Their actions paved the way, someday, for them to land here and assume ownership. That time wasn't yet, of course, but Centaurians were patient in one aspect: they set long-term goals with certain solar systems and planets, because it increased their strength in trade over time. If they had to wait a hundred thousand years, well, that didn't bother them. It gave the many species they populated the world with time to evolve and make themselves at home.

Torbar felt relieved as he lifted his hand to the Roman guards at the gates, his horse clip-clopping across the cobblestones and into the walled city. Looking up, he saw a rainbow to the east of the mighty city. That was a good sign.

Intuitively, he felt his rescue would come shortly. And when it did, he was going to utilize all his innate confidence and bravado, and convince Kentar that he should remain a Navigator, his family maintain their honor. Realizing he'd discovered the first clue to the Karanovo stamp, Kentar would instantly hail him a hero, not the imbecile he really was.

* * * * *

NOCTURNE™

Coming next month

TIME RAIDERS: THE PROTECTOR
by Merline Lovelace

Cassandra's psychic skills are the reason she's been sent to seventh-century China on a dangerous mission. Soldier Max is supposed to protect her, but when the crusade turns deadly, Max and Cassie are powerless to fight their growing attraction.

DANCE OF THE WOLF
by Karen Whiddon

On a quest to find his missing best friend, wildly sexy werewolf Jared's search leads him to mysterious Elena – the woman he recognises as his one true mate. Now their lives – and those of Jared's pack – depend on him winning her trust.

On sale 18th June 2010

TOUCH OF SEDUCTION
by Rhyannon Byrd

Like so many of his kind, tiger-shifter Aiden's past had shaped his view of humanity as cruel and petty. Until he met Olivia Harcourt, a woman with the power to inspire his deepest devotion – and determination to protect her from a dark fate.

On sale 2nd July 2010

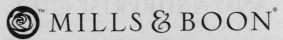

2 FREE BOOKS
AND A SURPRISE GIFT

We would like to take this opportunity to thank you for reading this Mills & Boon® book by offering you the chance to take TWO more specially selected books from the Intrigue series absolutely FREE! We're also making this offer to introduce you to the benefits of the Mills & Boon® Book Club™—

- **FREE home delivery**
- **FREE gifts and competitions**
- **FREE monthly Newsletter**
- **Exclusive Mills & Boon Book Club offers**
- **Books available before they're in the shops**

Accepting these FREE books and gift places you under no obligation to buy, you may cancel at any time, even after receiving your free books. Simply complete your details below and return the entire page to the address below. You don't even need a stamp!

YES Please send me 2 free Intrigue books and a surprise gift. I understand that unless you hear from me, I will receive 5 superb new stories every month, including two 2-in-1 books priced at £4.99 each and a single book priced at £3.19, postage and packing free. I am under no obligation to purchase any books and may cancel my subscription at any time. The free books and gift will be mine to keep in any case.

Ms/Mrs/Miss/Mr _____ Initials _____

Surname _____

Address _____

_____

_____ Postcode _____

E-mail _____

Send this whole page to: Mills & Boon Book Club, Free Book Offer, FREEPOST NAT 10298, Richmond, TW9 1BR